Climbing Jacob's Ladder

Volume One

The New World

Carole Love Forbes

This book is dedicated to the woman whose great enthusiasm inspired my interest in this subject in her class on 'Women in American History', at Antelope Valley College, Lancaster, California.

Annette Marks-Ellis

Author's Notes

Volume One of 'Climbing Jacob's Ladder' and the two volumes that follow, are works of fiction. Volume one, 'The New World' introduces two noteworthy women in early American history. I have woven my fictional characters, Bridget and Amanda, into their lives.

I have stayed to actual historical events and the lives of Anne Hutchinson and Margaret Brent. I have taken license in the lives of Margaret Brent's brother Fulke. All I found in my research materials was his name, so I have given him a fictional life. I have also changed the age of brother, Giles' Indian wife, Mary Kittomaquand, to fit my story. Giles actually married her when she was around eleven.

I was unable to find any information regarding little Anna Hutchinson's life, so I gave her a fictional life that goes through all three books. Recently I was told she was returned to Boston where she had a family, and may have living descendants. I hope they will forgive me for giving her a wonderful rescue and happy fictional life in these books.

There are several ways to spell Plymouth, one of which is Plimoth; however, I have chosen to use Plymouth as it is more familiar.

If you enjoy this book, please read Books Two and Three which will round out the two historical characters and follow the distaff lines of Bridget and Amanda. I will be introducing more American women of great valor in Book Three that goes through the Revolutionary War.

If you would like to know more about America's historical women there are internet biographies as well as books and articles available.

Carole Love Forbes

Prologue
~

London, 1623

To the clip-clopping heels of her high-top shoes, Bridget Wodehouse heaved a sigh of contentment. She was making it on her own in London, a feat few women could equal in 1623. She hoped Lady Redford would like her latest creation. Bridget couldn't help the feeling of pride she experienced that her millenary designs were gaining favor in high society. Bridget pictured the purple feathers she was going to try on Lady Mead's new hat, her mind engrossed with colors and fabrics. However there was no hurry on this order as Lady Mead was vacationing in the country.

The gown Bridget was wearing was of her own design. It was made of sturdy, fine wool, which helped keep out the encroaching cold fingers of wind. The neckline of her mauve gown was high, with a row of small colored buttons making their way down the front of the bodice. The skirt was plain and full, over a multitude of linen petticoats. Though not dressy, the long sleeves sported an insert of a complimentary knit pattern. She had topped this with a warm wool cape with a matching hood, which she held tightly to her throat against the London dampness. In its totality, the outfit flattered her blonde beauty.

The biting cold brought her mind back to the present. The fog had been worse than usual this day and thickened perceptively as darkness set in. Now, on her way home from Madam Adele's shop where she worked, Bridget felt very blessed.

A smile touched her pretty face. She loved her work, and was used to the walk to and from the shop. She had made this walk for almost a year. Her small flat was above a clock shop. She turned her thoughts to her suite of rooms. She had brightened it up by covering the few pieces of utilitarian furniture with sturdy fabric. She added bright touches with a knick-knack or two she had collected on infrequent shopping trips. The best thing about her new home is that it was in a good section of London, and was not far from the millinery shop.

However, she had left later than usual this night, having had to finish Lady Preem's straw bonnet. Suddenly, she felt a strong shiver run the length of her spine. She tried to ignore the niggling feeling that something was not quite right, and turned her eyes to the quaint shops that lined the street to gaze at the outline of intriguing merchandise shadowed by the fog. This was a respectable neighborhood, comparatively clean and free of slops, made up of small businesses, many with living quarters above.

She told herself that she was being silly, but in spite of this she quickened her step and tightened her grip on the bonnet strings with her left hand, using her free hand to pull her woolen cloak tightly around her. She was trembling now. She knew it was probably her imagination, but thought she heard footsteps behind her. Luke, Madame Adele's tailor, usually walked her home when she had to leave the shop late, but tonight he had been on the Tower Bridge shopping for new fabrics, and hadn't returned in time.

Bridget stopped, thinking she would let the other person go past her, but the footsteps also stopped. She pretended to look into the window of an apothecary shop but surreptitiously glanced behind her. No one. Blaming an overactive imagination, she heaved a sigh of relief and hurried on her way.

The fog was thicker now, bringing with it a damp chill that bit through Bridget's clothing. Through the fog she discerned the faint chiming of the curfew chimes from Lincoln Inn's Chapel. Pulling the cloak and her heavy skirt and petticoats a little higher so that they would not impede her steps, she lowered her head and put on speed, doggedly determined to get home quickly. Two more blocks and she would be safely there.

Suddenly her eyes opened wider, and fear sparked the same uncomfortable prickle through her whole body. Now there was no mistaking it. She heard footsteps come up quickly behind her. She started to run, searching windows for a proprietor who might still be working.

She ran faster.

"Oh, God, help me!" she moaned as she a large body looming up behind her. She started to open her mouth to scream, but a huge, gloved hand pressed over her mouth cut off all sound. A large, rough sack was thrown over her. Something hard came down on her head and she drifted, struggling all the way, into a deep dark tunnel.

Amanda McNeely, a child of the streets, sat guarding her small bundle of belongings and chewing on a moldy crust of bread that she had saved from the few meager meals tossed down by prison guards. The dungeon was cold and dark, the walls dripping dampness from the fog outside. The floor was strewn with what had once been straw, but now was a matted mess of dirt and excrement.

She had been in this squalid hole for almost three weeks, and had continually fought to be left alone in the crowded cell. The mere fact that she was a rare beauty, in spite of her condition, made her a target for the pest-ridden, pock-marked hags and diseased whores in the small prison cell. Her simple cotton frock was now torn and dirty and hung on her thin body like a sack.

"So, have ye made up yer mind yet, me fine lydie?" The raspy voice belonged to a singularly ugly hag known as Maggoty Marty. Due to the death of her one and only legal husband, Marty owned a small house in the slums of London. It consisted of four rooms, two at street level and the other two above them. She had, upon his death, started renting three of the rooms out to ladies of the night, on an hourly basis. She kept the fourth for her own use in the same occupation. She understandably catered to men who were too far gone on drugs or liquor to care about the condition of the body beneath them.

Amanda instinctively pulled back from the old woman, holding her thin hands over her nose and mouth for protection from the woman's body stench. "Go away, old hag. I told you before, I am not a prostitute. I have kept myself clean thus far, and I am not about to get involved with the likes of you!" Amanda pressed herself against the clammy, damp wall, turning her back to the ugly old witch.

"Ye'll be changin' yer tune before much longer in this dungeon. Me girls'll be getting' me out of this hellhole any day now, and with the money they'll be a'bringin me, I know I can get ye out, too." She cackled in morbid glee, "With yer looks, ye could be rich in no time, dearie."

Amanda closed her eyes tightly. She wished she could shut out the sound of the hag's voice, but the woman continued cackling in front of her for what seemed like forever. Finally, seeing no results from her tirade, Maggoty Marty wandered back to her corner. Amanda could not contain the single tear that squeezed its way from her slightly up-tilted eyes. It slid down a dirty cheek, leaving a clean white line to mark its trail.

Anyone seeing Amanda would have been surprised and troubled that such a young and lovely girl could be in this filthy, dungeon. Amanda possessed an inner beauty that lifted her above those around her. Her long, thick black hair was pulled back and tied with a thin strip of rag from her skirt. Her oval face was thin, but this only served to make her large violet eyes grab one's attention.

Amanda wondered what had happened with her mother's body. Blessedly the tears brought some healing. At last, she was able to grieve openly for her dear mother. She cried until exhausted, fighting her need for sleep as she felt the tension leave her body. She hadn't slept for such a long time, having been up night and day with her dying mother, and now fearing the hostile actions of her prison mates. She just wanted to be able to lie down on a clean bed and sleep.

As Amanda sat thinking of all that had happened to her in the last few weeks, the silence of the dungeon was broken by the cranking and creaking of the heavy cell door as the warder and three burly guards pushed their way into the crowded space. A middle-aged man, who had the craggy look of a seaman, followed them.

The warden, a rotund man in his fifties, looked at the assemblage of unholy inmates with disgust. With the air of one following orders he didn't agree with, he shouted, "Which of you 'lydies' want to go the New World and myke a new start for yerselves?"

There was a silence as the words sank in. "Captain Frye here is lookin' for six women to take as bondservants to the Virginia Colony. Well, let's hear ya. Who wants ta volunteer?"

With those few words from the warden, Amanda's slender hand flew up, and she took her first deep breath in a long time.

1

The Crossing - 1623

Bridget awakened, opening her eyes to nothingness. She put her hands up to her eyes to make sure they were open, fear of blindness her first terrifying thought. Her head was aching. Slowly she began to discern sounds, soft moans, weeping, scuffling near her and a creaking accompanied by motion. A ship. That must be it. She was on a ship, but why? Why was it so dark? She suddenly realized she was hungry and thirsty. Worse than that, she urgently needed to relieve herself. But, where... how?

"Oh, yer finally awake," a soft voice breathed close to her ear. In the dimness Bridget was able see a face. Her eyes, now adjusting to the dimness, made out a young redheaded woman, her round face painted with rouge and powder. She wore a gaudy yellow satin gown that had seen better days. It was very low cut, exposing large, round bosoms that threatened at any moment to escape their meager prison. Her face could not be considered pretty, as her nose was too short and turned up, and was covered with a generous sprinkling of freckles. A few faint pox marks proved her a survivor. Her eyes were the best part of her face, being large and blue-green. Her mouth was full and generous. Her smile lit up her face giving it a beauty it would not otherwise have had.

"I was beginning to think they had killed ya. I am Aggie Barrows. I guess we're sort of bunk mates, if there were any bunks."

"Where are we?" implored Bridget.

"We are aboard the merchant vessel *Atlanta* on our way to the New World. From the looks of it, you musta been waylaid. They dumped ya next ta me just after we boarded."

Bridget rubbed the tender bump on her head. "I remember now. I was walking home from the milliner's shop where I work when someone hit me on the head." She looked at Aggie. "Did you get waylaid, too?"

"No, dearie. I volunteered. I am afraid a lydie like you will be shocked at the lykes a me. I had a profession not worthy of the lykes a you. I wuz savin' me money to buy passage to the colonies, but one of me regulars caught on ta me. He beat me up and stole my savins', so I signed them papers where ya hafta work for six years and then yer free to make a new life.

"But...this is horrible. I have a good life in London. I don't want to be indentured. I have good friends who will be looking for me. I must go and see the man in charge." She started to rise but was still dizzy. "I have to get him to take me back."

"Won't do you no good, honey. We are too far out to sea. He ain't gonna turn around for nobody. Anyway, I've heard he is a heartless man. She paused, mistress...?"

"Oh, how rude of me. My name is Bridget Wodehouse." She gently rubbed the lump on her head. "There must be a way, Aggie. I can't go to the New World."

Bridget tried to hold back tears. Aggie put her arms around Bridget.

"Oh, don't cry, honey. I learned a hard lesson when I was forced into a life I hated. If you cry you become a victim. You can't let your feelings show. No matter what, Bridget, remember who you are, a lady. Never let anyone see anything but your strength."

Bridget brushed her tears away and managed a smile.

"Thank you, Aggie. I will remember that."

But, I am talkin' yer ear off when ya must be starvin'. I saved ya some beans and a biscuit."

Aggie put a hard biscuit in Bridget's shaking hand. "Nothing we can do now, honey, but make the best of it. You better eat."

"How kind of you to save me food. I am starving." Bridget pushed back a lock of long golden hair that fell over her forehead. Her usually sparkling sky blue eyes were dull and filled with confusion. Despite the dirt, her beauty was obvious. Her face was perfectly sculptured, her nose straight, and her lips full.

She accepted the small bundle of food Aggie offered her. She was still dizzy and her head ached so badly it was hard to move. She wanted to scream out her fear and frustration, but as Aggie had said, it would not help. She quickly finished the hard biscuit and then she started to squirm. "Aggie, even more urgent, I have not relieved myself for I don't know how long. Where do you go in this place?"

"I will show ya, honey." Aggie helped Bridget up and they made their way to a small storage room in an area called the aft. Walking was hard as the ship rolled and pitched. They had to crawl over the massed humanity on the floor of the cold, damp hold. Bridget was embarrassed at how public the wooden bucket was, but relieved herself.

As they made their way back to their spot, Bridget had to accept that the life she loved was forever behind her. However, she did feel more human since as her physical needs were met. Bridget's next query was about water with which to wash. This was not so easy. Fresh water was being rationed to the more than one hundred men, women and children packed into the rancid hold. The passengers were forced to wash in the icy seawater that was provided in large wooden buckets. Unfortunately, it left them with the pulling feeling of the salt on their flesh.

As the two girls made their way to the water buckets, Bridget was again shocked at the crowding and lack of facilities. The bulkheads of the ship were covered with hooks holding the meager belongings of the passengers. The floor was strewn with blankets and cloaks. Women and children lay close together to keep warm, using whatever they had to cover themselves.

The *Atlanta* left England on April 10, 1623, under the command of Master Algernon Fry, a merchant captain with an unscrupulous reputation. Not overly concerned with the welfare of his passengers, he was content to allow conditions to worsen. They had only been at sea for a day and already several people were violently seasick, lying in their own vomit, too ill to care. Bridget's heart went out to them.

After washing with the icy water, the two girls made their way back through the silent groups of huddled passengers. Suddenly, a woman let out a heartrending scream. Through the dark shadows, Bridget made out the woman who again screamed. She appeared to be in her mid-twenties and, upon kneeling down, Bridget realized that she with child. The woman was rolling on the floor, curled tightly in a fetal position, alternately moaning, then again crying out. Aggie bent down and took hold of the woman's shoulders, turning her gently.

"We have to get help for her," Bridget cried. Her hands shaking, Bridget tore a piece of white muslin from her petticoat and gently wiped the perspiration from the woman's brow. "Go and see if you can get a doctor, Aggie. There must be a ship's doctor."

Aggie whispered encouragements to the woman, and then headed for the stairs. The few women near them turned their faces away, trying not to hear or see what was happening.

Moments later, Aggie was back. "They won't let the ship's doctor treat the passengers unless it's a contagious disease. Ee's too busy with the crew. We hafta do it ourselves."

Aggie wasted no more time in talk. She examined the woman, whose pains were now coming every three or four minutes. Bridget helped the woman lie flat, while Aggie shoved a nearby cloak beneath her hips.

"I done this plenty 'a times with the girls at the house, them what didn't have enough money to get rid of unborn babies. It 'appens to the best of us once in a while."

Not much later, Mistress Warren Chester, was holding her infant son in her arms. The girls discovered that she was a widow who, out of desperation, agreed to go the New World as a colony wife.

"Thank God the man who has contracted for me knows about the child and has been kind enough to take on both of us," Mistress Chester explained. "My husband died in a factory fire eight months ago." She looked up at her two benefactors, tears of happiness in her eyes. "I cannot thank you ladies enough."

Aggie laughed. "S'pay enough to me ta have ya call me a lydie."

One other woman, Alice Southworth, joined them. She was quiet, soft-spoken, and in her mid-twenties with two small sons. She offered a piece of cheese and hardtack to the exhausted mother. Mistress Chester was young and strong and would have plenty of milk with which to suckle her son.

❧

Meanwhile, Ship's Master Algernon Fry, engrossed in completing the ship's logs, was interrupted by a loud knock on his cabin door. Putting his papers aside, he called out permission to enter. The door was pushed open by a husky young seaman.

"What is it Ox?"

"I have great news for you, sir. You will be so proud of me."

"Well?"

"I overheard you and the mate talking about missing a wife for the voyage. I knew how upset you were. You wouldn't want to lose the money for the fare, so I got permission from the mate to go ashore for a couple of days before we took sail."

"And?"

"And, I found the perfect girl! It was dark and she was alone, so I followed her."

"I don't understand. Why would you follow a young girl?"

"Well, I figured I could find you a pure woman, one who was young and sorta high class. I searched 'til I found this girl coming out of a fancy hat shop. An older man came out and stayed with her until they reached her home. I was a little upset about that, but watched the shop again the next night, and guess what?"

"I can't imagine. But I am beginning to get worried. Go on."

5

"Well, I was going to ask her to come and see you about becoming a wife in the colonies, but I was afraid my size would scare her. So I gave her a little tap on the head and brought her to the ship."

Fry leaped to his feet. His shock showed in his voice. "You kidnapped a woman? Are you insane? Kidnapping is against the law. Oh, my God! What if you had been caught?"

Ox's eyes shifted side to side as he followed the captain stomping back and forth across the cabin. "I grew up around here. I know all of the dark back streets. It was easy," he explained.

"Ox, you have outdone yourself this time. I have put up with your indiscretions since you were my cabin boy. I know you want to please me, but you never think before you act. This tops them all. How many times have I told you, when you get an idea, come and talk to me?"

"I was only trying to help you, sir. You been so good ta me. Gosh, I'm awful sorry, but I thought you'd be pleased." Ox let his chin drop to his chest.

"This time, I am very upset, Ox. I know your heart is in the right place, but you have done a very bad thing."

"Oh, sir, I feel awful."

"Was she badly hurt? What did you do with her?"

"I put her down in the hold next to a young gal I have me eye on. She's all right. Do you want me to bring her up here?"

"God no. If she has any brains at all she might figure out who had a motive to take her."

"Ain't you got to tell her she is gonna be a wife?

"I'll leave it up Pastor Paul to make that pronouncement to her when we reach the colonies. Just keep an eye on the girl and see that she makes it to Jamestown in fairly good condition." Fry dropped into his desk chair. "Oh, God."

"I'll take good care of her, sir. I'm gonna make you proud of me. I saved you that fare money, didn't I?"

The master nodded, sighed, and waved Ox out. "Makes one wonder why God didn't give you a brain to go with that body."

When Ox reached the door, he turned a shamed faced to his captain. "It's gonna work out all right, ain't it sir?"

"That remains to be seen, Ox. That remains to be seen."

Even though Bridget was shocked to learn how Aggie had made her living, she and Aggie became fast friends. Bridget understood Aggie's plight after hearing her story. Aggie had been the oldest of eight. Her poverty stricken parents had sold her into prostitution. Aggie had been happy that she could keep her brothers and sisters alive by sending money to her parents whenever she could. At twenty, Aggie Barrows looked young, but was already wise with age.

Although women could not legally own property, Aggie had always dreamed of having an inn of her own. Perhaps the New World would one day make her dream a reality. Aggie's brash personality and dockside language shocked Bridget at times, but her optimism, open manner, and loyal friendship, endeared her to Bridget.

A few days out, Bridget became curious about Aggie's resourcefulness. Aggie was the only passenger allowed to go up onto the ship's deck, and she always came back with small food stores, bandages and other articles with which she distributed among the women and children. Bridget finally got up the nerve and questioned her.

"Oh, I got me ways, dearie." Aggie hesitated a moment, then smiled. "Well, if truth outs, I got me a feller."

"A feller?" Bridget queried.

"A tiff, a sailor," Aggie laughed. "E's a real top, 'e is. 'andsome and strong. Name a 'arvey Andrews but everyone calls 'im Ox. Fact is, e's seeing to it that you and me get to go up on deck for a few minutes this afternoon. He'll meet us up there."

"Aggie, how wonderful." As Bridget straightened her clothing as best she could. Aggie slipped Mistress Chester a large crust of bread she had received from Ox. A short time later the two excited girls clamored up the slippery stairs and out onto the main deck, deeply breathing the fresh, clean air.

At a nod from Ox, the girls made their way to the railing and looked out at the clean sweep of ocean. Its surface reflected the bright blue of the cloud-free sky. The salty sea breeze was a luxury almost forgotten.

Suddenly a commotion broke out on deck. The girls whirled about see a group of dirty, ragged women in a noisy fray. The tallest one screamed, "Bitch. Yer no better than we are. Get yer nose outa the clouds!" A second woman joined in. "You weren't good enough to work for Maggoty Marty anyhow!"

Bridget gasped as she realized that two of the women were beating on what appeared to be a child. She started forward to intervene, but Aggie grabbed her arm. "No, dearie! We will only get in trouble, and it will not 'elp the poor wretch."

"But, they will kill her! Stop! Stop it!" screamed Bridget.

Ox rushed from behind the main mast to where the ragged women were grouped and pulled the two women away from a small girl. He looked over at Aggie. "Don't worry; I will take care of this. You two get below before you attract the Master's attention."

Bridget watched as Ox lifted the victim and pulled her away from the angry women. She saw she was a young girl. She could not have been more that fourteen or fifteen years old and was extremely thin and exhausted. Tears streaked her dirty face, and Bridget's heart went out to her. She wanted to take the girl in her arms and comfort her, but Aggie was tugging her toward the hatch. Reluctantly, Bridget followed Aggie down into the hold.

When the two girls were safely out of sight, Ox questioned the man who was in charge of the women left on deck.

"Why are these women up here? They should be in the hold," he scolded.

The young seaman looked disgruntled, "These are the women from the prison. I didn't think the master would want them in the hold with the better class women, so I took them down to the storage section until we were at sea. What should we do with them?"

"You better get them down in the hold before Frye finds out what you did." Ox warned. "But, who knows what kind of trouble they will make?"

Ox gave him a disgusted look, "Put them back on the starboard end, away from the other women then, but get them off the deck!"

The seaman pushed the prisoners toward the starboard hatch. Ox stopped him. "Hold up. Leave the young one with me. That should solve the problem."

The seaman was greatly relieved and pushed the young girl into Ox's arms. "Good idea, Ox."

Hours later, as Bridget and Aggie chewed thoughtfully on their daily ration of hardtack; Ox came below and summoned Aggie. When she returned, she had her arm around the young girl who had been attacked on deck.

"Ox got 'er free a those 'ags. They woulda killed 'er, they would. She can stay with us 'til we land."

"Oh, thank God," Bridget said, taking the girl's arm. "Sit her down here, dear." She turned to Aggie. "We have to clean her up, but first she needs something to eat."

"Ox gave me this." Aggie handed Bridget a sack of food.

"Oh, bless your Ox. He is a saint!"

Bridget peeled off one of her linen petticoats and helped the shivering girl into it. She had previously shared another of her petticoats with Aggie, and was now down to two that kept her legs warm.

From that moment on, Amanda McNeely became the third member in a friendship triangle. She cheered with Bridget and Aggie's companionship and loving care. Although the limited food rations precluded Amanda's regaining her lost weight, the constant fear had left her features, and as the dirt was washed away, Amanda's beauty began to show.

Amanda scrubbed her face and ebony tresses and face as clean as possible in the bucket of cold salt water.

As the days passed, Ox, in exchange for Aggie's occasional company, managed to get the three friends an old hammock in which they took turns sleeping. What he smuggled down to them in the way of food or other comforts, the girls shared with as many of the children as possible.

As the friends became better acquainted, they began sharing the stories of their very different lives in London. There came a day when Amanda learned to trust her friends enough to dig beneath her ragged dress and borrowed petticoat to bring forth her cherished treasures, a brush and hand mirror. When her new friends ooh'd and ah'hd, Amanda's eyes glittered.

"Oh, they are beautiful," sighed Bridget. "Look at that design. It is so unique."

"Yes," Amanda agreed, "My father was an actor as a young man, and he designed this dresser set for a production. The design was what he would have wanted for his family crest, if he had one. I have never seen another design quite like it."

"It's a pip, dearie. I never seen the lykes uv it neither. Must be worth a few bob, I would say. Silver is it?" asked Aggie.

Amanda ran her hand lovingly over the design on the back of the mirror. "I do not imagine it is silver, but it is worth a million pounds to me. I must preserve it to hand down to my daughter. No matter if it is real or not, it is the only family heirloom I have. Sadly, mama had to sell the bone and silver comb for food, but I saved the rest of the set."

Bridget covered Amanda's thin hand with her own. "How on earth did you end up in prison? It must have been horrible?"

Amanda leaned her head back against the damp bulkhead planks. "It is hard to believe how fast things can change. My life started out so good. My father, Michael McNeely, gave up an acting career when he met my mother. He became a seaman and remained one the rest of his life. He rose to the post of First Mate on a small ship that roved north and south of England for cargo."

"This is so interesting. Go on honey," Aggie said. Amanda continued.

"When my parents married, father set my mother, Elsie, up in a small flat. My mother told me many times how happy they were until Papa ran into a problem. He explained that the master had been killed, and that he had been promoted to ship's master. His merchant ship was forced to travel to the New World in order to make a decent profit for the shipping company. He left mama a sizable amount of money that he figured should last her until his return. Father went off to sea, not knowing that mother was carrying his child. She had not told him about me so he would not worry. She figured, a son would be a wonderful surprise for him when he returned."

Amanda shivered and Aggie put an arm around her. "Go on, honey."

"During her long months of waiting, mama spent the money wisely, and saved for my coming birth. Her one treasure, which she unpacked each morning and polished lovingly, was this beautiful hand mirror and brush set." Amanda traced the carvings on the mirror with her small, graceful hand as she spoke. "As you can see, it is carved with two angels holding their graceful arms out toward the beholder, as if to offer all the wonders of heaven. Then there is the interwoven crest on the sides. It was papa's wedding gift to mama. She treasured it above all else. She told me that before my birth she would hold the mirror to her rounded belly for her unborn child to see."

"This set will keep you safe and bring you much good fortune, my son," she explained to me, growing within her. "You must give it to your wife and then hand it down through the generations. Keep it always and guard it with your life, for it contains all of my love for you forever."

"Your mother must have been very lonely during all that time without her husband." Bridget said, "She was very brave."

"Oh, she was," Amanda said. She paused a few moments and then continued. "Eight long months passed until mother held me to her breast, a daughter instead of her prayed for son. After twelve months passed Mama's money was nearly gone, so she took me with her as she searched for work. When her money was all gone, my poor mother did not know where to turn."

The ship suddenly lurched and the gasps and cries around them interrupted Amanda. "Must be another storm," Bridget said.

Bridget gave Amanda a pat on her shoulder. "Keep talking, honey." Amanda waited until the passengers settled down before she continued.

"About six months from the time papa had set off to sea, a young sailor came to tell mama that their ship was now in dock, but my father was dead. The ship had run into bad weather on its way back to London and had wound up far out in the Atlantic. They ran out of rations before they made it to land, and were starving. They discovered later that papa had pretended to eat his share of the food they had, but, in truth, he had given most of his share to his men. Only five of the youngest seaman survived. The sailor pressed some money into mama's trembling hands and assured her that it was the Master's share from the small profits of the trip."

"That was kind of the young man," Aggie said. "Yes, he could have kept it and no one would have known," Bridged added. Amanda continued.

"That money lasted until I was nearly two years old. Mama then resorted to taking in laundry and mending, eking out a small but honest existence for the two of us. The food was always meager and our small flat had been exchanged for a damp, cold attic room in a part of London that had been taken over by the cities poor."

"By the time I was thirteen, my girlfriends were telling me that my beauty was the envy of all. My figure had filled out early; my breasts were round and firm, not wasted away as they are now." Amanda looked down at her chest and sighed. "My waist was tiny, and my hips full," She continued. "But, my best feature, so I was told, was my hair."

"To look like you would have been a blessing in my business," Aggie said.

"I did not think that beauty was a great reward, as I was constantly accosted by men of all ages," Amanda replied. "I stayed true to mama's wishes by jealously guarding my purity."

Amanda scanned her image in the silver mirror. She ran slim fingers over her dust-filled hair. "Do you think I will ever be pretty again?"

"Some decent food and a good scrubbing with scented soap and you will be good as new," Bridget assured her.

"Anyway," Amanda continued, "Mama dreamed of marrying me off to a well-to-do merchant. To this end she taught me to read and write, and with the help of papa's playbooks, I learned the basics of gracious living. I did not realize mama was ill with lung fever. Each day, she became thinner and weaker until she could no longer do the work for her small clientele. I took over the business, and cared for mama as best I could."

After a deep sigh, Amanda continued. "The week before mama died, I stayed by her side night and day. She was thin and gaunt, and her rich chestnut hair had grayed at her temples. I could not leave her to do any work so we soon ran out of food."

Bridget gently squeezed Amanda's shoulder. "You didn't steal food, did you? Is that why you were sent to prison?"

"I had no choice. I left mama propped warmly in bed and visited a few of her customers. I asked each for an advance to buy vegetables and perhaps a chicken to make broth for mama. Several of them were not at home and two claimed they had no money to advance us. In my desperation, and anxiety over Mama, I slipped a loaf of bread off the baker's counter, hid it under my cape, and headed swiftly back to our room."

"Oh, dear, I would have been too frightened to have done such a brave thing," Bridget said, shaking her head in disbelief.

"Oh, I was very frightened. I knew the penalty for stealing. At home I cut a generous slice of the soft crusty bread, poured water from a pitcher, and sat down to feed mama. I shook her gently, and felt a cold chill run through my body. I realized mama had died while I was out. I had stolen the bread for nothing."

Aggie caught her breath. "You did what you had to do, honey. If there is one thing I've learned is that nothing is bad if it keeps you alive."

Amanda fell silent and clutched the mirror to her breast, the pain of her memories etched on her face. Tears filled Bridget's eyes as Amanda continued her story.

"I sat there too shocked to move or cry. I had known the end was near, but my heart had not accepted it. Mama was gone and I couldn't even cry."

Amanda wiped away her own tears as she began to relive the horror that followed. "As I sat staring at mama there was a loud banging on the door, and a man's harsh voice was yelling, 'Open up in there! This is the watch!' This brought me out of my daze. I rose and stumbled to the door just as the man kicked it open. I jumped back, stumbled and fell against mama's bed."

"What...what are you doing?" I screamed at him. The night watch sneered at me. He grabbed my arm and pulled me to my feet. He told me the baker had seen me steal the bread and wanted me arrested. Then he told me that he had had his eye on me for a long time. He called me Mistress High and Mighty, and said that I would have to give up my hoity-toity attitude and face reality. He looked at my poor dead mama and told me that I was nothing but a poor girl no one to protect me and I had no choice but to go with him."

I questioned where he was taking me, and told him that I hadn't done anything wrong. I assured him that I would pay back the baker as soon as I got some sewing work.

He laughed at me and said I would not be doing any more sewing; leastwise not for anyone but him. I pulled my arm from his grip, but he quickly wrapped his arm around my waist and told me that I'd be taking care of him from now on. I couldn't believe I was being talked to that way. He said he needed a maid, and better yet, he would enjoy my young body."

Even Aggie was crying now, and more than a few of the others around the three friends had tears in their eyes as they listened to Amanda's story.

Amanda continued to shiver so Bridget draped part of her cape around her. Amanda gave her a grateful smile as she tucked the cape under her chin.

"He crushed me against his thick chest," Amanda continued. She closed her eyes, trying to make the memories go away. "The stench of his body nearly made me faint. Forcing me to the floor, he pressed his foul smelling mouth down on my neck and face, grinding his mouth into mine and causing my lips to bleed. As he held me down with his left arm, he tore at my clothing with his right." Amanda shuddered at the memory, but forced herself to go on.

"Suddenly I heard the deep bass voice of Master Wallace, the baker, yelling at the watch to let me go immediately. The baker then demanded that the watch get out. When I heard the baker's familiar voice, all the fight left me, and I drifted downwards into a deep, protective darkness."

"Oh, my god!" Bridget breathed.

"When I finally awoke, I found myself in that hellhole, Newgate Prison, charged with theft. I knew things like this happened, but I couldn't believe life would be that cruel to me. I feared I might be lost in that hell for the rest of my life," Amanda sighed. "The baker visited and told me that he understood why I had taken the bread, and therefore he had not preferred charges. But the watch who attacked me lied. He told the warden that the baker *had* preferred charges. That was why I was still in jail. The baker brought me the stolen loaf of bread, my few belongings and, surprisingly, mama's silver hand mirror and brush set, all of which were packed into a small bundle."

"Oh, thanks be," Aggie breathed.

"With great joy, I dug mama's mirror out of the bundle and held it to my heart. Then realizing the danger in that dungeon with women of the worst kind, I quickly stuffed it back into the bundle and tied it under my skirts. So far, I have been able to keep the set safe."

Amanda carefully re-wrapped her treasures and returned them to their hiding place beneath her skirts." So you see, the brush and mirror are all I have left of my family. You will keep my secret, will you not?"

The other passengers turned away, realizing they should not have been listening. Bridget and Amanda swore themselves to secrecy, and mentioned nothing more about Amanda's treasures as they faced the daily trials of the passage.

The weeks passed slowly, but the journey finally neared its end. Thanks to Ox, the three girls had managed to maintain their health as their ship approached a place called Jamestown, in the Colony of Virginia.

Other passengers had not been so fortunate. Many had faced daily sea sickness and had fallen ill. Several had died. Mistress Chester's infant son had not survived. He, and two infant girls, died of pneumonia, their tiny bodies now residing in the depths of the cold, uncaring sea.

As Bridget prayed for the end of this terrible voyage, she shivered with the realization that she was now totally on her own in a world that she could not begin to imagine. The only thing she was sure of was that the memories of this grueling passage would always remain with her.

2

Jamestown, 1623

Climbing the steps from the ship's hold for the last time, happy to breathe clean air, Amanda felt the reassuring weight of her bundle safely hidden beneath her skirt. She leaned over the railing, straining to see though the thick fog. An icy cold wind stung her cheeks, but it could in no way compare with the tingle she felt inside as her eyes scanned the open sea for a first glimpse of land.

Bridget huddled close to Amanda, her now soiled blue woolen cloak wrapped tightly around her against the wind. She could not help but smile. Exactly a month and three days after leaving London, they were finally nearing land. She experienced the familiar pang of fear and regret at having her familiar life torn away. She grabbed the ragged ends of the stained ribbons that held her hood, pulling it over her head and tying the knot tighter against the wind.

"It won't be long now, Bridget." It was a shout close to her ear, but the wind blew it into a whisper. Bridget nodded, and threw her arm impulsively around Amanda.

Seventeen-year-old Amanda's windblown inky tresses, freed from braids, blew freely in the breeze and framed the pale white delicacy of her skin. Her lips, now reddened by the wind, were full and soft.

Bridget's eighteen-year-old body had become almost skeletal, her newly forming breasts remaining small, but her good proportions lent promise of a slim but comely body.

Aggie leaned into the wind, her eyes also skimming the horizon.

"Blimey, but aye see nuthin out there. They are sure we are 'ere, are they?" A moment later the fog thinned slightly.

"Oh, there, look!" Aggie yelled, "Ain't those boats coming this way? Over there! You can 'ardly make 'em out through the fog."

Bridget looked where Aggie was pointing. Yes, there was no doubt now. Small fishing boats were appearing. As the morning breezes dispersed the worst of the fog, the harbor and several larger fishing boats came clearly into view.

"Land!" exclaimed Amanda. Amanda knew it would be good to feel solid ground beneath her feet again, but what would this New World hold for her? What type of person would she be indentured to? She turned to examine the faces of her two companions. An unexpected ache invaded her heart as she realized that with the longed-for landing, she would lose these two friends forever. Until that very moment, she hadn't realized how very dear they had become to her in their mutual adversity.

"Oh, Aggie, Bridget...we may never see each other again," sighed Amanda.

The three girls looked at each other, their parting now a painful reality. With much abandon and great affection the three joined in a warm, tearful embrace. Their eyes returned to the harbor as they neared the shore where a few wooden warehouses stood along the banks and a small community of brick and wood houses appeared in the background.

"Let's be 'onest, sweetings, we may never be together again, but nothing can end the friendship we have or take our memories away. They will always be in our 'earts," Aggie assured. They cuddled close against the cold as the ship sailed into the harbor. Aggie put a cold, bare, arm around Amanda's shoulder. Bridget lifted her cape, wrapping her two friends in its warmth.

As their turn came to disembark, they were jostled down a gangplank past dock workers unloading cargo from another ship. The harbor was brimming with activity, sailors and passengers embarking and disembarking from two docked ships. Some of the dock-workers sang as they worked, which seemed to lighten their burdens.

The male passengers set off in different directions, but the women were guided to a couple of groups on the dock. Bridget noticed a young pastor moving through the women in the group next to hers. She noticed that Alice Southworth was in that group and waved to her.

The pastor had a parchment roll and was checking off the women. Bridget watched as he stopped, rubbed his bald head, and then yelled out a name a few times. When there was no answer, the pastor hailed a young seaman who nodded and headed up the ship's ramp where he disappeared. A few moments later she recognized the ship's master, who had been pointed out to her by Ox. He and the pastor met and then disappeared behind a pile of boxes.

"Master Fry, explain to me the whereabouts of Judith Gogburn. Ahab Ward paid a healthy sum for her passage and has come all the way from Plymouth to claim his bride."

Fry had his answer ready, but nervously pushed a large hand through his graying hair.

"No problem, Pastor. Judith Cogburn was too ill to travel, but we found another young woman to take her place."

"Another woman? She is a Puritan?"

"I have been assured that she is a pure young girl."

"And she is willing to marry a man she has never met?"

"Well, not exactly. I figured you would be the one to tell her the marriage part."

The pastor looked closely at Fry. "I see you are up to your old games, Fry. Don't want to lose your payment, huh?" He heaved a great sigh. "I guess we will have to make the best of the situation. I will have to talk with Ward. He is not an easy man to deal with."

Fry breathed a sigh of relief as he followed the pastor as he moved around the boxes. "Which one is she?" the pastor asked.

Fry pointed. "She's in that group of indentures ...the one with the blond hair and the dark cape."

The pastor's eyes scanned the group until he spotted Bridget. "She's young enough, but she certainly doesn't look like a Puritan. Ward will be angry. He might not take her."

"What man would turn down a woman like her?"

"You have never met Ahab Ward." He directed eyes back to Bridget who was talking and smiling with a red-haired woman. He watched her for a long time and then turned to Fry. "All right. Have Ox pull her out of that group and slip her in with the wives."

The two men parted, the captain greatly relieved and Pastor Paul deeply worried.

The three girls were looking around at the scenery and chatting. Ox joined them and they greeted him happily, but when they learned that he had to take Amanda back with the prisoners, who would be sold at a separate auction, Aggie and Bridget were heartbroken. They bid a sad goodbye to Amanda. Ox gave Aggie a smile as he reluctantly took Amanda by the arm and led her to where the prison women were huddled against the cold. He was sadly aware that he was putting Amanda back with her enemies, but he had his orders.

When the tall woman who had beaten Amanda spied her, she let out a loud cackle. "So, me fine lydie, yer back with us. No man is gonna 'elp ya now!"

Amanda turned away from her evil gaze, grateful that she had been separated from her during the voyage. Whatever happened now, it had to be better than Newgate.

Bridget and Aggie were both surprised when Ox again joined them. He took Bridget's arm. "Sorry, miss. You have to go into another group." Both girls were confused and upset as they hugged each other and said their goodbyes. Ox led Bridget to a nearby group of women. She was angry. She demanded an explanation from Ox, who just smiled and gave her a pat on her shoulder before he departed.

With as much organization as could be achieved with so many confused and frightened women, three men wearing black tunics and workmen's aprons herded the groups of women into a large wooden storehouse. It wasn't much warmer inside than out on the docks, but they were protected from the wind. Long wooden tables with hand-hewn benches had been set with crude wooden bowls and utensils. Six women settlers, wearing plain warm dresses, aprons, and mobcaps on their heads, set large platters of food on the tables. With a great deal of pushing, shoving and yelling, the newly arrived women were finally seated.

The pastor then said a prayer, and the women dug into the first hot food they had eaten in many weeks. There were mashed potatoes, and long round vegetables with small kernels in rows, which Bridget learned was called maize. These vegetables were sweet and she could not get enough of them. There were also huge cooked birds, a kind Bridget had never before seen. The settlers called them turkeys and they were roasted to a tee, providing the most delicious white and dark meat.

When they finished eating, the indentures were led out to use the outhouses. Bridget caught sight of Aggie in that group, and decided to find out why they had been separated. When the workmen brought the indentures back, Bridget's group followed to take care of their needs. The two groups were then settled in different areas. Bridget watched as the pastor addressed the indentures. When finished, he came over to Bridget's group and explained that the prospective wives would be housed in several homes in the Jamestown Colony and would be provided clean clothing. Families had volunteered their services as many wives remembered how frightened they had been upon arriving in the New World.

The pastor, who introduced himself as Pastor Paul, explained that the 'ceremonies' of matching would take place at ten o'clock the next morning. Paramount in the minds of all of the women was apprehension about what these 'ceremonies' would entail. They were filled with suspense and visibly nervous. Tensions grew as the reality of marriage to total strangers hit them. Hope for a better life changed to fear and apprehension. Many of the women were in tears.

This was all Bridget could stand. She rose and approached the pastor. "Excuse me, sir, but there has been a terrible mistake made. I was kidnapped and put on that ship against my will. At best, I belong with the indentures. These women are prospective wives."

Pastor Paul cleared his throat. "You are where you are supposed to be." He rubbed his thin hands together and seemed very nervous and ill at ease. He looked away, touched by Bridget's despair, then faced her again. "I will meet with you before you leave the warehouse." He then turned quickly and walked toward the workmen, who quickly set up a small portion of the warehouse with straw mattresses and covers for the indentures.

The contracted brides were lined up, and the women who had served them dinner handed each a bundle of clean clothing. Just as Bridget reached the door, Pastor Paul approached her and pulled her aside.

"Now, young lady, what seems to be the problem?" he smiled.

"As I told you, I am supposed to be with my indentured friend," Bridget complained.

"Is your name not Bridget Wodehouse?"

"Yes, it is, but..."

"Then you are in the right group. You have been chosen to fill the place of a prospective wife who could not make the trip. It is a great honor."

"It is no honor to me! Indentures only have a few years to work. A wife is forever. I won't do it!" she spit out. "I have rights."

"As you must now realize, you left your rights behind when you left London."

"But, I didn't leave London because I wanted to. As I told you, I was kidnapped. Surely there is someone here who can help me." Her voice rose with growing fear. "I have money in London. I have friends who would do anything to get me back. They will pay my passage back to London."

"I am afraid Master Fry would not take you back without payment in advance. He is not an easy man to deal with."

"Can't we try? Can I talk to him?"

"Impossible! His ship is underway at this moment."

"Another ship then?"

"I seriously doubt that any merchant ship would take passengers, especially a lone young woman."

"There must be some way. I want to go home! Let me speak to whoever is in authority here."

"Unfortunately for you, I am the highest authority here."

"Are you telling me that I am being forced to marry a strange man because *you* say so?"

"Exactly," he smiled. "But your husband-to-be is a prominent man from Plymouth Plantation. You would be gambling on what kind master you might get as an indenture. Now I shall turn you over to Michael to take you to your host family." He turned to go, then turned back. "Tomorrow, be sure you wear the clothing we have provided you."

"This is a nightmare!" Bridget cried.

"You must calm down and accept your fate, young lady. You would not be here if it was not God's will. Go in peace and make the best of the new life offered you. Bless you, my child."

Bridget was housed with a young couple, Mathew and Sarah Judd, in their small one-room log cabin. Sarah was Bridget's height, but a little chubbier. She had soft brown hair pulled back in a bun at the nape of her neck. She was quite ordinary until she smiled, and then her round face and twinkling brown eyes lit up and she became quite pretty. Mathew had thinning brown hair. He was around five-foot-one, and had a paunch that jiggled when he laughed, which was often.

The Judd's slept in their overhead loft, so Mathew screened off a space in front of the fireplace and provided Bridget with blankets, a cot and a small table. On the table was a bowl of steaming water that had been heated in an iron pot in the fireplace. To provide more privacy, Matthew went out for a walk. Sarah offered Bridget the remains of a bar of perfumed soap she had brought with her to the New World.

"Oh, no, Mistress Judd, I couldn't accept such special soap," Bridget said.

"Do not worry about that, dear. I do not use such fancy things anymore. Sweet odors tend to attract mosquitos in hot weather. But it meant the world to me when I first arrived in the colony and I had my first bath in the New World. Please, it will make me happy if you use it," Sarah urged.

Bridget gratefully accepted the gift and as she scrubbed her skin with the sweet smelling soap. She rubbed her body with a linen cloth until she was covered with soft suds. She was in heaven. With a soft brush she scrubbed her skin red, and then scrubbed it again. Sarah brought her more water and she rubbed the soap into a lather and washed her hair until it squeaked. Another supply of warm water was used to rinse the soap from her hair. Toweling dry, she slipped into a warm flannel nightgown provided by her hostess and sat before the fireplace. Using one of Sarah's brushes, Bridget brushed her blond tresses until they shone with gold highlights. Soft little curls formed around her face.

With a big yawn, Bridget climbed beneath the cot's covers. She was asleep when Mathew returned and quietly removed the table and tub. He and his wife climbed to the loft, happy that they had been able to assist this delicate young girl.

The next morning Bridget awoke to the smell of fresh eggs, something Betty called side- pork, and mashed potatoes. She then lingered over a steaming cup of tea.

Noticing that Bridget seemed worried and unhappy, Sarah pulled her chair closer to her guest.

"Bridget, I know how frightened you must be. You see, I came over as you did, to be a wife. I was so scared when I met Mathew; afraid I would not please him, afraid he might treat me harshly. But it has worked out fine."

"But, I was not supposed to be a wife. I was kidnapped and dumped on a ship, and I am told I have no recourse."

"That is terrible," Sarah commiserated. "But it does not change the facts. All I can say is that you have to be very brave and make the best of what has been thrust upon you. The wisest thing you can do now is try to impress this man. It might turn out to be a love match."

"That will not be easy in the dowdy dress they have given me. It is far too big."

Sarah suddenly perked up. A smile lit her face. She could not let this young girl meet her new husband in the provided garments.

"I have a gift for you, Bridget. I will get it." Sarah returned from the loft carrying a gown and undergarments. After a short argument, Bridget finally agreed to try on the gifted clothing. She was surprised and pleased at the obvious quality of the gown, which had once been fashionable. There was a bodice and skirt of emerald green velvet, with a high neck and long sleeves. It was trimmed at wrists and neck with a narrow band of dark fur. There was a shift and petticoats of fine cotton, and warm stockings. She decided her own shoes were still serviceable. A green velvet bonnet with two plumes, one black and one emerald, topped off the outfit. Sarah also gave Bridget a long black velvet cloak with a hood trimmed in garnet velvet.

"I will never be wearing the likes of these again. Someone should enjoy them," Sarah sighed.

Bridget thanked her host effusively. She had not worn clothes like these since her parents were alive and they felt wonderful. Now that she was clean and dressed nicely, a strange sense of calm settled over her.

❧

Pastor Paul chewed his nails as he waited for Ahab Ward. Ward was on time and as he approached, Pastor Paul pulled himself together. This would not work if he showed any sign of weakness.

"Good morning, Master Ward. Fine day, isn't it?" said the pastor, smiling.

"It would be a lot better if I didn't have to get here earlier than expected. Is there a problem?"

"Unfortunately, your promised bride, Judith Cogburn, became quite ill and could not withstand the harsh sea voyage."

"Are you telling me I am to return to Plymouth without a wife? Do you have any idea how embarrassing that will be? I have made two expensive trips to Jamestown, and have paid a large sum of money for a good Puritan woman to keep my house and give me sons."

"So you explained when we first met, Master Ward. But we cannot circumvent God's wishes. And as God's servant I have found you a wonderful young, healthy woman who is willing to take Cogburn's place."

"A substitute wife?"

"Well, sir, you did not actually know the Cogburn woman, so you should be happy to accept this other girl. We will not have another ship arriving for a few months, and I know you are anxious to get back to your work and your home."

Ahab frowned as he thought over the pastor's argument. "I have your word that she is a Puritan then?"

Pastor Paul bit his lower lip, said a prayer for forgiveness, and lied. "Most assuredly, however, her Puritan clothing was quite soiled from the trip. We put her in a plain dress. I will have her here in an hour. You won't miss your ship back to Plymouth."

Jacob was not a happy man, but he accepted the pastor's words and set off for the inn for a heart-warming, tankard of ale.

The next morning Bridget sat by Sarah's fireplace in her new outfit while Sarah tended to chores. Mathew had agreed to take her to Pastor Paul when the time came. As she gazed into the flames, her mind wandered back to the life from which she had been torn. She remembered her first day in London. It had been very exciting. Like most country girls, Bridget had long dreamed of going to the city. Her father, Sir John Wodehouse, had arranged for his wife and daughter to stay with friends while they planned a magnificent ball designed to find a suitable husband for Bridget.

Bridget's father was the third son of an Earl so she had been gently, if not richly, reared. She had looked forward to her introduction into London society. Her father, who had always preferred country living, had settled his wife and daughter in a manor house in the country, and seen to it that his daughter was educated by a tutor.

Bridget's parents had been determined their golden-haired daughter would have a happy life and a good marriage. To this end, they had saved money for years, and in the summer of Bridget's sixteenth birthday, they had set off for London to stay with long-time friends, the Count and Countess of Knollwood.

Bridget pulled her gaze from the glowing flames and looked down at her hands resting on the velvet skirt. Her eyes quickly turned back to the glow of the firelight and thoughts of her story-book life. Her mind continued reviewing her life.

Tragically, not long after arriving in London, her mother and father had been caught in a smallpox outbreak. Fearing for their daughter's wellbeing, they had sent a message to Bridget telling her to continue her stay with her best friend, Anna Walkins. They chose to remain in London to complete preparations for her coming-out. This proved to be a fatal mistake. Her parents were stricken with the pox and, in spite of the best care, had died.

Bridget remembered how grateful she had been when the Knollwoods arranged for her parents' bodies to be secretly transported out of London and sent back to their home for proper burial. Her parents had been quietly interred in the family cemetery, thus escaping the fate of hundreds of men, women and children whose remains were dumped unceremoniously into the large burial ditches that were hastily dug around the city during these epidemics.

Bridget felt the grief well up inside her. She felt a great burden of guilt, knowing her beloved parents had died planning her coming-out.

Following the private funeral, she had lain in a bed at Anna's house for two days, drifting back and forth between silent sorrows, tears, and healing sleep.

～○

When Bridget awoke, she had found that the pain had lessened enough for her to address concerns about her present situation. Bridget had known she could not continue to impose on Anna's family, and she knew she would never be content to remain in the country. She was now a young woman on her own.

Bridget listened as Anna's father brought up the Wodehouse estate. Walkins had explained that the daughter of his best friend was soon to be wed and he was looking for a house to present them as a wedding gift. Walkins promised to contact this man on the morrow. He knew his friend would like the Wodehouse property and could afford to pay cash.

Relieved, Bridget had agreed and within the week had found herself with enough funds to start her new life. She would go to London to the Knollwoods.

Bridget had known that Anna's family would never agree to her going to London alone. Without telling them of her plans, one week later Bridget left the Walkins home, leaving money to pay for her stay, and a note telling them that she was going to the Knollwood Estate in London and would be fine.

She had left in the middle of the night, stopping at her home to pack a few clothes. She lit the fireplace in her room with a tinder box, and lit a candle in the fireplace flames. She had reluctantly entered her parent's bedroom. Tears filled her eyes, and she wanted to run, but she knew she needed to be sensible. She opened the secret bottom in her mother's dresser drawer. Her mother had revealed its location to her. Bridget pulled out the cache of money and jewels. It was for a rainy day, her mother had said, and Bridget had never known a rainier one. She blessed her mother's foresight. She had pulled herself together and departed her childhood home for the last time.

The coach to London left as the sun rose. She knew that when she received the funds from the manor house, she would be financially secure.

Upon reaching London, Bridget had headed straight for the home of the Count and Countess of Knollwood, where she was greeted lovingly by the two kind people. Countess Maria threw her arms Bridget and held her closely, expressing sorrow for the loss they all shared.

Bridget was shown to a guest room and allowed to rest. A sumptuous feast was being served that night for the Knollwoods' friends, but Bridget begged to stay in her room, where she had been served a light, but filling dinner. Following a hot bath she felt better.

Sarah's humming brought Bridget momentarily back to the present. She watched her hostess as she busily swept the floor with her homemade broom. Bridget's thoughts soon drifted back to the things she preferred not to remember.

It had come as quite a shock when the Knollwoods had explained that all her parents' money had been spent on merchant's debts for her coming-out. The Count had offered to take her on as his ward and see to it that she had her coming-out. He explained that he and the Countess wanted to allot Bridget the dowry that would have gone to the daughter they had been denied. He explained that Keithly and Arthur, their family barristers, had set funds aside for her in a special account."

The Count had then retrieved a folded document from a small-keyed-drawer in a table near his chair, and handed it to Bridget. He explained that the document would be her proof and contained the address of the barristers. When she needed funds she should to contact them.

Realizing how important the document from Knollwood was, Bridget had folded it into the tiniest square possible, and stuffed it into the golden locket given her by her mother. She knew that she would never take the locket off.

Bridget had lovingly thanked the Knollwoods. That night as she lay abed, Bridget was sorely tempted to let these kind people take care of her and arrange a comfortable marriage, but something inside made her balk at the idea of being put on an auction block to find a husband. She hated the idea of being subject to a man, especially a strange man. How could she know what to expect...kindness, cruelty, indifference, or even worse...boredom? The young men of her village had not helped allay these fears, as she had found them vulgar, uneducated and boorish.

Bridget was anxious to find what London had to offer. She stayed in her room for two days going over possibilities, and assessing her skills and talents. The most obvious was becoming a governess or a tutor. However, the thought of what her life would be in service made her decide against it. She planned to save the proceeds from the sale of her house to purchase her way into a business. She touched her locket. There was always the money from the Knollwoods', too, but she would keep that for an emergency.

The next morning she had dressed in one of the outfits she had designed, and was given permission to use the coach to go shopping. The countess insisted she take a maid with her. Bridget asked the coachman to take them past notable millinery shops. After observing several, she had asked him stop in front of a charming shop near London Bridge. She directed the maid to wait, and spoke to the owner, Madam Adele.

Bridget was startled as she felt a touch on her arm. It was only Sarah, so she let out her breath.

"Bridget, dear, you were so far away. Are you all right?"

"I am fine. It is just the first time in so long that I have had some quiet time to myself. I guess I was reliving my life," Bridget smiled.

"Oh, I would love to hear your story."

"I had come to the time when I started my apprenticeship in a fashionable London millenary shop."

"How exciting. Can you share it with me? I lived in the country, and have never been to London. Was that your home?"

"No, my family lived on a country estate. It was only after they died that I decided to go to London. I wanted to do something I would enjoy and excel in. I remembered my first love, which was working with fabric and design."

"Oh, how wonderful," Sarah exclaimed. "But weren't you frightened being by yourself?"

"Yes, but I was also excited. That was what I wanted to do with my life. Since the age of thirteen, I had designed and made all of the hats and gowns my mother and I wore. I was much lauded for my talents."

Sarah rested her chin on her hands enjoying Bridget's story. Bridget continued.

"I had set out to look for work, and soon I was hired as an apprentice by Madame Adele, whose wealthy clientele were accustomed to being pampered. I sold my mother's jewelry and invested in her shop. Madame had agreed that I would be considered for an important position, but I had to start at the bottom, learn the business, and prove my abilities. I was in heaven."

"Oh my, Bridget, I can see why you are resisting your fate here. But please continue."

Bridget smiled. "I rented a small room in a good neighborhood, and with the salary I received, I was quite comfortable. I worked hard to impress Madame. I knew the money my god-parents had given me was safe with the Knollwoods' barristers, and I invested the funds from the sale of my parent's house with them, too. I pictured myself as a partner in Madam Adele's one day. I know it was an impossible dream, but I held it in my heart."

"Too bad there isn't some way you could go home," Sarah sighed.

"I tried, but Pastor Paul made it clear there is no way."

"Then you must make the best of your new life. I will pray for you." Bridget smiled her appreciation. As Sarah went back to her chores, Bridget thought about Amanda and the story of her past that was so sad. She prayed that Amanda would find a better life.

Matthew came in the door and joined them. "Ready to go, Bridget?"

"I guess I'm as ready as I will ever be," Bridget sighed.

"I put all of your things in your bundle," Sarah said as she handed Bridget the bundle. You may find some use for them." Bridget hugged Sarah. "Thank you so much for being so kind and listening to my story,

Sarah." Bridget took Mathew's arm and stepped out to face her future. She swallowed hard, hoping to rid herself of the lump in her throat.

⌒⊙

As Bridget joined her group she saw Amanda and Aggie being led away. She waved until they spotted her and returned her greeting. So much was happening that she soon lost track of them. She later learned that most of the indentured servants were sent to the Maryland Colony where they were auctioned off to the highest bidders.

Bridget's attention was drawn as Pastor Paul called out her name. She slowly moved toward him, resisting the urge to run.

When Pastor Paul turned and saw Bridget, she witnessed his face contorting with surprise and chagrin. "Oh, dear Lord, where did you get those clothes? This is terrible!"

"Mistress Judd gifted me with this beautiful gown," Bridget said, as she ran her hands down the front of her dress. I realize it is past it's time, but at least I look more like myself."

"Where are the clothes we gave you? I told you how important it was for you to wear those clothes."

"They were too big for me. I looked awful. Why would you want me to look like that?"

Pastor Paul stood staring at her for a long moment. "What happened to that dress?"

"I have it here in my bag."

Pastor Paul took a deep breath. "Well, I guess there is no time for you to change now. Follow me."

Bridget walked beside the pastor, her steps tentative and lacking energy. Suddenly a tall man loomed before her. He had his back to her.

"There...there is Ahab, your new husband," the pastor told Bridget as he pointed to the man she was staring at.

Her future husband stood erect. He was at least six-feet tall, and was well built, with broad shoulders. He was clothed in a long black

32

belted tunic with a wide white collar, knee-high pants, hose and black shoes. His hat had an extra tall top and a large brim.

When he turned to face her Bridget's heart nearly stopped. He had to be at least forty years old. He had a black beard touched with gray. His piercing, steel-gray eyes peered from beneath shaggy black brows. A long, slightly beaked nose, hung rigidly over his nearly lipless slash of a mouth.

Bridget let her eyes slide upward until she looked straight into his cold stare. Her knees buckled. She was saved from falling by Pastor Paul. The tall man stared her up and down.

"Are you all right, Mistress? Have you heard what I've been saying?" Pastor Paul asked.

Ahab looked at Pastor Paul, then sneered and turned his attention again to Bridget. Bridget swore that she heard a deep growl as the tall man took in his breath. His expression was relentlessly judgmental as he took in her clothing.

Ahab returned his hateful gaze to Pastor Paul. "This is your idea of a wife, Pastor?" he said through clamped teeth. "This is what you call a Puritan woman?"

Pastor Paul took a deep breath. "She is a pure young woman. Her own clothing was soiled and, unfortunately, her hostess provided her with this gown. You will be pleased when she is once again in her own clothing. Remember what we discussed. You are fortunate to have such a decent girl who is willing to become your wife."

Pastor Paul turned his attention to Bridget. "This is your new husband, Ahab Ward of Plymouth Colony." Bridget managed a slight curtsey. Ahab said nothing but continued to stare critically at her.

"I have not yet made up my mind, pastor," Ahab said.

Bridget was hurt to see the evident anger on this cold man's face. Long moments sped by as he continued to inspect her with distaste.

Suddenly she felt anger roiling up inside her. How dare this old man criticize *her*. She wished she had some way to get her money in London, but she had no idea how. She felt strangled. She wanted to scream, but she remembered Aggie's words about knowing who she was. She took a deep breath and lifted her chin. She would bluff it out.

"Your appearance is truly of a sinful nature," Ahab grumbled. "Are ye a Christian woman?"

"Yes, sir," Bridget affirmed stiffly. Ahab scowled. "Ye do not look it."

Bridget opened her mouth to retort, "I have..." but frustration stopped her words.

Pastor Paul intervened. "She is more than willing, sir. Such an innocent young woman will need a good husband in this unforgiving land."

Ahab stared at Bridget. "Tell me yourself. Are you willing?" He stared coldly into Bridget's eyes. She felt the weight of circumstances facing her. Because she had no choice, she took a deep breath and nodded her head in agreement. Pastor Paul began to breathe again.

"I'll go and fetch Mistress Southworth and her boys for you now, sir. The other women and children going to Plymouth with you have already been taken to the inn." With this, the pastor turned and fled.

Bridget was pleased that Mistress Southworth was coming with them. As least she would know someone in Plymouth Plantation.

Ahab growled, "If ye are coming with me to the colony, ye had better make yourself presentable, woman."

"I don't...don't know what you mean, sir," Bridget ventured. "What is wrong with this lovely dress? It was a gift..." Ahab interrupted, "Such clothes are worn by the European courtiers, sinners and blasphemers all."

"This outfit..." Bridget began. Ward again interrupted her. "The women of Plymouth do not wear such frippery, or flaunt their hair in public. We consider it sinful, especially when hair is that unholy color. Fallen women wear their hair colored like that. "Take off that feathered monstrosity and cover your hair immediately!" he barked.

"I don't have..." Bridget started.

"In my world, women speak only when spoken to. Ye will kindly learn your place." Bridget opened her mouth to protest, then, seeing Ward's expression, quickly closed it.

At that moment, Pastor Paul approached with Alice Southworth and her two small boys. During the voyage Alice had been friendly from time to time with Bridget, but mainly stayed to herself and cared for her sons. With the morning light shining on Alice, Bridget was impressed with the young mother's dignity. She gave the impression of height by her excellent posture and quiet poise. Her outfit was of good fabric, but plain in design and color. Her dark hair was neatly covered with a muslin cap. Her eyes were hazel and her expression free of artifice. Her features were even, except for a nose that was straight, but slightly longer than beauty accepted.

"May I introduce Mistress Alice Southworth, Master Ward," Pastor Paul said. He then turned to the woman. "Ahab Ward has been kind enough to offer you and your boys his escort to Plymouth Colony where you will meet with your contracted husband, Governor William Bradford."

"This is very kind of ye, sir," Alice said with a quick curtsey. Turning to Bridget, she smiled, "Isn't it wonderful to stand on firm ground again, my dear? I am so glad you will be going with us." Bridget smiled, but she felt such panic that she secretly touched the pastor's arm. He looked at her sternly and shook his head. "You are very blessed, my dear."

Ahab took Bridget roughly by the arm and led her toward the docks. "We must be off now. We have a long, hard trip ahead of us!" Alice raised her eyebrows at his rudeness, then shrugged and followed him, herding the two boys before her.

Ahab stopped and turned to Bridget. "Where are your belongings?" Bridget held up the bundle Sarah had provided. "This is all I have. I was not expecting to travel."

"And you, Mistress Southworth?" Alice held up her small reticule. "I also have a canvas bag over there." She pointed to a pile of luggage and Ahab followed her and retrieved her bag.

When he joined Bridget again, he growled, "We'll be staying in an inn near the docks until our ship is ready to sail. I will appreciate silence while we walk."

And silence he got. Alice looked sideways at Bridget, who gave a small shrug. They settled into a swift walk. The air was filled with many scents, notably the smell of fish. What struck Bridget most was the vastness of sky and the clean freshness of the cold air. In contrast to the crowded, narrow streets and ever-present stench of London, it seemed a fairyland.

The docks were busy but not crowded. A few seamen labored at loading and unloading another ship docked in the harbor. Bridget looked for the *Atlanta,* but it was far out to sea on its long journey back to England. With it went her last chance of going home. She turned her face from the ship and forced her attention back to the docks. Since she had been unconscious when she was hoisted aboard ship in London, Bridget had never seen a port town before and found everything about it fascinating.

"Quite different from London, isn't it, Bridget?" Alice smiled.

"I would say so," Bridget said, returning Alice's smile.

Bridget was impressed by the size of Jamestown Colony and the beautiful woodlands surrounding the plank wood houses. The clear blue sky generously sprinkled its color over the calm bay. This was indeed a *New* World, so different from any place she had ever been or even read about. If it were not for the prospect of marriage to the man striding before her, she might even be happy here.

The Settler's Inn was small, and the innkeeper and his family friendly. That evening after a hot dinner, the women and children retired to their accommodations. A Puritan woman, Mistress Digirie Prust, and her sister, Edna Allerton shared a room with Bridget. Their children slept on a straw mattress near the door. Ahab spent the night on a bench on the main floor in front of the huge fireplace.

The next morning Bridget opened her bundle and brought out a wrinkled gray dress with white cuffs. She put it on, then added the long apron which when tied thankfully helped the dress fit her small waist. There was a wide collar that was pointed in front which attached at her neck. Unfortunately, knowing Ahab's thoughts about her hair, there was nothing to hide her blond tresses. Fortunately Mistress Prust provided her with a white cap called a coif. With her hair pushed neatly under the coif, Bridget was ready to face the day. She was beginning to take an interest in what her new life would bring.

Ahab looked her over as she came down the stairs and then turned his face away. After a quick breakfast, they boarded a small merchant ship for their journey north. Thankfully, it was a much shorter trip. The women and children shared a cabin with a double bunk, which, though crowded, was heaven compared to the stinking hold of the *Atlanta* on their journey from England.

When their new ship, the *Westwind* arrived at Plymouth, Bridget's heart sank. Sarah had warned her that the colony was primitive, but this place made Jamestown look like paradise. She was surprised to find that a tall, strong palisade surrounded the colony. Most of the trees had been cleared back from the high wooden walls. They were ushered into the settlement through gates which were usually kept closed as a caution against hostile Indians. The largest building was built of slats of wood and was easily recognized as the meeting house and church. It was topped by a large wooden cross.

There were seven plank houses and four larger buildings, which served as storage buildings all built in the summer of 1621. The rest of the domiciles were huts or small, one-room cabins. There were even a few living places dug into a hillside.

As Ahab and his party passed through the gate, it was closed behind them.

Bridget grew too curious to remain silent any longer. "Why are the gates kept closed? Are we in danger here?" she asked Ahab.

Ahab scowled at her. He was not accustomed to women asking questions, but he decided a warning about the savages would serve.

"The local tribe, the Wampanoag Indians, have signed a peace treaty with us, but since the death of one of their kind, an Indian named Squanto, no one knows if they can still be trusted. They are strange, unpredictable and godless creatures," said Ahab.

"You mean they might attack us?" Bridget asked.

Ahab ignored her second question, which Bridget considered rude.

Alice Southworth came up next to Bridget. "Bridget dear, I was not aware you would be coming to Plymouth to be a wife. You must be excited."

Bridget smiled. "I thought I was to be an indenture, but was chosen to replace Ahab's intended wife who was too ill to travel."

"Well, I am so happy for you. I have not met my new husband, but I hear he is a respected and Godly man."

"I am happy for you, too," Bridget smiled.

Ahab moved beside them. "Ladies, if you can stop talking, let me enlighten you as to what you can expect. Although all prospective wives are married by proxy before they take ship, they also go through a formal ceremony in the church to confirm the unions in the sight of God. This sacred ceremony will take place tomorrow morning. Oh, here is Governor Bradford now."

William Bradford was a middle-aged man with a shock of gray hair and a short, strong body. Bradford quickly whisked Alice and her two boys away to their new home. Ahab attended the unloading of supplies that he had purchased for the colony in Jamestown, leaving Bridget and the other ladies alone for a short time.

The sea air was crisp, but Bridget could feel the beginnings of spring in the air. The sky was deep blue and as cloudless as it had been in Jamestown. She was fascinated by how *much* of the sky one could see. However, England had a charm of its own and she suddenly realized how she missed the green meadows of her country home.

When Ahab returned he took the remaining group for a noon meal at the home of a woman named Gertrude Brown, who was very talkative. Through Gertrude, the group learned about Plymouth colony, including the fact that the original population had consisted of forty-one males and their wives, children, and servants who had come over on the ship *Mayflower*. Bridget hoped she would see Gertrude again. Her mind was full of questions about her new home.

When the other women were taken to the church to meet their new husbands, Ahab led Bridget to his home where he turned his space in the loft over to her.

Ahab settled in a hard chair with a blanket. At least she was safe from him for the night. As she unpacked her bundle, the newness of the experience momentarily quelled her fears. She clasped her fingers over her mother's locket, and took a deep breath. She was ready for the challenge before her.

Part One

BRIDGET'S STORY
In the Northern States

Lineage chart:

Book One starts in 1623 in London, England. The North covers Jamestown, Plymouth, Boston, and New Amsterdam.

Bridget Wodehouse (b.1605)

Jacob Ward

Twin Sons (b.-d.1624)   **Rachel Ward** (b.1625)

Aggie Barrows, (b.1603) **Friend**

Historical Characters: Residents of Plymouth, Anne Hutchinson & Family

3

Plymouth Colony, 1624

The contractions were not yet too painful, but coming closer together. Fear gripped Bridget. So many things could go wrong in childbirth. She was also worried about how Ahab would react.

"Please God, let it be a strong, healthy son," she prayed. "Ahab will never forgive me if anything goes wrong this time," she thought as her pain eased.

Bridget tried to find a comfortable spot on the stuffed mattress in the loft. Although Ahab had gone to fetch Gertrude to assist in the birthing, Bridget feared Gertrude would not arrive in time. Bridget knew she had to keep her mind busy on other things to keep from screaming, so she thought back to her early days in Plymouth Plantation. Paramount in her mind was the delicate relationship between herself and her husband.

After her wedding in the cold church building, her life had taken on an uninspiring pattern. With her neighbor, Gertrude Brown's help, Bridget did her best to learn the ways of the colony wives, but Ahab was never impressed. Fighting back the growing pains, she forced herself to review those first months.

The winter of 1623 had been better than the first two winters in Plymouth. Food stores had been more plentiful, but it had been extremely cold and pneumonia had been rampant. Food had been rationed fairly among the first comers and their families, the biggest share, as usual, going to the children.

Ahab worked hard for the colony and for his home. He was gone much of the time on hunting trips and exploratory jaunts with Miles Standish, the military leader of the colony. When he was home, he spoke only to read from his prayer book and give her directions for the day. Once, she had dared ask him why the book mainly dealt with hell-fire and sin. Ahab had angrily explained that it was not for the congregation to interpret the passages, only to study what the church leaders outlined. That was the last time Bridget expressed her doubts about his religion, but, in her heart, she longed to hear more about God's love, and less of sin and sorrow.

Bridget felt a tear begin to form in her eye. It was not a tear of physical pain. It was a much deeper pain that had lived with her from the first night of her marriage to Ahab. He had been kind knowing that she was a virgin. He had explained what was about to happen and warned her there would be pain. But, then he took her with little interest and no tenderness. Before he fell asleep, he yanked her mother's locket from around her neck, and told her to get that object of the devil out of his house.

Bridget had lain quietly beside him until she was sure he was sleeping soundly, then got up and retrieved her locket. She sequestered it beneath the folds of her green velvet gown at the bottom of a small trunk that had belonged to Ahab's first wife. In the first months, she had hoped she could turn Ahab's dislike for her around, but this was not to be.

She couldn't have known what turmoil and self-loathing went on behind Ahab's dark brows or what made him close his heart and mind to her. This singularly taciturn man continued to criticize her every move, treating her like a clumsy servant. At night, he would turn to her, lift her woolen nightshirt and quickly take her. It was clear that all he wanted to do was plant his seed in her.

It would have eased some of her grief had she known that in the deepest recesses of his heart Ahab hid an attraction for her that he prayed daily to conquer. He had sworn to love no other woman than his good wife, and the pain of his guilt made him lash out at Bridget at every opportunity. She was too beautiful to be trusted. She was not of his religion. The devil had sent her to test his faith. Indifference was his refuge.

Bridget's labor contractions were increasing in frequency and strength. Pulling her mind to the present she pushed the covers off and raised her knees hoping to lessen the pain. As the pain eased, her mind returned to her memories.

For Bridget, learning to embrace the life of the colony was a daily struggle. But with the help of Gertrude, and Alice she had persisted in her efforts. She thought many times about escape, but fear of the unknown in this danger-filled country had kept her in Plymouth.

Bridget slowly became competent in her daily chores, which started at dawn. Ahab expected Bridget to make all of their clothing. She was glad that she knew how to sew, but was unhappy that the clothing was so plain and unfashionable. All of the colony women made their clothing from fabrics imported from England.

Fortunately she had gained expertise. The garments she made were strong and sturdy. Cooking, cleaning and preparing food for storage had taken up the majority of her days.

Catching her breath after an especially long pain, Bridget wondered what happened to Ahab and Gertrude. The pains were getting closer together. Keep thinking!

Bridget had been grateful that many of the tasks required of the colony women could be shared. Bridget loved the occasional quilting bees. The ladies went to the homes of different women each bee. Bridget had loved their first bee held in her cabin.

Holding back the scream that was forcing its way to her lips, Bridget clenched her teeth and forced her mind back to that quilting bee.

Bridget had worked hard to clean and tidy her home. She remembered the ladies who had participated. The first to appear at her door had been Gertrude, carrying a bowl of salad greens. Then Elizabeth Howland arrived. Elizabeth was in her thirties. The warmth in her gray eyes enhanced her plain face. Desire Minton and Mary Chilton came together. Priscilla Mullin Alden was late, but once there, her smile had brightened up the cabin. Priscilla had admired Bridget's house, lauding its size and flattering Ahab as a builder. Priscilla seemed younger than she was because of her childlike enjoyment of life. Having married John Alden in 1621, she was then the mother of two young children.

By the time Bridget's guests were seated around the large wooden trestle table, the sideboard was loaded with sweet and savory dishes, and the basic fabric was laid out.

Desire had suggested that Bridget select the subject, so Bridget suggested small diamonds of different colors. They all agreed. Desire was in her late twenties. She was tall for a woman; around five-foot two, and she was on the chubby side. Desire had decided to return to London due to the hardness of the life, and to please her family. Bridget smiled remembering Priscilla saying that she couldn't imagine living in the same town as a king.

The women had worked steadily laying out the pattern pieces to fit their design. As they worked they talked and laughed and it did Bridget's heart good. It took a number of meetings to complete the whole pattern. Their final meeting found the sewn-together pieces ready to be spread on a cloth backing to make into a quilt. They then attached the four sides of a quilting frame with coarse twine. The frame was then spread over the tabletop and four chairs and the ladies sewed the quilt together with small, even stitches.

When the quilt was finished, the women presented it to Bridget, who was surprised and thrilled. The final bee had ended late in the afternoon. After the ladies left, Bridget had picked up the quilt and held it close, murmuring into its soft folds. That day had been a milestone for Bridget. The terrible feelings of being a fish out of water would never again be as bad.

The contractions were coming closer together now. She had to work harder to keep her mind busy and push back the fear and pain. Where was Gertrude? The child was getting impatient.

Bridget again forced her mind back to her early days in the colony. In addition to quilting, there had been an occasional feather-stripping party. The colony's geese were gathered, and their feathers stripped from the quills and sorted accordance to their size and softness. This would determine their use. The feasts they had shared when the work was done were joyful.

Bridget's thoughts were interrupted by a strong, sharp pain. She fought back a scream. She adjusted her swollen body until the pain subsided, then forced her mind once again to her life with Ahab.

Bridget's pain-tortured mind took her back to the day, ten months before, when she had given birth to her first offspring, two beautiful twin boys. Though premature and small framed, they had seemed healthy. Ahab had been in seventh heaven. She had never seen him so happy. He had even softened toward her, sparking a burgeoning hope that he might learn to care. He had turned to her more frequently in the night, displaying a tenderness she had not suspected in him. He even smiled and hummed while working around the cabin. It had been like stepping out of the darkness and into the light.

Their twin sons had been born in December of 1624. Ahab had named the boys Jacob and Micah. They had been happy for those few months before the boys died of pneumonia, Jacob first and Micah quickly following. Everything that had happened to her since the fatal day she was kidnapped paled in significance to the loss of those two brief lives. Their tiny bodies were buried in the hard New England soil.

Bridget had needed to share her grief with Ahab but the night the boys died, Ahab had gone mad, yelling and railing at her, calling her a witch. He had blamed her for their deaths. She could not convince him otherwise. What she did not know at the time was that Ahab blamed himself more for letting his feelings get out of control. He had known from his first sighting of Bridget that she was the devil's tool, but he had let himself be confused by the fact that the Lord had given him not one son, but two. In Ahab's mind, their deaths were God's punishment for his slip from piety.

Three months later, driven by pressure from the governor to increase the colony's population, and by and his own desperate need for a son, Ahab made the painful decision to try again. He found no solace in the cold matings, and turned from whatever comfort Bridget tried to provide. Perhaps, after the birth of this new son, Ahab would realize that she was not evil and they could be happy again.

She could not hold back a yelp as another sharp pain shot through her groin. Where, oh where was Gertrude? Bridget screamed as a stronger pain racked her slight body. She could hear her own voice calling out for help.

"Oh, my dear girl, I am so sorry!" Gertrude exclaimed as she burst into the cabin. "I was not at home when Ahab came for me. How far between?"

"I don't know, but they are pretty close together," Bridget gasped. "This one is..." A scream stopped Bridget's words as the biggest pain yet split her groin.

"Do not worry, dear. I have set a bucket of water to heat in the fireplace. Your husband will bring it up as soon as it is ready. Now, let us see to this babe." Gertrude set about her preparations, cooing to Bridget all the while.

A full hour later, Bridget smiled down at the pink and lovely infant girl in her arms. "Oh, Gertrude, in my secret heart, I was praying for a girl. I have given a lot of thought to her name. She shall be called Rachel in honor of Ahab's mother. Perhaps it will help his disappointment and anger at me for failing him again."

"I do not see how he could resist a little beauty like this," Gertrude said. "I will leave ye to suckle her now. I have to get dinner, but I will be back to check on ye later. I will bring you some stew, so just rest. Do ye want me to tell Ahab about Rachel, or...?"

"No, Gertrude, dear. Thank you so much for everything, but I should be the one to tell him."

"All right then, dearie. God Bless all of ye this day."

Bridget could not take her eyes from her tiny daughter. "Everything will be different now, Rachel. Just wait and see. We'll be happy, the three of us together. I will keep you alive no matter what it takes. You are mine, and I love you with all my heart!"

And, things *were* different, only not for the better as Bridget had hoped. The moment Ahab gazed upon his tiny daughter; he made up his mind that he would never accept her. At that moment, all of the hatred he had felt for his wife was transferred to his girl-child.

Ahab lifted his eyes from his daughter and turned them on his frightened wife. Bridget felt his stare as she would have felt a huge icicle passing through her heart. She watched him as he turned his back on them and climbed down from the loft.

Ahab placed a cot near the fireplace. He never set foot in the loft again.

Bridget had finally accepted her fate. However, she worried about eleven year old Rachel. She had been renounced by her father and had few friends her age. Ahab ignored Rachel unless she made a mistake, and then he treated her harshly. However, Rachel and Bridget were bolstered by the love they had for each other. This morning, Rachel was enjoying one of her rare chances to be on her own.

Rachel let a rare laugh escape as she ran through the forest at the edge of the compound. She knew that Tepho was close on her heels and would soon catch up with her, but the joy of running free kept her moving. Her long auburn hair flew behind her as she ran. Her cap had come off and was being held on her shoulders by the knot at her neck. She was dressed in the fashion of Plymouth Colony women.

"You are as slow as the sea turtles on the shore, Onnashu." Tepho told her. He was not even breathing heavily as he caught up. He grabbed her by an ankle and tumbled with her onto the damp, leaf-covered ground.

Rachel knew her father would punish her severely if he even suspected her closest friend was a young Wampanoag boy from the tribe that had befriended the first comers

Rachel had always been fascinated with the Indians who had befriended the First Comers. Rachel also loved to hear Tepho tell stories of the early days, before the white settlers had come to his world.

Rachel rolled over in the cool leaves, her hands behind her head, and gazed up through the flickering lights and shadows of the branches and leaves that formed a ceiling above her. Tepho flopped down beside her, and followed her gaze.

"When can you come again, Onnashu?"

Rachel smiled at the name he had given her. It stood for 'fire hair'. He had bestowed the name on her on that first day they met, more than three years before. She had wandered away from the compound in search of berries. The time had slipped by too quickly and she had found herself at twilight not knowing where she was, or how to get home.

She had helplessly floundered around, and was having a hard time keeping tears at bay, when she heard someone laughing.

She could see no one. Perhaps it was a wild animal. She had been warned not to go into the woods for this very reason. She did not want to admit her fear, but there it was.

Rachel had decided that doing something was better than doing nothing, so she started to run.

A voice had warned her that she was heading in the wrong direction and called her 'Onnashu'. She had stopped and listened, thinking it must be her imagination. She could remember it all so well now.

A young boy had stepped from the brambles and stood quietly at a distance. He had told her not to be afraid, that he would not hurt her.

Rachel had stared open mouthed at this unexpected apparition. He had not spoken again for a few moments, giving her time to come to grips with his strange appearance.

Even then Rachel had thought that this young native boy was the most handsome male she had ever seen. He was slim, but every muscle in his body was firm. He had a certain grace about him, as if any movement he made was well mastered.

She had stammered when she asked him who he was. He had smiled and told her his name was Tepho and he was from the tribe of Massasoit. He told her that he could see she was from the place of the white man and was lost. He had reached out his hand to her and said he would take her home.

Rachel had gazed in awe at the boy. She had seen Indians in Plymouth, but she had never seen an Indian who looked like this one.

His head was shaven at the bottom, and the remaining hair was pulled up on top of his head. This young Indian had golden brown hair, and startlingly deep blue eyes. The breach cloth covering his waist was pulled down at one point to reveal skin much lighter than that of the rest of his body, indicating that the dark coloration was more a product of the sun than of heritage. She had wanted to ask him many questions, but he had been intent upon leading her home.

Tepho had remained out of sight as Rachel rushed out of the woods and through the back gate to her house. Bridget gave her in a welcoming hug. She had been very worried. Since that meeting, the two young people had met secretly whenever Rachel could sneak away from her duties.

Back at home Rachel asked her mother about the Indians who visited the Colony. Bridget fixed a cup of hot tea and sat down at the wooden table. Rachel cuddled near her on the bench as Bridget told her about them. As usual, when alone, they used 'you' instead of the first comer's 'ye'. That morning, her work done, Bridget felt like talking. She relayed the story that Gertrude had told her in the early days.

"We will consider this part of your history lessons. The first comer's left England on August 23rd, 1620, and landed in New Plymouth on November 11th, 1620. As you know, their ship was called the *Mayflower*. Their first winter was extremely harsh and many died of sickness and starvation. They were helped through the first two winters by neighboring Indians who taught them to fish and plant maize. Of course, the colonists were afraid of what the Indians could do to them. But this problem was solved when a peace treaty was signed with Massasoit, Chief of the Wampanoag. An English speaking Indian named Squanto was an immense help to the first comers."

"Do you know the whole story of Squanto, Mother?" Rachel queried. I have wanted to know more about him."

"Yes, dear. Squanto had an interesting history. He was kidnapped by some adventurers, and sold into slavery in Spain. He was subsequently sold to a Captain Dermer of the Newfoundland Company. Dermer took him to London to meet a man named Sir Fernando Georges, an adventurer who wanted to populate New England. There Squanto learned to speak English. Squanto then talked his way onto Georges' ship to return to Massachusetts in 1619."

"I am glad he got to come home," Rachel sighed.

Bridget smiled. "I am too, Rachel. Would you like to hear more about early life in Plymouth?"

"Oh, yes. Do we have time?" Rachel asked.

"Your father won't be home until dinner time and the stew is ready," Bridget smiled.

"I have not told you about my first year here. It was 1623. The lean years were almost over, and the harvests had begun to be plentiful. The October holiday, which had begun in 1621was occasionally repeated. As we still do, the women brought food for a hearty repast, including roast goose, wild turkey, cold venison, hot biscuits and gingerbread. There were several types of squash, maize, carrots, turnips, onions, beans and yams. There were berries, plums, gooseberries, and raspberries. Also on the tables was an abundance of oysters and clams introduced to us by the Wampanoag. Oysters are now a common staple for the settlers."

"I love the October holiday," Rachel smiled.

"The fun did not stop there," Bridget explained. "Just like now in the evening we had a big party. The adults danced to the fiddlers, and they drank gallons of cool, sweet cider. Then the children were taken home and put to bed."

"That's the part I didn't like," Rachel said. Bridget continued.

"The harvest festival that first year was very special because we were able to add beef to our diet. A man named Edward Winslow had brought over three heifers and a bull, the first in the colony, and the herds rapidly grew. There were also a few horses brought over on the *Mayflower*." Bridget stopped to take a sip of tea.

"There were also house raisings where the men under your father's direction, built cabins. Sugar making time and corn husking parties rounded out the good times."

As her mother talked, Rachel's mind turned to her friend, Tepho. She wished she knew more about him.

Bridget fell silent as she watched her daughter's eyes began to droop. The girl worked so hard, and she was so willing. Her loving nature healed Bridget's heavy heart. Bridget prompted Rachel to take a short nap, so Rachel lay down on the rug in front of the fireplace. Bridget took up her embroidery. She was content.

Three days later, Rachel had a chance to slip out and meet Tepho. As she walked toward their meeting place, a large hollow tree near in a clearing, she enjoyed the serenity of the forest. Suddenly, as were all his appearances, Tepho stepped from behind a large tree. "I was hoping you would come today, Onnashu." His familiar voice warmed her.

"I finished my chores early. I wanted to talk to you."

"Is everything all right with you?"

Rachel smiled. "I am fine, but my mother told me about the early days in Plymouth, and now I want to know more about you and your people. Can I ask you some questions?"

"Speak, little one. I will do my best to answer your questions."

"Tell me the philosophy of your people, Tepho. Is it so different from that of our church fathers?"

"I have been told about the beliefs of the colonists. What those people believe is very different from what we believe. But, you are not as they are, Onnashu. You have a gentle spirit. The woodland animals follow you because you are not mean in your heart. You know how to love. It is almost as if you were born into the wrong body."

"I do know there is little love with my people. We are taught of sin and punishment. I am fortunate my mother is not like them. She believes that God is good and loves us. Of course, this is a secret between my mother and me. If my father ever found out, I cannot imagine what he would do."

"Your people are confused. They think they can own the land, and can kill and destroy at their slightest whim. We believe we are caretakers of the land and the animals, and we have great reverence for all the Great Spirit has created."

"I think we are a lot alike, Tepho." He smiled and nodded.

Rachel did indeed feel part of the verdant woodland that Tepho and his people loved so much.

"I fear it is time, Onnashu. You came late so it is time for me to take you back. Your father will be returning for dinner."

Rachel closed her eyes, reluctant to face the truth. She wished she could stay here in the woods. She didn't want to go home. She had lived in fear of her father all of her life. She didn't know from one minute to the next if she would be punished. This left her in a constant state of anxiety. Her mother did her best to protect Rachel, but Bridget was also a victim.

Rachel reluctantly rolled onto her knees and rose, shaking the leaves from her gray gown. "You are right, Tepho," she sighed. "But, it is hard to leave this beautiful spot."

"The next time you can come just leave your feather in our tree, and I will meet you."

Rachel's whole demeanor changed as they slipped back through the woods. The boy always hated to see this transformation. She was his Onnashu of the woods. He knew he would always love his 'fire hair'. Since he first saw Rachel three years ago, his heart had been hers. He now studied every feature, every movement of the girl who strolled beside him. Her skin was smooth and clear, if a little too pale. He admired her gold-flaked eyes, but he especially liked her hair which was the color of autumn leaves.

As they reached their appointed meeting place, Rachel's steps slowed. Finally, she stopped and looked up at Tepho with sad eyes. She never knew when they might see each other again. Tepho took both of her hands in his and gave her a reassuring kiss on the forehead.

"Do not grieve little one. We will be together soon again, and I will have a surprise for you."

"A surprise! Oh, what is it?" Rachel asked.

"It will not be a surprise if I tell you. It will give you something to look forward to until we meet again." With that he kissed her hands and vanished into the trees.

Rachel stood for a moment looking after him, then turned slowly and walked to the back gate near her home. It was seldom guarded, so she quietly slipped in.

⌒◠

Bridget turned from the cooking pot as Rachel entered, greatly relieved that the girl was safely home.

"Rachel, I thought you would not get back in time. Your father is due any minute. Get your apron on and help me set the table."

Rachel donned her apron and started doing as her mother asked, but her spirits were low and her movements slow as she put two trenchers on the table. She and Bridger shared one but Ahab insisted on one of his own.

Bridget, noting her daughter's distraction, moved to her and put her arms around her. "Perhaps I am not being wise to let you go with Tepho. You always seem so sad when you return."

"Oh, no, mama, it is not being with Tepho that makes me sad. It is coming back to a father who wishes I had never been born. What have we done to make him hate us so?"

"He cannot help how he is, sweeting. He is a product of his religious beliefs, and of the hard life he has known here in the colony. I gave up trying to change him years ago. I have learned to have a thick skin. I grieve for you, who have not the years, nor the wisdom to withstand his coldness."

"Would he love me if I were a boy, mama? I heard one of the women at church talking about Ahab Ward being stuck with a woman who could not bear him sons."

"He is fortunate to have a living child. Many of the parents in Plymouth would be overjoyed to have a child as strong and as beautiful as you. You must not feel as if there is anything wrong with you, Rachel. The problem is in your father's blighted spirit."

"Maybe I should try to act more like his church friends." Rachel suggested.

"You and I agreed long ago that living among these people does not mean we have to adhere to their religious beliefs. We must be brave enough to be ourselves. I admit it is hard to say 'ye' all the time, but we must pretend to be like everyone else."

Rachel nodded, satisfied. As Rachel finished setting the table, Bridget watched her daughter's face. Bridget's heart went out to her. If there were only some way to escape this awful place. Thoughts of escape were never far from Bridget's mind. Though it seemed an impossible dream, she had schooled Rachel daily. She was grateful for her father's insistence that she have a good education with a tutor. Meanwhile, she had Rachel near her.

Life was much been better for Bridget since Rachel had been born. Loving and being loved lifted a burden from her soul. When Ahab was not home, she and Rachel would sit and discuss subjects dear to their hearts. Rachel also took advantage of the books Bridget borrowed from Alice Bradford.

Rachel also helped her mother sew clothing for friends and neighbors. A couple of changes Bridget had made to the standard design of the settlers clothing had actually been approved by the Church council, so her dressmaking was in now in much demand.

Collars were now deeper and more pointed. Cuffs were much longer, but still starched to pristine stiffness. The main change was the addition of a short peplum ruffle at the waist which hung over the apron, and a dressier ruff around the collar. Colors like green, blue and rust were also a welcome addition. However, Ahab insisted his wife and daughter wear the same beiges and grays, with no modern fripperies. Somehow designing, even in this small arena, filled a space in her heart that had been left in London.

One week later Bridget's chances for escape began to improve. She had been discussing a better education for the colony children with Alice Bradford, who was her good friend and confidant. Alice had borne the governor two sons and was expecting another child in the fall.

Alice helped Bridget many times during her years in Plymouth. She was, of course, subject to the strict rules of the church and her husband's governorship. Alice was only allowed access to books of high moral character, and she was not above lending one to Bridget when she could. Alice realized how hard Bridget had worked to become one of the community, but being much more open minded than most of the colonists, she saw Bridget's side of her miss-matched marriage.

As the women sewed and talked, Alice took note of the ravages Bridget's marriage had wrought. Where had the beautiful, delicate blond girl in the green velvet dress gone? The weary lackluster woman who sat near her was devoid of animation and her shoulders drooped with worry and unhappiness. It was obvious to Alice that Bridget still did not belong in Plymouth. This was neither her world nor her religion.

Alice, brought up with the harsh demands of her religion, found great solace in its teachings, but, her heart went out to Bridget. She had marveled at Bridget's strength and her ability to remain a kind and giving person. Alice had seen many women destroyed by the hardness of colony life. A number of women had either returned to the continent or sickened and died.

Alice pulled herself back to the present. She poured steaming tea into Bridget's cup and added a drop of honey. Bridget smiled her thanks.

Alice rose from her chair, laid her sewing hoop down, and made a quick survey of the room, checking doors and windows to make sure they were alone.

She returned to her seat and resumed sewing. She spoke in a soft voice, not looking up at Bridget, "Have ye ever thought of leaving Plymouth, Bridget?"

Bridget looked up quickly, pricking her finger on her needle. Had she heard what she thought she had heard? She reached for a napkin from the luncheon tray and wrapped it around her bleeding finger.

Alice looked into Bridget's startled eyes. "It is not impossible, ye know. I could help ye."

"Help me?" Bridget breathed.

"I know this comes as a shock to ye. After all, I am the wife of the governor, but, I am also a woman; a woman not entirely devoid of pity or understanding. I cannot help but compare ye to Dorothy."

"Dorothy?" Bridget questioned.

"Dorothy was the governor's first wife. Ye have probably heard the rumors that she drowned herself. No one knows for sure, of course, but in my heart I feel, although the church denies it, that she probably did."

"But, why would she do such a horrible thing?" Bridget asked.

"Dorothy, from what I have heard, was a city bred girl, used to money and the easy life. She was slight of build and delicate. She fell in love with the wrong man. This life was too much for her and I believe she walked into the ocean on purpose. I would not like that to happen to ye, Bridget."

Bridget was amazed. "Oh, I am much too strong for anything like that, and I have my daughter," Bridget assured.

"Therefore, your hell has no gate. Bridget, I have watched ye for years now and seen ye struggle with our way of life and our beliefs. Your dedication to the community has touched my heart, but under the surface your pain is evident. Are ye really content to live the rest of your life with a husband who dislikes you?"

"Ye know divorce is not possible, Alice. Fate tricked me into this marriage, and I can see no way out. I can bear it, but I do worry about Rachel. I wish I could give her a happier life."

Alice lifted Bridget's chin and looked deep into her eyes. "Listen to me, Bridget. Gertrude and I have discussed this many times, and we know we cannot leave ye and Rachel trapped here. Only those who chose our teachings can find true happiness in our way of life. The Church must be strict in order to make our New World a better place than the old. But, ye do not belong here and there is no reason ye should spend the rest of your life in misery. Ahab is a good Christian man, but too many deaths and too much sorrow have soured him, making him a poor husband and father."

Bridget sighed. "He hates Rachel for not being the son he wanted. Nothing she does can please him. He is constantly punishing her for small infractions, so much so that she does not know *what* to do. It has nearly paralyzed her," Bridget sighed.

"I know, my dear, and no child should be raised in an atmosphere of hatred. Gertrude and I think we have come up with a way to get ye and Rachel away from here. The only problem is what ye would live on when ye leave," Alice frowned. "We thought if we could get the two of ye to Jamestown, perhaps, ye could get a position as a governess. Jamestown is now a big colony and it is not that far away by ship."

Bridget's heart leaped. "But I have money, lots of money. It is being held for me in London by my godparent's barristers. I could somehow get in touch with them, and have them transfer my money to a bank in the New World."

Alice could not hide her surprise. "Ye have money of your own? But, my dear, I do not understand."

'My parents' were minor nobility in England. They died long ago so I guess I would be called 'Lady' in England. My parents depleted their small fortune on a coming-out ball for me just before the plague took them. However, my godparents, the Count and Countess of Knollwood set up a dowry for me, which was due me on my eighteenth birthday. I do not know if they are still alive, but I have kept the papers proving my inheritance."

"Why, my dear, I had no idea! Ye have solved the last piece of the puzzle. I can get a letter smuggled out of the colony and on a ship to England for you. A certain sea captain has managed to get books to me from time to time. He is a good friend and will keep our secret. Keep your chin up for a little while longer, Bridget. We will get ye and Rachel out of here somehow. When we do, I would advise ye to use your title. Although we are far from England, a title is always impressive."

⌒૭

Three months later, Bridget and Gertrude discussed the last minute details for Bridget's and Rachel's escape from Plymouth Plantation.

"I have a little coin that I brought over with me from England," Alice said. I want ye to take it to tide you over until you have the money from your barristers."

"Oh, no, Alice. We could not ask that of ye. I do have a little money in my trunk. Ye and Gertrude have done so much already," Bridget argued.

"You will need all you can take, dear, and I have no need of it. The governor provides well for our family, and since we are learning to deal with the winters, the colony is thriving and there is plenty of food stored for everyone. We have learned our lessons well. There will not be a repeat of the year ye first came when Weston had all of those greedy young men shipped to the colony. They ate up most of our winter stores. They were a bad lot for certain." Alice gave Bridget a hug. "Please take the money my dear, for the girl if not for yourself."

Bridget could not hold back the tears. "Consider it a loan then," Alice urged.

Drying her eyes, Bridget took Alice's hand in hers. "You have been such a good friend to me. I do not know what I would have done without your kindness. There is no way Rachel and I will ever be able to thank you. We will miss you and Gertrude terribly."

Bridget realized that she had dropped the 'ye's', her mouth dropped open, her hands quickly flew up to hide her lips.

"Do not worry about the 'ye's', dear. Gertrude and I both know that ye and Rachel use the 'you' when ye are alone. It is of little importance in the long run. Besides, it will make it easier for ye to fit back into your own world."

Alice then pressed a small purse into Bridget's hand. "Gertrude and I have made an arrangement with my friend, Ship's Master Christopher Johnson, to take you on his ship. He helped the First Comers many times with food and supplies. He will get ye and Rachel to Boston. It has a large seaport and Master Johnson has an office there. Ye can stay at an inn until ye get your funds from London, and then he will take ye both on to Jamestown."

Back at the cabin, Gertrude helped Bridget check her baggage.

"It all seems so unreal. I cannot believe it is actually happening," Bridget sighed.

"Have ye finished redoing the green gown?" Gertrude asked. "Ye will need it when ye reach Jamestown. I have heard they are more fashionable than Plymouth," she grinned.

"It is strange holding the gown in my hands again," Bridget smiled. I had wrapped the dress and my mother's locket in wool treated with herbs, and hid it in my trunk. Fortunately the fabric did not deteriorate, nor did the bugs get it, so it will do. It was still much too large, so I took it in and brought it up to date from that fashion plate you gave me. I am sure I will not disgrace myself."

"I made an outfit for your Rachel from a woolen cape I brought with me on the *Mayflower*. It was a gift from my sister who had not chosen the Puritan way of life. Its red color is not acceptable in Plymouth, but there was enough for a small cloak and hood to keep Rachel warm. But, you must hurry now. Ahab is due back from the hunt by dinner time."

"Oh, Gertrude, thank you so much. Rachel will be thrilled with her new clothes. I will help her get dressed now. What time will we be leaving?"

"I do not know for sure, but ye are both to meet me in front of the storehouse in half an hour," Gertrude said. "By that time I should know the exact time and place."

A half hour later, armed with Gertrude's directions, Bridget and Rachel slipped out of the cabin and through the back gate heading toward the woods. When they reached the reassuring protection of the trees, Rachel pulled away from Bridget.

"What are you doing, child? We cannot tarry now. Ahab may return sooner than expected, and we have to be at the rendezvous in twenty minutes. Bridget checked the old pocket-watch Alice had given her. "We must not miss the man with the horses."

"It won't take a minute, mama, but I must leave a note for Tepho. He won't know where we have gone."

"Rachel, darling, we are going very far away from here. You will never see your friend again. There is no time for notes!" Bridget admonished.

"Tepho can read, so my note will be my goodbye. I won't go another step until I leave my note in our secret tree. It is not far from here. It will only take me a couple of minutes."

Bridget, knowing how much Tepho had meant to Rachel during the past three years, was torn. She finally let go of Rachel's hand, and the smiling girl ran quickly toward her secret tree.

A mile away, Ahab's hunting party was on its way back to the colony with a good store of fresh meat. Ahab, his musket over his shoulder, was leading a horse carrying two deer and three rabbits. He was tired and anxious to get home to hot food. He suddenly became aware of someone moving up beside him. He recognized the man as one of Standish's men; a rat-like character named Jem Hanks. He instinctively pulled away from Hanks, but the man pushed closer, his voice raspy as he whispered. "If ye could use a little information, I would be willing to trade it for some of that venison."

Ahab looked at the man, his distaste obvious. "I doubt any information ye have would be of any interest to me."

"This information will. It has to do with yer daughter," Jem hissed.

"My family is of no concern of yours. Be about your business, man!"

"Ye had better reconsider, Ward. You will be mighty sorry if you don't."

As much as Ahab wanted to ignore the man, his curiosity got the best of him.

"Go on. You have your deer," Ahab grumbled.

Forty minutes later, the hunting party arrived at Plymouth. Ahab unloaded Hanks' deer in the square and headed for his cabin. He breathed freer when he saw a small light in the loft. He knew Bridget was caring for Gertrude's children, but Rachel would be in bed. However, a short search of the cabin revealed that it was empty. His anger grew as he gabbed up his musket and pushed through the back gate and into the woods behind his cabin.

～◯

Back in the woods, Bridget was pacing in a small clearing. Half an hour had slipped by and Rachel had not returned. Bridget was anxious and frightened. She did not dare call out for fear of being heard. Bridget jumped as a masculine hand touched her arm.

"Woman, where have you been? You were supposed to meet us fifty yards back in the forest. "Let's go!"

The burley looking man was dressed in animal skin trousers and dark tunic. He smelled of the woods, and campfires. 'We cannot wait any longer, Mistress." One look into his earnest eyes assured Bridget that he was a man to be trusted.

"My child is not with me," she whispered. "She had to go back for something. I cannot leave without my daughter. We must wait!"

"I'm sorry, Mistress. We go now or not at all. The captain has to cast off in exactly two hours. We will barely make it as it is."

"Then I cannot go! I cannot leave my child behind!" Bridget wailed.

"Look lady, I know how you feel, but is too late to change the plans. You cannot go back looking like that. From what I hear your husband can be violent. Who knows what he might do to you. Come on, lady, let's go! We will worry about your daughter later."

Bridget turned and started toward the edge of the woods. Before she had gone three steps, she felt a heavy object come down on her head for the second time in her life. The dark night became impenetrable.

5

Boston, 1636

Bridget struggled up through a haze of pain to find herself again aboard a ship. She was in a lower bunk in a small, clean cabin. She gingerly touched the top of her head and felt a large bump. It was painful to the touch and her head was throbbing.

She sat up to discover she still wore her green velvet gown, which, although slightly wrinkled, was presentable. She rose and splashed her face with the icy cold water in a bowl on a small wooden table. Avoiding the bump on her head, she smoothed down her hair. Where was she?

Realizing she was hungry, she was about to open the cabin door when someone knocked. She opened the door to see a tall man who looked in his thirties. He wore an immaculate outfit, which looked like that of a seaman. His dark blond hair was slightly receding. His face was attractive, with lines earned by smiling. His eyes were sky blue and boasted a twinkle.

"Mistress Ward! You are up. I hope you are feeling better in spite of your unfortunate accident."

"Accident, sir. I think not!" Now that she was fully awake and alert, the memory of her second abduction flowed back to her. "I was kidnapped and brought aboard your ship. I take it you *are* the master of this ship!"

"Yes, Mistress. Ship's Master Christopher Johnson, at your service. I came to see if you feel well enough to join me at mess. You must be famished," he stated with a shy smile.

"The only thing I want is for you to turn this ship around and take me back to Plymouth!" Bridget demanded, hands on hips.

"Sorry, Ma'am, that would be impossible. I have a deadline to make in Boston. Once I make that deadline, unload my cargo, and load a new one, we will set sail for Jamestown."

"But, my daughter! We must go back for her. She is the whole reason we were running away. I cannot leave her behind. There is no telling what her father might do to her."

"I know how distraught you must be and you have my sympathy, but I also have a business to run. If you will be so kind as to join me for dinner in my cabin we can discuss your daughter's situation," he offered.

"Perhaps you can stop at some port along the way so I can get ship back to Plymouth."

"Mistress Ward, that makes no sense at all. We have you free now. There is no going back. If you did go back it would make things worse for both you and your daughter," he parried.

Realizing the weakness of her stand, Bridget looked into his kindly eyes. Taking a deep breath, she took his proffered arm and they started down the passage toward his cabin. Smiling at him, she said. "Please call me Bridget." He nodded.

The ship's cook had prepared a savory meal, and despite her churning emotions, Bridget enjoyed the food. After dinner she and Johnson talked at length about Rachel's plight. Bridget tried again to convince the master to turn back. She couldn't believe she had been waylaid again with no one to help her.

"All right, you can't turn back, but is there no port where you could let me off?"

"Bridget, that is ridiculous. Think. We have half of your problem solved. You are free, and we will get Rachel free as soon as we can." he said sincerely. "I will continue working with Alice and Gertrude, and I promise to get Rachel away from Plymouth and back with you as soon as possible. In the meantime, you can correspond through Gertrude."

"But, you have your business to run. When will you be able to do all of this?"

"I will fit this in, believe me. And when at sea, I will find other ways to keep you in touch with your daughter. Alice and Gertrude will see to Rachel's welfare."

"I am sorry if I sound ungrateful for all you have done, but I think I had better leave the ship in Boston. It is not that far from Plymouth. I can await Rachel there."

"If you are determined to stay in Boston, I must warn you. The church officials are very suspicious. If your husband traces you there, they would be only too happy to turn you over to him."

"I shall take my chances. When Rachel is with me again we will go on to Jamestown."

"You will need money to live on until then." He handed her a small pouch, but she refused it.

"You are very kind, but I have money to last until I can get in touch with my barristers in London. Alice and Gertrude loaned me a sufficient amount."

Johnson reluctantly returned the pouch to his pocket, and smiled at her. "You are a stubborn woman, Bridget. If you insist on Boston, so be it. I do have an office in Boston Harbor. I do shipping there for the British East India Company. And, I know a woman who runs a small boarding house. If she has room, I know she will take you in, and she knows how to keep her mouth shut," he assured her.

"Is Boston a large port?" Bridget inquired. "I need a local barrister in order to send for my funds in London."

"We can take care of that, too. Now, you need to get some rest. I shall see you to your cabin." He smiled down at her so warmly that Bridget could not keep from returning his smile.

Bridget's first disappointment came when she stepped off the ship in Boston. Contrary to her hopes, Boston was just a larger version of Plymouth. She felt very conspicuous in her green velvet gown, and got many disparaging glances from the citizens. They were dressed like she had in Plymouth. Boston was definitely not going to be her permanent home.

Over lunch in a nearby inn, Johnson gave Bridget a history lesson. John Winthrop had established Boston, and many of the successes of the Plymouth Colony had been instituted in Boston. It had a large harbor which brought the riches of the Old World to the new. In London, King Charles had just been forced to call parliament into session due to a Scottish invasion.

After lunch, Bridget and Johnson took a carriage to his barrister's office not far from the wharf. It was a company that catered to sea captains and shipbuilders and it was highly recommended by Johnson. They were ushered into the office of the manager. He was a portly, cheerful man who wasted no time in reviewing Bridget's information. He assured her there would be no problems with transfer of her money to Boston. He was familiar with her barristers in London and assured her they were highly respected.

Once more ensconced in their hired carriage, Bridget sat quietly, hardly noticing the unimpressive homes they passed.

"I expected you to look a little happier, Bridget. Do you not like Boston?" Johnson asked.

"Well, frankly, sir, I was hoping to get out of Separatist territory. These people seem no different than those of Plymouth," she replied. "The worst is that John Winthrop is here in Boston. I do not trust that man. He is a fanatic when it comes to his religious beliefs."

"I am sorry. I guess I should have warned you when I saw what you were wearing."

"It would have been helpful. Fortunately, I kept the best of my colony clothes as work clothes. They are in my baggage. Hopefully your friend will have a room for me, and I can change into my old clothes.

Like you said, I certainly do not want to be conspicuous in case my husband has people looking for me," she volunteered.

"Good idea. I am pretty sure Mistress. Beggley will be able to put you up."

"We can drop you off at your office, Master Johnson. The driver has your instructions, and I know you are neglecting your duties," Bridget smiled.

"I would feel terribly remiss if I abandoned you at this juncture, Bridget. I will accompany you to Mistress Beggley's."

Bridget started to protest, but Johnson put his large hand over her cold ones and shushed her. "No, no. My job is not finished until you are safely established. And, please, call me Chris."

They then sped away from the harbor district. Mistress Beggley's establishment proved to be a two-story building near the commons. She was a pleasant, slightly overweight lady in her late thirties. She was happy to see Johnson, and after a short meeting; assured both that she did have room for Bridget. After Chris left, Bridget settled into a pleasant room overlooking a small garden at the rear of the house. She dropped, exhausted, onto the small cot and was soon asleep.

When Bridget awoke, the sun was streaming into the room and she could hear birdcalls. She realized she had fallen asleep in her clothing and felt grimy and disheveled. She quickly slipped out of the green velvet dress, her petticoat, and chemise and freshened up by pouring water from a pitcher into a large basin which had been provided. The water was cold, but there was a small bar of scented soap on the dresser so she was able to clean off the grime and perspiration. She wished she could wash her hair, but not in cold water. Later she would ask Mistress Beggley for a basin of hot water.

She carefully folded the green velvet dress and placed it at the bottom of her satchel with a sigh. Perhaps one day soon she and Rachel would be wearing their finery in Jamestown. Then she knelt down by the bed and did something she did not think she would do. She prayed.

"Dear God, Boston is not the answer. I so wanted to get away from these people and their unloving beliefs, but, I am grateful to be away from Plymouth and I know you will bring my child safely back to me soon as you can. I thank you and promise to make the best of what you have provided."

After she had donned her dark blue colony clothing and tied on her cap, she left the room in search of Mistress Beggley. However, at that very moment her hostess came bustling up the hall toward Bridget's room.

"Oh, my dear, ye are awake. I looked in on ye last night with a small dinner, but ye were fast asleep. Ye must have been exhausted. Come, I have a nice breakfast waiting for ye in the kitchen."

Bridget followed eagerly, her stomach rumbling. She could hardly believe she was finally away from Ahab. She felt a lightness she had not felt for years. Her thoughts turned back to Rachel. "I am so sorry I failed you, Rachel. I wish I knew what you were feeling and thinking. I hope you don't hate me for not coming back," Bridget sighed.

Two weeks later, Mistress Beggley came bustling up the hall and knocked on her door with quick, sharp taps.

"Bridget! Bridget, dear, let me in. There is not much time."

Opening the door, Bridget ushered her in. "What is the matter, Mistress Beggley? Are you all right?"

"I am afraid we are in trouble, my dear. Two men came here today asking questions about a young woman who had run away from her husband."

Bridget's heart started thumping. "Oh, Mistress Beggley, you think they are after me?"

"I think I convinced them that the woman staying with me was a much older woman, a widow from London. But, we have to get ye away from here before someone else describes ye to the authorities."

"Why are you helping me, Mistress Beggley?" Bridget asked.

"My life has not been an easy one, and I know how difficult it is for a woman to survive in a man's world. I was sold to a Puritan man, too, and forced to the Separatist way of life. Though I did not love my husband,

I gave him three children. His death from lung fever left me with their support and this house. My boarders' rental payments helped me raise my children. So ye see, my dear, I have survived, but my life is now tied to my home and my children. I have to stay here. But, ye do not."

"But, Mistress Beggley, I need to be here in case my daughter gets away from Plymouth. Besides, I have nowhere to go."

"I know, my dear, but there is no point to your being caught and returned to your husband. I have a place for ye to go, if you will agree to it."

"Where is it?"

"The best place for ye would be a more liberal colony, a place where ye could live the life you were born to. That place would be New Amsterdam."

"New Amsterdam? But I don't know anything about the place."

"I do not know all the facts either, but my older brother lives there. He says the colony was started early in 1624 as New Netherland, and it is a big one. It goes all the way from the Hudson River Valley north to Ft. Orange. I think the man who started it was May or Mey, and he brought about thirty families. About a year later, a fort was built and the settlement of New Amsterdam was constructed at the tip of an island they call Manhattan. This new settlement was under the control of a Dutchman called Willem Vergulst, who took Mey's place as governor. About a year after that, they changed governors again when a man named Peter Minuit arrived with a new group of settlers. Minuit took over control as head of all New Netherland, and from what my brother tells me, Minuit bought the island of Manhattan from the local Indians. He paid about sixty guilders in Dutch money. My brother says he got a very good deal."

"Sounds interesting," Bridget said.

"Oh, my yes, and someday when my children are on their own, I am going there to be with my brother and his family."

"It sounds wonderful, but how on earth can I get there?"

"One of my roomers, a Mr. Hazlett, goes there every month to do business at Fort Amsterdam, and as luck would have it he's due to go again tomorrow morning. I do not know if ye have any money, but I am sure he would not charge ye over much to take ye there in his supply wagon. He sells lumber to the four forts on the island and other prominent builders here in Boston. I have spoken to him and he has agreed to take ye."

"Then New Amsterdam is a thriving colony?" Bridget queried.

"Well, it is fairly new, but the Dutch seem to be progressive people. Now, are you sure you will be all right by yourself?" Mistress Beggley worried.

Bridget assured her mentor that she had money to pay her passage and gratefully agreed to travel with Master Hazlett. She wrote a note to Christopher Johnson telling him she had to leave Boston and was heading for New Amsterdam. She promised to let him know her whereabouts when she was settled. Somehow she knew she could trust Chris to keep the escape lines open for Rachel.

Bridget's second note was to her barristers, telling them to have a substantial letter of credit made out for her and transferred to a responsible barrister in New Amsterdam.

Having taken care of all of her connections in Boston, she bid a fond farewell to Mistress Beggley, giving her a few coins, which Mrs. Beggley was hesitant to accept.

Bridget and Mr. Hazlett were soon bouncing along on a westbound road out of Boston facing an extremely long and tiring trip to New Amsterdam. Although the wagon that carried the large load of lumber was large and strongly built, it became uncomfortable after a day of travel. The road was just a two-wheel path honed out by the passage of many wagons.

They traveled overland south. After three days of riding on a hard wooden seat and sleeping on top of the piles of lumber, Bridget wished that, despite the danger, she could have traveled to New Amsterdam by ship. However, she knew the church authorities kept a close eye on the comings and goings at the port. She was lucky she hadn't been stopped when the captain's ship had landed.

Dozing on her seat in the wagon, Bridget was awakened when the wagon came to an abrupt halt, and Hazlett yelled to someone, "Wake up ye lazy bugger! We got a load to get across the river."

Bridget got down from her seat gingerly and studied the terrain. They were on the bank of a wide river, which Hazlett identified as the Great North River, or as some called it, the Maurice River. Haslett greeted a grubby looking man who rubbed his eyes and pushed back a hank of graying hair. As the man rose slowly from his old wooden rocking chair, Bridget sized up the landing.

There was a small log cabin, a large woodpile, and a rickety wooden dock and a large wooden raft. A yellow hound dog slowly rose from the porch near the man's rocking chair. He shook himself, and then trundled over to Bridget. Bridget, being a lover of dogs, rubbed the hound behind the ears. The morning was chilly, but the sun was shining, and she took a big breath of fresh air. She admired the beauty of the trees and shrubbery, and the sparkling water rushing past.

Bridget and the hound waited inside the small cabin, warmed by a crackling fire in the fireplace, while Hazlett and the ferryman loaded the wagon onto the large raft.

The ferryman, Woody, was kind enough to fix them a small lunch of beans and rice, with a steaming hot cup of tea. He was not one to do special favors for his customers, but this time there was a beautiful young woman to consider. Besides, the hound liked her, and that was good enough for Woody.

The ride across the river, seated on a pile of wood, was an exciting experience for Bridget. What she would find on the shores of Manhattan Island, only the Creator knew.

6

Fourteen-year-old Rachel peered with longing through the window in her loft as a hawk flew lazily toward the woods behind the cabin.

Spring was making its much awaited appearance in Plymouth Plantation. The icy winds were giving way to warmer breezes and the birds reappeared a few at a time. The trees began their yearly budding. How many people had wished they were birds so they could fly free of their earthly bonds? she wondered. There was now a jail in the colony, but she knew no one confined in that jail was more a prisoner than her.

So many new colonists; so many new homes, she sighed. The high fenced wall had long ago been toppled. New storehouses had been built. Everything in the colony had expanded. With each ship that landed the population of Plymouth grew.

Rachel could hardly believe how the colony was thriving. People with every manner of skills added to the population. There were now over two thousand settlers in Plymouth and the Massachusetts's colonies were becoming a pattern for new colonies in the New World.

All of this was happening outside the Ward cabin, while its lone occupant was held captive within. Rachel was allowed to go to church, but at all times eyes watched her every move. Ahab, determined that Bridget would never see her daughter again, had hired men, including Jem Hanks, to watch the cabin. The wharves and any spot where escape might be possible were also watched.

In spite of her virtual imprisonment, Rachel was blossoming into a lovely young lady.

Fortunately, Ahab's stays at home were less frequent, which could not please her more. She had abundant time to herself, and Gertrude saw to it that she was not too lonely. Ahab allowed her to take care of Gertrude's big brood on occasion, and she also cared for Priscilla Alden's growing family. Rachel had an immense love of children, and her greatest joy was being around them, though she feared she would never marry and have children of her own.

Alice Bradford found that Rachel knew how to read, write, and do her sums, so she had asked her to tutor some of the colony children. She did find confidence and a feeling of accomplishment in teaching.

It was two years since her mother had escaped. Rachel missed her terribly. She also missed Tepho who's death lay heavy on her shoulders. That awful night still returned in nightmares.

She had been foolish to go back with the note and feather for Tepho. If only she had listened to her mother. But her thoughts had been centered on her friend. The foliage on their special tree shielded a small hole where they had hidden their messages. She had planned to hide the message and rush back to Rachel, but as she had turned to leave, Tepho himself had appeared.

Rachel had been surprised that he was there so late at night, and asked him why. He told her that the Great Spirit told me something was wrong. She had explained that she was leaving him news that she was leaving Plymouth with her mother. He had been shocked, asking her when she would return. She had sadly admitted, never. He asked where they were going, but Rachel had no answer for that. She realized time was passing and began to fidget. She told him she would miss him, but must hurry.

Suddenly she had heard her father's loud voice. He had screamed at Tepho, calling him a filthy Indian. Rachel had twirled to see her father moving from behind the trees. The expression on his face had been something out of hell. Rachel had yelled at her father telling him that he did not understand; that Tepho was her friend.

Ahab had shouted that he could not trust her for a moment and ordered to her to get away from the Indian. Tepho had tried to calm

Ahab, assuring him that he would never harm Rachel, but Ahab turned from the boy. Having noticed the outfit Rachel was wearing, Ahab had demanded an explanation. She didn't know what to tell him so she remained silent. Ahab then accused her of running away with a savage Indian.

Rachel could not give her father a good explanation. If she let on she was escaping with Bridget, Ahab would catch her mother, and would have every right to beat her severely. Rachel knew she had to stall until her mother could escape. She prayed that Bridget would have the strength to leave without her.

Ahab had grabbed Rachel arm, causing her to let out a scream of pain. Tepho then advanced toward them, righteous anger strangling him. He raged at Ahab to let her go, and had shouted that she would be better off with his people.

Ahab had then put his bearded face close to Rachel's and angrily ordered her to go home to her mother, vowing that that he would take care of the savage. As Ahab pushed his daughter sideways, she had lost her balance and fell. Tepho grabbed Ahab's throat, and they struggled, man against boy. Tepho was in good shape for a sixteen-year-old, but had not the bulk or hardened musculature of his adult opponent.

Ahab hit the boy hard on the jaw, and Tepho had flown through the air, landing hard on the ground, his head hitting a stone. Rachel had pushed herself up and tried to go to her friend, noting blood seeping from his head, but Ahab had angrily pulled her back. He had then lifted the slight girl in his arms and headed quickly for his cabin. Rachel remembered how hard she had struggled to get free to go the Tepho. She had screamed for Ahab not to leave Tepho alone for fear he might die. Ahab just grunted.

Ahab had kicked open the cabin door dropping her hard on the floor. He then ordered her to fix him dinner. His anger against Rachel had not subsided, but he would wait until morning and confront Bridget for failing to keep track of Rachel's movements. After they ate in silence, Ahab found an old hemp rope and tied Rachel's ankles to the bed in the loft. The bile had gathered in his throat when he thought about his daughter and that filthy redskin. He paced the floor for hours awaiting Bridget's return from babysitting at their neighbor's house. He had finally decided she was staying the night. His temper had cooled as he took up his prayer book and found some solace.

All hell broke loose the next day when it was discovered that Bridget was nowhere to be found.

In the years since Bridget had made good her escape, Rachel had never spoken of her mother. She had been made to pay a price which was more than any child deserved. She was brought up strictly by the rules of the Plantation, which meant the rules of the church. Although she was forced to listen to the dire threats and doom and gloom predicted by the minister, she was of stout heart. Her faith in her mother's loving God maintained her. She had learned to escape into herself. Most of her waking thoughts were of her mother. She read the letters that Christopher Johnson smuggled in to Gertrude so many times that she could recite them by heart. Somehow she got through the days one by one.

Of course, Tidbit had helped. The first time Rachel has set eyes on the wriggly little puppy, her heart had been lost. She could hardly believe that anything so tiny could really be alive. Tidbit was a creature of mixed heritage, born to Gertrude's terrier, Spot. She was the smallest of six, the runt of the litter, and Rachel's heart went out to her. She tentatively touched the pup's satiny head.

"Oh, she is so tiny...and so perfect!" she exclaimed.

"That she is," Gertrude smiled. "She is a rare one that pup. She knows already that she is special. Smart as a whip she is; puts her siblings to shame."

"I'd give anything to have a puppy like her," Rachel sighed.

"She is yours...if your Pa will let ye keep her." Gertrude smiled as she picked up the tiny pup and handed it to Rachel. "Of course, she cannot leave her mother for another couple of weeks, but then..."

Rachel's shoulders slumped. "He will not let me have her. I know it."

Gertrude put her arm around Rachel. "Well, ask him anyway... maybe he will."

It had taken over a week for Rachel to get up the nerve to mention the pup, which she had already named Tidbit, to her father. As she had expected, he refused her request.

For once in her life, Rachel did not instantly accept her father's will. She continued extolling the merits of the puppy, explaining that a good watchdog would be a great asset when he was away on his travels. Much to her surprise, Ahab finally agreed to see the pup.

She led her reluctant father to Gertrude's yard and proudly picked up Tidbit, holding the tiny creature in the palms of her hands.

"What is this?" Ahab exploded. "Ye call that mouse a watchdog? Girl, ye are out of your mind!" At this, he turned and headed back to their cabin.

The next day, Rachel had the surprise of her life. She heard her father's heavy step and the door bang open. "I do not have an idea what ye want with this mouse, but here ye are. Ye better take care that it does not get in my way." With that, Ahab pulled his hand from beneath his shirt and deposited the tiny puppy into the hands of his astounded daughter. "Ye have to take her back to the bitch until she is old enough to eat on her own, but she is yours." From that day, Rachel's life took an upward swing. She had what she had not experienced since her mother's escape...love.

Rachel later found out through Gertrude that Ahab had been complaining about the pup at a council meeting. Governor Bradford had placed an aging hand on Ahab's arm, smiled and said, "Why not let the girl have the dog, Ahab. What harm would it do?"

Now that Rachel had something to love, the boredom of her every-day chores, even the whole feeling of life in Plymouth Plantation, changed. Tidbit made everything fun. Gertrude observed the change in Rachel with satisfaction. Gone were the drawn features, the large eyes filled with sadness and loss. In their place was a radiant young woman, whose laughter brought delight to all of her friends.

The tiny dog grew to about the size of a house cat, but she had the strength and energy of a young pony. The two played together. Tidbit even learned a few tricks, which brought proud smiles to the face of her mistress. Her best trick was to stand on her tiny back legs and dance around as Rachel clapped her hands.

Each day was brightened with some touching or funny occurrence. The two were inseparable, held together by the strongest bond in the universe...mutual love.

Ahab ruled that Tidbit must stay outside the cabin in a lean-to Rachel had devised. However, when Ahab was away from home, Rachel would sneak the tiny dog up to her room in the loft, where they would sleep cuddled together. As winter set, in Ahab relented and the loft became their special little world.

Rachel often worried what would happen to Tidbit when she escaped, for escape she would, in time. She prayed that her rescuers would let her take her dog as she could no longer imagine a life without her Tidbit.

One morning, while she was playing with Tidbit, Rachel saw her father's man, Jem Hanks, watching her. She knew Ahab paid Jem to keep an eye on her when he was not around. She had learned to hate this unkempt, foul-mouthed man. Just the thought of his eyes on her made her cringe.

So far Jem had kept his distance, but Rachel could feel that his interest in her was more than that of a guard. This made chills run up and down her spine. She watched him out of the corner of her eye, hoping he would go about this business. Instead, Jem started walking slowly toward her, looking around furtively to see if he was being watched.

Rachel felt her throat tighten with fear as she picked up the dog and backed toward the cabin.

"Nuthin' to be afeared of, Gal. Just checkin' in to see if yer behavin' yerself."

"I am...we are just fine, Master Hanks. We are not going anyplace. You can tell my father all is well," Rachel said bravely.

"Ye have grown into a mighty purty girl, Missy. Guess you must get real lonesome in this old cabin." He smiled, displaying an array of decayed teeth.

"Please go away now!" Rachel grew more frightened by the moment.

Jem just smiled, eyeing Rachel up and down as he pushed open the gate, again checking to see if anyone was around. As he walked slowly toward Rachel, she warned him. "Ye better get out of here. My father is due home any minute, and he would not like ye being here."

"Wrong, Missy. Your Pa's busy with the guvner. He won't be home for an hour or two. Ye better start bein' nice to me. I won't hurt ye none. Just want a little friendly touchin'. That ain't askin' too much now, is it, missy?"

"If you don't go right now, I will start screaming," Rachel warned.

Jem just laughed and moved closer to her. "All the folks around here are at the meetin' at church. It's just you and me, missy," Jem grinned.

His lanky arms reached out for her, and she felt his bony hand gripping her skirt. She tried to scream, but no sound came out.

It was at that moment that Tidbit went into action. The little bundle of fur flew from Rachel's arms and landed on Jem's chest. Tidbit, yipping her loudest, grabbed at Jem's throat.

Rachel screamed in fear for her dog. She lunged forward, reaching for Tidbit, but she was too late. Jem grabbed the pup from his throat and tossed her across the yard, where her small body hit the fence with a frightening thump.

By this time Gertrude, returning early from the meeting, heard the commotion and came running toward the cabin. Jem turned and fled the yard, escaping into the woods behind the cabin. Gertrude followed him a few feet, then came back into the yard and slammed the fence closed. She watched as Rachel moved quickly to Tidbit to help her. The tiny heroin had been too small to survive such a blow.

Ignoring the tears that ran down their cheeks, Gertrude and Rachel buried Tidbit in a beautiful spot near the cabin. They prayed over the little dog with the big heart. In total shock and grief, Rachel made a vow that she would not stay a day longer in Plymouth. She knew that without Tidbit, she could no longer stand her bleak life. She knew she had to go now, with or without anyone's help.

Rachel learned that Ahab had tracked Jem Hanks down and nearly beat the life out of him. He had sworn that if he ever saw Hanks again he would kill him. Jem had skulked away nursing bruises and a broken nose and had not been seen since. Rachel was surprised, but decided her father's actions were meant to impress the Colony. She knew he did not love her or Tidbit. From that moment on, her mind was occupied only with plans for escape. She had finally given up on any of her mother's or Gertrude's plans to get her safely out of the colony. She knew she had to find her own way.

As she lay in her cot in the loft, she determined that the biggest obstacle was finding a way past her father's watchdogs. Escape by ship would have been the easiest, but she had been stopped every time she got close to the docks.

No, her only hope was to find the camp of Massasoit and beg his help. She knew Tepho's people would assist her and protect her. She only hoped they had not blamed her for Tepho's death.

That night she laid awake making plans. She knew she had to make her move before Ahab returned from leading Governor Bradford's expedition to his mining holdings at Buzzards Bay.

The most frightening problem was finding her mother. She had learned that a Master Johnson could be found in a town named Boston. He would know where her mother was.

The next morning, Rachel put her plan into action. Ahab had burned the outfit Gertrude had made for her first escape attempt, so she decided she'd use some of her father's clothes. Rachel found an old pair of Ahab's knee-high trousers which would only need a little shortening. The waist was way too large for her, but with her mother's sewing needle and some wool thread, she managed to take the waist in six inches on both sides. They were still a little loose, so she found an old piece of rope to tie around her waist to hold them up. It didn't matter if the shirt was too large, as it would hide her budding figure. She would wear her own cotton hose and sturdy shoes, and take one of her father's hunting jackets. She was lost in its bulk, but it would keep her warm.

Hiding her long auburn hair was the next problem. Rachel searched through her father's belongings until she found an old knit cap. She tied her hair up in a topknot, and stuffed the cap down over it. She was pleased with the results. All that was left was to tie her few personal belongings into a bundle, along with the type of food which would not soon spoil. This included some hard tack, ham, and a few slices of smoked turkey. She had a small cache of money Bridget had sent her through Alice. She hoped it would keep her until she reached Boston. On a whim, she added a bottle of Ahab's ale to her store.

That evening she ate a good, hot dinner, then relaxed in a chair before the crackling fire. All she had to do now was wait. At three o'clock in the morning, she awoke with a start. Panic gripped her as she realized she had fallen asleep. She had no way to know what time it was other than the moon was still fairly high, and the sky comfortingly dark. Was it too late to leave now? If it got light before she was far enough into the woods, someone might catch her. On the other hand, most everyone should now be asleep. Hopefully this would include her watchdogs.

She decided to take the chance. Dressed in her makeshift outfit, Rachel gathered her bundle, slinging the rope handles over her shoulder. After perusing the area around the cabin, and being sure she was not being watched, she stealthily stepped out of her past on the way to a new and unknown future.

She breathed a sigh of relief as she went further and further into the woods. She would use Tepho's message tree as a starting point. She had been to Massasoit's camp only once, and was not sure she could find it again.

At the tree she stopped, not being able to resist the temptation to check for a message, but found none. The faint hope that Tepho might have survived had found a spot in her heart, but was now sadly laid to rest.

꒰꒱

Now that Rachel was alone in the forest at night, she questioned her decision. In her mind she had been so sure but the reality was frightening. She could still turn back. She could be in the warm comfort of her cabin, cuddled beneath the covers.

But there was her father's wrath in Plymouth, and her mother waiting for her in Boston. No, she would not be a coward. She owed that much to her mother. She now had it within her grasp to make her promise to herself a reality. She decided to keep going. When she got deeper into the woods, where the chances of being apprehended lessened, she bedded down for the night.

Morning was quick in coming. Rachel awoke to the songs of many birds. Leaves rustled in a soft breeze. Her spirit soared. After eating a small snack, she gathered her belongings and set off again. She remembered Tepho's explaining how Indians marked trees to guide them. As he spoke, he had marked the trees on the way to Massasoit's camp to show her how it was done. All she had to do was find those old markings. However, in two years, the underbrush had grown thick, nearly obscuring the old Indian path.

Rachel dug out her hunting knife and cut away the foliage around the larger trees until she found Tepho's faint markings. Her heart beat faster as she experienced the joy of accomplishment. She uncovered subsequent markings along the way and made good progress through the woods.

When the sun was directly overhead, she stopped and ate a few bites of food to renew her strength. It should not be too far now. She was grateful for Tepho's trail guides, and was thankful she had not tried to take this journey in her heavy skirts.

As evening grew closer, she finally reached her destination. She literally flew the last few yards to Massasoit's camp. When she stepped into the open compound she was struck by the absence of movement or sound. Massasoit's people were hard-working, and the camp should be bustling. The silence frightened her. As she walked around the camp, she found only empty shelters, cold fire pits, and a few broken tools.

All Rachel heard was a loud, steady drumming, which she finally realized was the beating of her heart. They were gone, all of them. What was she to do? Exhausted, she finally put her blanket down on the dirt floor in one of the dwellings and dropped off to sleep.

Rachel was rudely awakened as a strong, angry hand tugged her off the floor with a painful jolt. Her sleepy eyes flew open. A tall Indian, with stripes of white paint on his angry face, stood holding her by the arm.

He dragged her out onto the ground. Her mind, sluggish from sleep, couldn't grasp why she was being treated so harshly. Indians had always been kind to her.

Another Indian in similar paint and armed with a bow and arrows, joined them. The two Indians talked back and forth in a strange, guttural language. The second Indian looked very closely at her face. He grinned evilly as he pulled Ahab's woolen cap from Rachel's head, releasing a waterfall of shining auburn curls.

Her fear increased rapidly as she realized her predicament. These were not Massasoit's Indians! She had heard to too many tales of Indian atrocities not to realize that she was fated to either die or become a concubine to one of these savages.

The first Indian let go her arm, threw her to the ground, and retrieved his weapons from the ground. By then Rachel's arm was stinging in pain. When released she lay there holding her aching arm, not daring to move. Screaming would only prompt more violence, and who would hear her out in this wilderness?

A third Indian, who looked about Tepho's age, finished his search of the village, and joined the duo with the helpless girl at their feet. They argued back and forth. Finally the tall Indian prevailed and they prepared to leave the village. They pulled Rachel off the ground, tied her hands together with a rope and dragged her behind them.

A fear such as she had never known chilled her body and numbed her mind. She must find some way to escape. She needed a miracle.

They traveled a long time. Rachel's wrists were raw from the ropes. Her mind was filled with images of what torture and shame might be in store.

When they finally stopped, Rachel was again shoved to the ground where she watched as the younger Indian tied her feet together at the ankles. The tall Indian made a small fire, and pulled something out of his leather pouch that looked like pieces of flat brown wood. He distributed it to his friends, who chewed on the nasty-looking twigs with relish.

The younger Indian caught her looking at him as he ate, and spoke to the tall Indian who grudgingly pushed a piece of this wood toward Rachel. She looked askance at it, but the young Indian nodded for her to eat it. She awkwardly lifted it toward her mouth, but was immediately sickened by the terrible smell. She guessed that it was a form of jerky and she knew would need her strength, so she bit into the stick. To her amazement it was not as bad tasting as she expected. She finished it off quickly, and watched as her three captors settled down for the night. She hoped they would sleep deeply, so she would be able squirm out of the ropes and sneak away.

She knew not where they were headed, but she must be many miles from home by now. She waited a long time, feigning sleep, until she felt it safe to make her attempt. However, the moment she moved, the young Indian awoke and jerked at her ropes, which he had attached to his ankle. Surprised, she yelped at the pain in her ankles. He reached across the fire and sent his fist into her jaw causing an explosion of pain and lights.

Rachel awoke to a bad pain in her jaw and loud screams and the sound of fighting. Her captors' were being attacked. She found her stinging wrists were still tied together. The rope that was tied to her feet was pulled taut, so she moved toward its source only to discover that the rawhide was still attached to the lifeless body of the young Indian.

Rachel felt bile coming up from her stomach as she saw the blood covering the young man's torso. She gathered her courage and pushed his body until the rope pulled free. She sat up, fearfully trying to see what was happening. Silence descended as the battle ended. It was too dark now to see much. Whatever was happening she did not have much hope. She feared that at best, she would only change captors.

Rachel knew she must now move. She had to escape. She pulled herself up painfully, and reached for her cap only to find that it was covered with the young Indian's blood. She dropped it, and pushed herself awkwardly to her feet. The rope around her ankles fell free but the rope on her wrists was still cutting off her blood supply. She would worry about freeing her wrists when she was clear of danger. She grabbed her blanket and pouch with both hands and ran, plunging into the forest. She was breathing heavily when she finally stopped and leaned against the trunk of a large tree. Gasping to catch her breath, she dropped her blanket and small bundle at her feet.

"You are still fleet as the deer, Onnashu! I feared I would not catch up with you."

Warm strong arms closed around her. She thought she was dreaming that she was in the safety of Tepho's arms, and that he was not dead but here to protect her.

"You are not dreaming, little one. Tepho is alive and well."

"Tepho?" she gasped. "Is it really you? I thought my father had killed you."

"No, my little Onnashu, I am very much alive. No white devil could kill a warrior like your Tepho. We must get back camp. It is cold and you have been hurt. I am so sorry, little one. Sorry I let this happen to you." He cut away the remaining ropes.

"But, you did nothing…" Rachel found she could talk no more. She felt such happiness to be safe in her friend's arms that she relaxed against him as he lifted her gently into his arms and took off at a run.

She would have been amazed at the joy he experienced to having her in his arms. Thoughts of her had lived within him day and night. He did not know what fate could hold for a beautiful white girl and a half-breed Indian, but there was enough happiness in his heart to make up for whatever the future might bring. He smiled down at the girl in his arms. "We go to Massasoit's new camp."

As they traveled, Tepho cleared up the mystery of his return from the dead. On the fateful day of Ahab's attack, his friends had missed him when he did not return by nightfall. They went in search of him. They found him unconscious and stopped his bleeding with deerskin rags. Back at their camp, Tepho had quickly healed. He told Rachel that he had returned to their tree for several months after his healing, hoping she would leave a message. He finally gave up, thinking she must have escaped with her mother after all, so he returned to his camp.

A great burden of guilt lifted as Rachel realized that she had not caused her friend's death. "I'm so sorry," she explained. "My father had me watched all the time and…and I thought he had killed you. Thank God you are all right."

In a large clearing, Tepho and Rachel met five of Massasoit's braves. They all set off for the new village. Tepho let his friends go on ahead so he could have more time alone with Rachel. They traveled by day then lay awake for hours after eating a small supper. They shared the stars shining through the trees as they talked about their lives since their parting. They found they still shared the rare gift of mutual caring. Tepho slept the first night huddled close to Rachel. Rachel had never before felt warmth like that of Tepho's strong young body next to hers.

Fortunately, they did not encounter any other hostile Indians. When they reached Tepho's village, Chief Massasoit greeted Rachel warmly, explaining that he had been warned about the encroachment of the Narraganset Indians into his territory. Chief Massasoit had decided to temporarily move his camp to set a trap for the Narraganset.

Rachel now understood why the enemy had been greeted with an empty village when they attacked. The main band of Narraganset warriors had departed, but the three renegades had returned to see if they could find any hidden valuables. Instead, they had found Rachel. Thinking their chief might want her; they had taken Rachel and had set out after the main band of warriors.

Tepho and his warriors had been watching from hiding when Rachel was taken. They had followed the renegades until they set up camp for the night and quickly killed them.

Chief Massasoit and his council discussed what would be best for Rachel. Massasoit knew where Boston was, so Tepho volunteered to take Rachel to her mother. The council agreed, having great trust in Tepho's skills. Rachel was taken by the women and dressed warmly in Indian garments for the trip. Massasoit gave Tepho directions to the place called Boston.

After two nights with the Wampanoag, armed with water, jerky, maize meal, and Rachel's bottle of ale, she and Tepho started their journey to Boston.

The journey was a long one on foot, but the two young people treasured every moment of it. They passed many trees and plants that Rachel had never before seen. She was touched by the beauty around her. She knew in that moment that her mother had been right. The world was a wonderful place, and only a loving God could have designed it.

One night, by a small fire, Tepho told her about his mother. "My mother was white skinned. She was the first child to be born in her small colony. When she was but a babe, she and her parents escaped an Indian attack in their small outpost in Virginia. Her father had been wounded, and he died on the trail north. My grandmother, with my mother in tow, kept running, hungry and frightened, living off the land with berries and whatever small game she could trap.

My grandmother was a very brave woman. As she and my mother traveled, she carved messages on rocks from time to time to let her people know where they were headed, but no one ever came after them. As they went further north, a hunting party of Massasoit's warriors found them and brought them to our old village. My people had not had any contact with white people and were fascinated by my grandmother and my mother. They decided to keep and care for them. My grandmother became very important to the tribe. She taught them English, and showed the women the skills of the white women. Much loved, she died in her sleep when she was very old.

In the meantime, my mother had grown into an attractive young girl. She and my father, Great Mountain, fell in love. My mother died giving him a second son, Rehan. I grew up as one of the people. The whites call me a half-breed. I would never be accepted in your world."

The closer they got to their destination, the more Rachel's heart sank. She secretly wished that this trip with Tepho would never end. He kept her safe, and slept at night with his firm young body at her back to keep her warm. She did not know the name of the feeling she had for Tepho, but she knew that she was happiest in his presence. She would have been shocked to know that her feelings were echoed and magnified in the heart of the young half-breed who was her friend and protector.

As she slipped off to sleep, she missed his soft whisper "I will not let you go, Onnashu. I will find you again."

7

Rachel and Tepho tried to hide their sadness behind brave smiles as they reached the outskirts of Boston. They were forced to face separation. Rachel had known Tepho was special to her, but not until this moment had she realized she loved this young Indian.

"Well, my little Onnashu, this is where it ends. I will now have to live on memories of you...your beauty, your wits, and your gentleness. The Great Spirit blessed me by sending you to me and now I know you go to a better life. But please know that you will always live in my heart."

Then to Rachel's surprise and joy, he lifted her chin and forced her to look into his eyes. She recognized the love that had lain hidden there for so long. Then his mouth moved slowly downward until his firm lips rested on her warm mouth. Tepho gazed into her eyes for a long moment, then turned and walked back into the woods. He did not venture a backward glance.

Alone now, Rachel felt cold and frightened. Boston was unbelievably big. Rachel could not conceive of so many houses...so many people. She was surprised to note that the clothing they wore was similar to that worn in Plymouth Plantation.

As she walked toward what she hoped was the center of the city, her thoughts kept returning to Tepho. She remembered how he had explained that there could be no future for a white girl and an Indian. Society would never allow a marriage between them. Her mother would be heartbroken if her daughter had to live as an Indian, an outcast from society.

Rachel felt a tingling go through her body when she remembered his kiss. She did not know his was a white man's kiss, as Indians did not touch mouths. He had learned the difference when his white mother had kissed him on the lips when he was a baby. Rachel walked on.

Bridget couldn't be happier with her home in New Amsterdam. The locals, nearly all Dutch, were cheerful, friendly and proud of their settlement. She learned from Mr. Hazlett that thirty families had settled permanently in the colony. This group consisted of five patron-ships by the year 1630. In 1628 there had been only one family, the Rensselaerswyck's who settled near Albany, and were totally successful.

The thrill of having money was uplifting. Bridget had written to Alice and Gertrude to assure them she was safe and returned their loans.

Though the settlers' houses were primitive, the people clung to their European lifestyle. The patron-ships were built around a large fort built in 1626 on the lower end of what was named Manhattan Island. The fort had a large windmill which ground grain from the local farms. The grain was brought to the mill by these farmers, or by Indians who carried the grain down the river on canoes.

The Dutch West India Company, backed by the Dutch government, had chartered the colony. The river itself was named after the explorer Henry Hudson, who had sailed into Half Moon Bay in 1609. Bridget was told that the governor was working on importing more families.

Bridget was pleased to note that fashion gained greater importance as more and more wealthy Dutch and Europeans made New Netherlands their home. Thus it was the perfect time for her talents for fashion design to succeed. Since regaining her health and self-confidence, she felt she was starting all over again although she was now a mature woman.

New Amsterdam had the flavor of the Old World, but was very clean and new. Upon her arrival from Boston, she found that her funds had arrived safely. Mr. Hazlet's niece, Martha, had allowed her to stay in her home while she looked for a place of her own.

Then she ran into the problem of property not being sold to a woman. She settled for a little white lie. She told the property owner that her husband, a German Baronet, had sent her ahead to buy a house. She had even written a document to that effect and signed it Baron Edward Wodehouse. The property owner, impressed by the title, finally relented and sold her a small two-story wooden house in the area of Fort Amsterdam. It was backed by the river.

This day was a very special. This afternoon would see Bridget on board Christopher's flagship for a short visit to London.

The trip would make it possible for her put her property in her own name. She had claimed her husband in London was very ill. They didn't know it yet, but the Baron was about to die and leave all his worldly goods to his dear widow. Bridget hated telling so many lies, but her future and Rachel's were at stake.

At age thirty-three, Bridget was lovelier than ever. Her blond hair glowed; her skin was firm and her cheeks rosy. The only lines on her face were small laugh lines at the outer edges of her sparkling blue eyes. Her figure had rounded and her breasts filled out, giving her a pleasing figure.

Bridget had been doing some last minute shopping at the country store and now headed home. She had set up a small millinery shop in the front of her two-story home. Taking advantage of her title, as Alice had suggested, she named her shop Baroness Wodehouse's Fashion Salon. She had begun with millinery only, but since the popular hat styles in New Amsterdam were, in her estimation, not too attractive. She had expanded into gowns of her own design and her business grew daily.

Bridget's gowns were in the height of Dutch fashion, and she had made an elegant wardrobe for herself. She had contacted Madame Adele in London shortly after her money arrived and Madame Adele had kept her informed on the latest London fashions. She saw to it that Bridget was supplied with the most exquisite and expensive patterns and fabrics. She also recommended Bridget's shop to any of her clients who were moving to the New World.

Bridget loved New Amsterdam. Being part of New Netherlands, it was situated between Virginia and New England, and boasted of a large and busy seaport. When she had first arrived, she had enquired at the harbor about Christopher Johnston. She was told that he had a small office and warehouse under the auspices of the Dutch East India Company, in the Port of New Amsterdam

She had left her address with Chris's office clerk, and when he had arrived in port he visited her. Over dinner, he explained his business to her. Shipping in the New World is ruled by a Board of Trade. Chris's shipyard was situated along the coast north of Boston where his company had access to good standing timber for building merchant ships. Most of his business was transporting produce from the Massachusetts fishery. His merchant boats carried dried codfish to ports in Spain and the West Indies. The profits of the Massachusetts fishery went to support the colony, but the shipbuilders and merchant traders also made a good profit. His warehouse in New Amsterdam held other saleable products like firewood, cider and salted beef and pork.

Christopher had kept her apprised of what was happening with Rachel. Several attempts had been made to get Rachel out of Plymouth but so far all had failed.

This morning Bridget was wearing a warm coral wool gown. It had the popular wide collar and gull sleeves. Her overskirt was a deeper shade of coral. Her bonnet was in the Dutch style with a high conical top and a full brim.

Bridget was now accepted in business circles. More and more businesses were being imported from the Old World. There was now a counting house, and a brewery where a fine beer was brewed with barley and wheat. There was even a tavern and a wooden church. There were many religions and many languages in Nieuw Amsterdam, as the Dutch spelled it. There was a grudging religious tolerance in the Colony. Being a woman on her own, she did not have entree into the circles of the better class of women like Vrouw Greta Rensselaerswyck who reigned as the wife of the patroon at Fort Oranije on the South River.

However, she was working on getting into higher circles where she could charge bigger prices for her designs. The title of Baroness gave her some stature and it was her main attraction. Though her success was built on lies, she was doing what she wanted to do and was secure in doing it. Her only sadness was the continuing fact that Rachel was not sharing her freedom and luxury. She had been two long years now without her daughter. She missed her terribly.

Bridget had written a long letter to her old friend Anna Walkins soon after she was settled, and had been corresponding with her ever since. She also kept up her correspondence with the Knollwood's, and wrote regularly to Rachel through Gertrude.

After a shopping trip to purchase ribbon, thread and buttons, Bridget decided to walk the short distance to her house. She slowed as she approached the front door of her home. She was pleased with the displayed in the front window, where a beautiful plum colored day dress was hanging. Several ready-made hats in the Dutch style sat on the floor near it.

She unlocked the door and stepped into the cool interior. Bridget removed her hat and cape, settled her pouch purse on a chair and went to her fabric cabinet. She placed her recent purchases of threads and buttons away in a drawer, and prepared the work that needed to be done before she left on her trip.

She carried a bolt of pink silk to the cutting table. Lady Van Dorn, a recent arrival from Holland, needed a gown for her daughter's coming-out in the spring, and her assistant, Claire Doorn, was going to make the dress. Bridget couldn't help but picture Rachel wearing such a gown.

Bridget was glad that her house backed up to the Hudson River. There was traffic on the river at all hours of the day and night, and

Bridget loved the hustle and bustle. There was a long narrow back yard leading down from the house to a dock and a small cabin which held garden supplies. She worked with a local gardener to plant flowers and shrubs in as colorful array. She wanted to erase forever the memory of her life in Plymouth.

In the rear of her house, there was a kitchen and a small family room. There was also an enclosed veranda. Just behind the dress shop there was a living room. All the rooms, though not spacious, had many small diamond-shaped windows. She was happy that hers and Rachel's rooms on the second floor both faced the garden. Her home pleased her, but, as much as she loved her new life, she found it lonely.

As her business grew, the upkeep of both house and the business had become too much for her so she had hired an assistant for the shop; a Dutch girl named Claire Doorn, a quiet young woman of twenty. She also hired a woman in her early thirties, Letty Brown, a misplaced English woman, to act as housekeeper-maid.

When in town, Christopher would visit and occasionally take her to dinner in one of New Amsterdam's taverns.

She was excited about her upcoming trip to London. Claire entered the shop from kitchen, "Oh, madam, you'll never guess who was in this morning." Unable to contain her enthusiasm, Claire continued before Bridget could speak. "Mevrouw Van Dyke was here! She's absolutely the queen of society in Swanendael. There won't be a lady in the colony that won't want your designs if she likes the work!"

"That's wonderful, Claire. Is she coming back, or do I have an appointment to go to her home? Where exactly is Swanendael?"

"It's on the South River. She left directions and said you should call on her at your earliest convenience. I didn't tell her you were leaving for London today. She said you should bring some sketches and fabric samples."

Hearing a faint tapping on the front door of the shop, Bridget turned. "Oh, that might be Chris." She hurried to open the door.

The tall good-looking man smiling down on her was a very familiar and welcome sight. "Chris!" she smiled.

"Good morning, Mistress Bridget. Thought I'd come by and take you to the docks. The *Goodfellow* is ready for boarding. I take it you are packed and ready. I brought one of my seamen to pick up your baggage."

"I was hoping you'd come. Oh! I can hardly believe I'm really going to see London again."

"There is no doubt about that, my dear. Your stateroom is ready and waiting. The ship departs at two o'clock. I only wish I was sailing with you, but my business takes me to Boston."

"And you're positive I won't miss word about Rachel?" Bridget asked.

"Don't worry. Her escape has been planned for the end of May. You'll be back way before that." Jones eyed Bridget with his usual admiration. "You look positively glowing today, my dear."

"I am. It's going to be so wonderful to see the Knollwood's' again. The Count is advanced in age. I might not get another chance to thank him for giving me this great life. I want to bring back the latest fashion plates so I can get new design ideas. Most important, I have some papers to sign for my barristers."

"Would it be all right for me to go see Mevrouw Van Dyke's to take her order?" Claire asked.

"Oh, I would love that." Turning to Claire, Bridget gave the girl last minute instructions on the upkeep of the shop. "I trust in you Claire. Meet with Mevrouw Van Dyke and take her measurements. Establish what she wants in the way of design and fabric. Tell her it will take two weeks, and you can do the sewing. If she asks about me, tell her I am in London and will be back with lots of exciting fabrics. Do you think you can handle all of that, Claire?"

"Oh, yes, Mistress. Have a wonderful trip and do not worry about anything. I will do a good job for you," Claire vowed.

"I have no doubt of that, Claire. When I get home my daughter will be coming to live with me. You will like her." Bridget tucked her gloved hand over the Christopher's arm, and they headed for his waiting coach.

Bridget's ship had one stop before heading for London. It took her south, back to the place where she had first stepped foot in the New World. She was excited to see how much Jamestown had grown in the interim. As she stood at the ship's rail enjoying her view of the southern colony, Christopher joined her.

"How about my taking you to lunch at the Settler's Inn? I hear the food is very good."

"I guess we have plenty of time. That will be lovely, Chris. I'll get my hat and purse."

Entering the Settler's Inn, Christopher led Bridget to a small table in a secluded corner and waved to the serving girl. He ordered a light lunch of chicken with a mixed green salad, and then sat smiling at her.

"Whatever are you staring at Chris?" she asked. She was flattered because she already knew the answer.

"I'm looking at a very beautiful woman."

"Thank you, kind sir. It always makes a woman feel better to be admired by a good-looking man."

"Touché, Mistress."

A mature woman approached the table with a pitcher of beer. "Oh, here is our hostess." Bridget smiled.

"A little welcoming gift." the woman smiled. Then she stopped and stared at Bridget.

"My God! Bridget?

"I beg your pardon," Bridget replied.

"It's me, Aggie! Don't you remember, on the trip from London?"

Bridget's eyes flew wide open as she recognized her old friend. "Aggie! I can't believe it."

Bridget jumped up and hugged her old friend. Happy tears glittered on their cheeks.

"Whatever are you doing here? You don't live in Jamestown, do you?"

"No, I live up north, but am on my way to London on a business trip."

Aggie pulled away. "Sit down, sit down. Enjoy your lunch, and if you have time before your ship leaves, we can catch up." Chris, who was enjoying his ale, was happy the two friends had found each other. Aggie excused herself and went to make sure that Bridget and Chris's luncheon was top of the line. When Chris finished eating, he attempted to pay the bill but Aggie adamantly refused.

"You are my special guests. I'm going to get my husband to take over for a while so we can visit."

"This is wonderful," Chris smiled. I had no idea you two knew each other. Let's eat, Aggie, and then I'll head back to the ship. Bridget, I'll pick you up in time to embark."

"Oh, thank you, Chris. That will be wonderful."

Aggie smiled at Bridget. "I am so glad to see you with Chris Johnson. He is a wonderful man."

"And he is a wonderful friend," Bridget shared.

"We will go up to my sitting room and catch up. Bridget shared her adventures with Aggie Suddenly Aggie remembered something. She revealed to Bridget that Amanda was living just outside of Jamestown. Bridget was amazed and happy, and promised to visit Amanda on her return from London.

When Chris arrived to take Bridget to the ship, the ladies bade each other a fond farewell. Bridget gave Aggie her address in New Amsterdam, and Aggie promised to keep in touch now that there was a post.

With the good feeling of an old friendship, Bridget set out to meet even older friends in London.

As Rachel continued her search for Bridget, she felt lost and abandoned. She felt no part of the people around her. Her mother would make everything right, but first she had to find her.

She finally found a man who looked approachable. He gave her directions to the Port of Boston where she hoped to find Master Christopher

Johnson. To her surprise and relief, the man had taken her to the port in his wagon. He didn't feel it was safe for her to be wandering around Boston by herself, especially dressed as she was.

She was eyed by passing pedestrians, and she was acutely aware that her Indian garb set her apart. The kind man with the wagon let her off near the wharfs where she was welcomed by the smell of the sea. After several tries she located the correct warehouse. She entered a wooden building that was very large and was full of trade goods. There were several men sitting on stools at high desks.

Rachel gave her name and asked for Christopher Johnson. She was ushered into a small neat office that was warm and cozy with a small wood stove in a corner and two windows. She sat on a chair before the large desk, and pulled out a biscuit from her satchel. She noted the bookshelves behind the desk. She had never seen so many books. Slowly the books dissolved before her as fatigue finally caught up.

Chris rushed into his office, his heart beating wildly. Yes, there she was, Rachel Ward. The girl was slumped in his large, hard-backed chair; her head tilted sideways, the remains of a hard biscuit in her open palm. His heart went out to her as he contemplated all that must have happened during her escape. His relief was apparent on his face.

He took off his heavy wool cloak and draped it over Rachel, careful not to wake her. She was very thin and small half dark circles underlined her eyes. He turned as his clerk entered with the manifest of current cargo and Chris whispered, "You can put that on my desk, Tibbons. Right now, I need you to run over to the inn and bring back a good hot breakfast...eggs, bacon... Wait for it and bring it back here, please." Taking a quick glance at the sleeping girl, Tibbons accepted the coins and set off on his mission.

Rachel awoke slowly, dragged back into consciousness by a wonderful aroma. As she sat up, a tall, blond man with a kind face smiled at her.

"Who are you?" Rachel questioned.

"My name is Christopher Johnson, and we have been waiting for you, Rachel." Rachel smiled hesitantly. Chris pushed a mug into her hand. "Drink it. It's very delicious, and will warm you."

Rachel took the mug and breathed in the rich aroma again. "What is it?" she asked.

"It's called chocolate. I picked up a small supply in Spain. It is very expensive and reserved for the rich. They wouldn't let me import it, but did allow me this small sample which I reserve for very special occasions. Ancient People in the lower Americas, the Olmec, used it in its original form, which is quite bitter. I was told that a warrior named Cortez introduced what they called xocolati to Spain. The Spanish added sugar and a flavoring called vanilla. It is really special. Try it." Chris pressed.

Rachel sipped the hot brew and found it sweet and delicious. As she quickly finished off the chocolate, Chris placed a small table covered with delicious dishes in front of her. She did not need any urging to dig into this feast. She ignored the growls of approval coming from her stomach.

Chris watched as she ate. He wished there were some way to notify Bridget. He had sent a letter to her in London when Gertrude had told him the girl went missing, and he knew she would be worried sick. He would send a short note to Gertrude in Plymouth letting her know that Rachel was with him.

In the meantime, he had to get Rachel installed somewhere, and get her some decent garments. He decided to take her to the nearest inn and establish her there.

Chris bundled Rachel up in a warm blanket, and established her in his personal carriage. While they were seated in his carriage, Rachel quickly outlined her flight from Plymouth, telling him about Tepho and his assistance, but leaving out the personal connection. He marveled at her courage and determination. She was much like her mother.

"But, where is my mother?" Rachel inquired. I thought she would be here."

"Unfortunately, your mother does not live in Boston. She has a home and dress shop in New Amsterdam. She had to go to London on business. It is lucky I was here when you arrived. We had been planning your rescue for May."

"My rescue?" Rachel gasped.

"Yes, my dear. We finally figured out a way to get you safely out of Plymouth, but you found your own way out. I appreciate your telling me about your adventure." Chris smiled. "However, when you disappeared from Plymouth, I sent a letter to your mother on one of my ships. It takes a long time to get a letter to England, but I'm sure when she received it she took the first ship available to return. We never dreamed that you would make it to Boston on your own. We owe a debt to your friend Tepho. But for now, let's get you settled.

Chris installed Rachel in a small, clean room at the nearest inn. Rachel slept for two days. Chris inquired after her many times, and finally asked the innkeeper to send him notice when Rachel came downstairs.

So it was that when Rachel did descend the stairs, Chris was there to greet her. He had ordered a sumptuous breakfast. Now very hungry, she enjoyed the breakfast, and when she was filled, tried to hide a small burp. Chris brought her up to date on mother's adventures and her shop in New Amsterdam. Rachel took it all in with wide eyes. She realized how much her mother must have changed, and it disturbed her.

Chris provided Rachel with some spending money, so she could purchase fabric to make herself a new outfit for her stay in Boston.

"I shouldn't be taking money from you, sir." You have done enough for me already," Rachel said.

"Don't worry about that, my dear. Your mother has provided me with plenty of money for your search and rescue. Anything you need just let me know."

So, Rachel settled down to wait.

The innkeeper's wife went shopping with Rachel. They chose some soft blue wool to make a dress, and some unbleached muslin for underpants, chemise, bodice, petticoats, a coif and an apron. Rachel also purchased several books.

Time hung heavy. Rachel thought about her mother, but mostly about her lost love, Tepho. She remembered so many things about him, and sorely missed him. No matter how busy she kept her mind, his handsome face kept appearing before her eyes. She couldn't help but wonder why she seemed fated to lose everyone she loved; first tiny Tidbit, then Tepho, and now her mother. These losses left her with a heavy heart.

By the end of the second week, with no news of her mother, time was weighing heavy. She was tired of reading. She was regaining her energy and zest for life and nothing seemed to fill the lonely hours. She was used to hard work and did believe the Puritan claim that idle hands spawned an idle mind. She finally hired a carriage to take her to the docks to see if Chris had any information on Bridget's ship. When she arrived at his office, he leaped up and greeted her with a warm hug.

"This cannot be the same waif I found sleeping in my chair two weeks ago." He held her away and took a good look at her. In his eyes, she was lovely beyond compare. She needed to put on a few pounds, but her cheeks were rosy, and her auburn hair shinning with gold highlights. Her smile was sparkling, showing off full pink lips and straight white teeth.

"Come, you look so lovely in that new dress, that I am taking you to lunch at Harvest House to show you off. We have much to discuss."

As an excellent lunch of salmon filet, fluffy rice and sliced tomatoes in vinaigrette filled her stomach, Rachel broached the subject most on her mind... Bridget's return.

"We are hoping Bridget made the *Good Fortune*, which is due in Boston in three weeks. I'll come for you when the ship docks and we can greet her together. I cannot wait to see her face when she sees you."

"But, what am I to do in the meantime?" she complained. I don't want to sound ungrateful, but I'm not used to being idle and frankly I'm going a little crazy sitting around the inn."

"How would you like to fill the time?" he asked.

"I would like to find some work somewhere."

"But you are only fourteen."

"I have worked hard all my life. I am very dependable." she defended.

"But, your mother would not like it. When she returns, she will want to take you home to New Amsterdam.

Rachel took her stand. "Until she is back I need to keep busy. It is what I want."

"Doing what?" he sighed, relenting.

"I enjoy children and I'm good with them. I have tutored children in Plymouth and could be of some help to a mother who might be overworked."

Chris looked at the young girl in a different light. "You would really be willing to work in someone's home...you mean, like a governess?"

"No, as a tutor. Mother gave me a good education and I love teaching. It would be just until mother returns." The lift of her chin and the firm mouth told Chris she was indeed serious.

As he looked at Rachel in her new outfit he noted how different she was from Bridget.

Her mother's blond, blue eyed beauty contrasted with Rachel's dark and quiet dignity. Rachel had a surprising serenity that belied her harsh upbringing, though he also noted a touch of melancholy. He took a deep breath and searched his mind.

"I do know one woman who could use some help. She teaches things of the soul, and she has a large brood to tend. She may be able to use a temporary tutor. I will get in touch with her."

Rachel smiled her gratitude. "Oh, would you? Thank you so much. I will be forever grateful."

"I will call on her tomorrow. Oh, by the way, her name is Anne Hutchinson."

Rachel was looking forward to her upcoming interview with Ann Hutchinson. She had washed and pressed her blue outfit with a flatiron she borrowed from the innkeeper. She had heated it in the public fireplace and laid out her new dress on a bench. She had also ironed her bonnet and apron. She was satisfied that she looked like a tutor. She tucked her hair under her coif, and adjusted her skirt and matching bodice.

At exactly eight forty-five in the morning Rachel set off to her interview, feeling a mixture of excitement and trepidation. At nine o'clock she rapped on Mistress Hutchinson's front door. As she waited she took stock of the brownstone house. It had two stories, with six gabled windows in the upper stories. The brass knocker she used was worn from much usage.

Just as she was about to knock again, a girl of five or six opened the door. "Ye must be the teacher lady," she beamed. "Come in, Mistress. I'm Anna. Come right this way, Mistress." The young girl darted before her, leading her into a large library. The walls were lined with books of all descriptions. Rachel hoped she would be able to use this wonderful library if she was given the position.

The room was intriguing. It seemed to be set up for meetings, having three rows of hard-backed mahogany chairs set up in front of a huge desk of the same wood.

Rachel turned her attention to the little girl who was staring at her intensely. Anna smiled, and Rachel was impressed with the beauty of her smile which remained even when she spoke. Her eyes were large and dark brown and they sparkled with good humor.

Anna indicated an overstuffed chair near the desk, and Rachel sank into it.

"My mother will be here in just a minute. She's with one of her church people."

"Oh, is your mother a minister?" Rachel asked

"No. She can't be a minister cause she's not a man. She's just interested in God." With a nod Anna turned and left the room in search of her mother.

Rachel was tempted to leave, fearing her new employer would turn out to be another stern religious taskmaster like her father. Just then little Anna stuck her face around the doorjamb with a wide grin. "She'll be right here, mistress."

As the child again disappeared, Rachel decided to stay.

A few minutes later, as she was inspecting a bookcase, she heard a warm, deep voice. "Ye must be Christopher Johnson's friend...Rachel, isn't it?"

Rachel turned to see the most imposing woman she had ever met. Though small in stature, there was a quality of strength and power that seemed to flow from her. She was not a beautiful woman, being sturdily built and plain of face. It seemed like there was a light coming from her face, a light that reached out and touched one and made everything seem better. Rachel was surprised to see that Mistress Hutchinson was in the family way.

The woman continued. "Christopher tells me ye have had a rough time of it. It is not easy being a woman in a man's world, but we are winners, are we not, Rachel?"

Hearing these few words spoken from the heart, Rachel relaxed. As they continued to talk, Rachel fell more and more under the spell of Anne Hutchinson. Little did she know just how much this woman would come to mean to her.

Anne did ask one question. "Some of my children are older than you, Rachel. Is that all right with you?" Rachel smiled and nodded. "I may be young, but you can trust me to start your children on a good education."

"I have taught them the basics. I am sure you have lots more to offer." Anne said.

The rest of the interview went well. By the time Rachel left the Hutchinson home she felt wanted and needed. However, she was very curious to know more about Anne Hutchinson.

That evening when she talked to Christopher, he admitted that Hutchinson's bold spirit and her ready wit had made her stand-out in the community. Chris laughed. "I'm afraid you will find out just how unconventional her teachings are, but I trust you have a mind and opinions of your own."

⌒◦

Rachel sat at a round wooden table in the small room she shared with little Anna, who was sitting on her bed dressing her rag doll.

Feeling she was being watched, Rachel turned her attention to Anna. Rachel smiled, and was gifted with bright smile in return. "Ye are pretty," Anna offered.

"Well, thank ye little one. And so are ye," Rachel returned.

By the following week Rachel had become fairly well acquainted with all of the children. Each maintained a personality of his or her own. With such a large family, life at the Hutchinson home was hectic, to say the least.

The Hutchinson's had brought eight of their children with them from Alford in England on the *Griffin*. Faith, Bridget and Mary and the first William had died as infants. Susanna, age sixteen and Elizabeth, age eight, both died of illness in the same month in 1630.

Edward and Richard were adults and did not live at home. Edward, age twenty-five was married to a woman named Sarah, and he worked with a minister named Joseph Cotton.

The younger children ranged in age from five to eighteen. The youngest girl was little Susanna, Anna to the family, who had greeted

Rachel on her first day. Anna was five and everyone's favorite, though they all tried not to let it show. Anna was a merry soul, always asking questions and eager to try out new things. She was mature for her age and her small round face expressed her intelligence. Anna's hair was auburn, and she preferred to wear her hair in long braids, which she tied with pieces of bright colored woolen yarn.

Zuriel was the baby at age two, and he was a quiet little boy. He had dark brown, unruly hair, which he didn't like anyone to touch. He liked to play with a set of blocks his father had carved for him, and preferred playing alone.

Katherine was eight. She resembled her brother, but unlike Zuriel, she liked playing with the other children. She was not happy unless she was making believe with her doll, and playing house with her sisters. Her hair was also dark brown, and she wore it properly tied up under a bonnet. Rachel found that Katherine learned best when the lesson was explained in fairy tale parables.

William was six. He was called William Two because he was named after his older brother who had died at age fifteen. William, called Willy, was tall for his age, husky in build, and enjoyed doing outdoor chores. His hair was dark like Anne's and he had hazel eyes. William had a great love for music. He hummed to himself most of the time, and received many dirty looks from his siblings when they were trying to concentrate on their lessons.

Samuel was ten, and the rowdy one. When lesson-time came, it was always Katherine's job to round him up from some wild game and drag him, complaining loudly, into the classroom that was set up in Anne's meeting room. Samuel had his father's light hair, which insisted on curling around his face. He found this too feminine and embarrassing. He resembled his father, William, in everything but his eyes, which were a light shade of blue, like Anne's.

Francis, who did not study with the other children but sometimes sat in on history lessons, was eighteen. He was tall and built strongly because he did most of the heavy work around the house. He had a serious demeanor, but when he did smile it lit up the room. His wavy hair was the color of wheat. His rather long face was saved by the strong jaw that supported it. His eyes were a darker blue than Anne's, his nose long and straight.

Most of Rachel's time was spent with the children, but she did find herself around Anne occasionally and she admired this kind, giving woman. Anne never stopped. She worked around the house in the mornings, and spent time with her children every afternoon, sharing what they had learned during their classes with Rachel. She held meetings most evenings.

Many a time Anne, heavy with child, was called away to act as midwife to women in the Massachusetts Bay Colony. She never refused her help and was much loved by the women she nursed and also by those who regularly attended her classes. Through Anne's teachings, women who had been relegated to house servants began to recognize their humanity.

One evening a woman stayed after a meeting. She was also with child and was distraught because she already had five children to care for and educate. Anne took her into the parlor, and sat with her on a settee in front of the fireplace. The woman thanked Anne for allowing her the time, but she could not contain her emotions. As her thin body slumped, tears started flowing. Anne called Rachel to bring in some hot tea, and when she brought in the tray, Rachel had quietly slipped into a chair in a dark corner in case Anne should need anything else.

Anne poured two cups of steaming tea while she waited for the woman to calm down.

"My dear, my dear," Anne murmured. "Please do not cry. There must be something we can do. Here, hot tea is always comforting."

Refusing the tea, the woman who was named Helen Glass cried, "No! No. I have sinned. I am so ashamed. I asked God not to give me this child. I had no right to ask God to keep a soul from being born. I shall never be forgiven."

"I do not believe that at all, Helen," said Anne.

"The church teaches us that all life is sacred. I have broken His law by being so weak. It is just so hard. I feel I am not strong enough to care for so many children properly. But, I had no right to ask God to withhold his blessing of another child," Helen sobbed.

Anne moved closer to Helen and put her arm around her. "My dear, remember what we have learned in our classes. Our teaching abhors the condemnation of the church on matters in which they should have no say. We know that God is a loving father, and surely a loving father would not condemn ye for turning away from such a heavy burden."

Helen Glass brushed tears from her cheeks, and sniffled. "Lord knows I am trying to be the best mother I can, but I get so tired. I think sometimes that I am going to collapse, but I have to keep going. My husband is never home, so I *have* to see to the children."

"I know, my dear. I am blessed to have Rachel Ward to help me. I know ye cannot afford help, but we must ask ourselves if God would give us more than we can handle. Sometimes we are stronger than we think. We know that God would not condemn ye for what ye asked, but the church does, and we have to live under their commandments."

"But," Helen sniffed, "if they even suspected I had asked such a thing of God, I would be excommunicated."

Anne smiled. "Then we must thank God for not letting them know. This goes no further than this room. Most important, we must remember our own Covenant of Grace. Because God loves us so much, he gives us His forgiveness in the form of grace. He loves us and wants us to be happy."

"I guess my faith waivers a little. Grace is so new to me. I do not know if I really understand it."

"My dear, Grace is easy to understand. It is the way God shows us his love. It is the strength, the armor, and the peace of God. Grace is everywhere present. Every breath we take is filled with grace. Everything we touch is filled with grace; everything we smell is fragrant with grace. It is wise to seek a deeper understanding of grace. Each person will understand grace a little differently than the next and this is good. The Father's grace is unique to each person," Anne explained.

"So, what am I to do? How can I handle this burden?" Helen asked, feeling calmer. She picked up her teacup and took a sip.

"With God, there is always a way. The thought that comes to me right now is that your oldest girl, Emma, should come and take classes with Rachel for a while. Rachel can show her what and how to teach the young children, and this will lift part of the burden from your shoulders," Anne suggested.

It seemed like a light had come on in Helen's face. For the first time, she smiled. Her shoulders straightened as hope replaced despair. "Oh, could she really do that? That would be so wonderful. God *is* good!"

Helen grabbed Anne's hand, and gave it a squeeze. "I'm so sorry I lost faith. I'll be fine now. I know that with Emma's help, I will be able to take care of my children who I love with all my heart. Oh, Mistress Hutchinson, how can I ever thank ye?"

"Seeing ye smile again is all the thanks I need," Anne assured. "I will get Francis to take ye home."

In the weeks that followed, Rachel saw little of Anne. It seemed that there were legal problems of some kind, regarding her religious teachings. The children were good pupils and quite well behaved. The older children were supportive of the younger.

Rachel wondered at times, why she had been hired. Her main job, it seemed, was keeping the little ones company while their mother was away from the house or having her weekly church meetings. Rachel taught the younger children their rudimentary lessons in reading, writing and arithmetic, and occasionally assisted the older children in their lessons, but she felt she was not doing enough.

Helen Glass's daughter, Emma, did come and join in the classes as often as she could and said her mother seemed much calmer and happier.

Rachel attempted to assist the older children in house cleaning chores, but Anne had objected. Anne was concerned that her young ones have chores and keep busy looking after each other so they would not feel neglected or unloved. Both Hutchinson parents were very loving and attentive.

The house itself was roomy. The Hutchinson's had been granted ten acres in the best area of Boston. Their two-story house was located at the corners of Sentry Street and High Street. The house had a large brick chimney which opened on to several rooms. The library, where Anne held her meetings, was spacious. There were several bedrooms which were shared by more than one child.

Rachel didn't see much of Anne's husband, William, as he had his business to run. Mr. Hutchinson, who was in textiles, had built a lean-to on the ground floor where he kept his textiles and conducted business. He did spend a half-hour every evening with his brood, and Rachel, feeling this time should be for him and the children, went early to her room and read.

As Anne's problems with the church escalated, Rachel became more and more curious as to the reason for Anne's trouble. Some of the mystery was solved when Rachel had finally found a few minutes with Anne's husband.

"So ye are curious about our Anne. Well, my dear, that is understandable. My wife is a very interesting person."

"I feel so bad that she is in trouble with the Church. She is such a good woman. It does not make sense to me," Rachel said.

William sat in a carved wooden rocking chair, and motioned for Rachel to sit across from him.

"Well, my child, it is a long story, but I think ye deserve to know it. Anne's story starts with her parents. Back in England, Anne's father, Francis Marbury, was an Anglican minister. The Anglican Church had its birth when Henry the Eighth was on the throne. Henry broke away from the Catholic Church in order to justify his many divorces and marriages. In 1571, Anne's father, Francis, was teaching in a church in Northampton. He had been arrested and sent to jail for his opposition to political appointments to the pulpit. When Francis was released, he courted and married Anne's mother, Bridget Dryden, and they settled in Alford."

"Oh, my mother's name is Bridget," Rachel interjected. William continued.

"Francis taught and preached at St. Wilfred's. When his quarrels with the Anglican leaders resumed, Francis was forbidden to teach. Francis wrote down the story of his trials with the Anglican hierarchy and published it. Anne, then a child, learned to read by following her father's adventures in his book."

"I'm afraid I don't know much about the church's teachings. I merely attended church on Sunday's in Plymouth," Rachel sighed.

"Well, Anne's mother, Bridget, ran a busy household, giving birth to more than thirteen children. She was a skilled midwife and assisted other women in the community with birthing their young. As my Anne grew up, she went with her mother on these missions and learned the skill of midwifery."

He fell silent for a moment.

"I hear she is a wonderful midwife." Rachel offered. He nodded and continued.

"Anne's father finally moved the family to London, where he experienced several satisfactory appointments. He died in 1611 leaving a will with a strange demand. He stipulated that his female children must stay with their mother until they were married.

"My Anne was a little past marriageable age, but she finally accepted my proposal. I made my living as a textile merchant in the town of Alford, so I took my bride back there where we lived for the next twenty-two years. During those years my wife also gave birth to thirteen children, eleven of whom blessedly survived childhood."

He breathed a deep sigh. "Anne, while on her trips to the market, had many opportunities to listen to a new young minister called John Cotton. This young minister believed that the Anglican Church was in error when it taught that people should only be judged by how well they followed the rules of the Anglican Church. Cotton believed and preached that people should not be judged on their actions. Their faith in God was what counted. He called this teaching the 'Covenant of Grace'."

"Oh, I have heard her mention the Covenant of Grace," Rachel said. Hutchinson smiled.

"My Anne believed in his teachings and did her best to spread them. She felt that people should answer to their own inner conscience and not to the church."

"And do ye also believe what John Cotton preached?" Rachel asked.

"Oh, yes indeed, Rachel. We both strayed from the Anglican teachings. It was not long before Anne and I were taking short trips to listen to John Cotton. My younger sister met and married another young minister, John Wheelwright, who also sided with John Cotton. Not long after my sister married, John Cotton took ship to the New World on the *Griffin*. One year later, in 1634, my family and I followed in his wake, also on the *Griffin*."

"Ye wanted to be near John Cotton and his preaching?" Rachel enquired.

"Yes. We hoped for a new start and a new understanding of God's will in this country. But trouble started again even before our ship docked in Boston."

"Why could ye not believe what ye wanted to believe? Why should the Anglican Church be so upset?"

"Ye will see as I continue my story." Hutchinson answered. Rachel smiled, her eyes glowing with interest.

"On the *Griffin*, we traveled with a minister called Symmes, who was prone to give four or five hour sermons on the evils of not obeying church rules. Anne loudly protested, and swore she would prove Symmes wrong when we reached the New World.

"So, did she do what she threatened?" Rachel asked.

"Unfortunately, she did not have the chance. You see, Symmes got back at Anne shortly after we settled in the Massachusetts Bay Colony. All residents of the Colony had to be members of the Anglican Church and had to go through an examination by the clergy to join. I had no trouble becoming a member, but Anne was forced to wait a week, and then go through another examination by the Governor. This was only the start of Anne's troubles with the church. From that point on Anne has been forced to live her life on the defensive."

"It is hard to understand that they were mad at her because she did not believe what they wanted her to believe. But, I guess it was like that in Plymouth, too. That's why my mother left." Rachel explained.

"Well then, young lady, ye should understand what my dear wife has had to put up with."

"But, what is it that Mistress Hutchinson believes that angers the church leaders so?"

"Since ye are so interested, Rachel, just come to Anne's meeting tomorrow evening and judge for yourself."

"Do ye really think it would be all right? All those people are so much older than me and so important looking."

"Do not worry, Rachel, ye can just slip in the back of the room where it is a little darker."

Rachel finally agreed and went up to her bed that night wondering what great things she might learn at Anne's meeting.

Bridget's visit to London was rewarding. She was surprised to see how little change there was in the sprawling old city. First, she visited her old friends and benefactors, the Count and Countess of Knollwood, only to find that Count Knollwood had died the month before of lung fever at age sixty five. Bridget was saddened, but glad that she could spend some quality time with the countess. She told the amazed old woman of her abduction, journey across the sea and of her life in Plymouth Plantation. Countess Knollwood could hardly believe that anyone could survive such primitive conditions.

"You were very brave, my dear. I'm sure I would never have survived, and having to leave your child behind when you escaped...Oh my!"

"My friends in Plymouth are helping me. I will get Rachel back, never fear. They have a plan to get her out this coming May."

"I am so happy you escaped that awful life. My husband would have been, too. We both loved and missed you very much, you know. It was horrible not knowing what happened to you. You were as dear to us as our own child would have been."

They had parted with Bridget's promise to return soon. During the two months that Bridget was in London, she visited the old woman often, and came to know her better. She also visited with her old friend, Anna Walkins in her old home town. She was now Anna Heybridge, and was happily married to the Lord Mayor. She was also the proud mother of a girl and boy.

In London, King Charles was sparring with a man named Cromwell. Both men had obviously forgotten the Magna Charta. Bridget had a bad feeling about this controversy but was glad she did not have to be involved in English politics.

Bridget's mornings were spent making the rounds of fabric houses and shopping for feathers, laces, ribbons, etc. with Madame Adele. They went over the latest designs from Paris, and modified some of them to fit into the Dutch mode of Bridget's world of fashion in New Amsterdam.

Bridget had steeled herself to walk the route she had taken that fateful evening when she was waylaid. The old fear that had caused so many nightmares seemed to close in around her as she stopped on the actual spot. At first, it seemed like her heart stopped beating, and then she experienced a great anger rising up inside of her.

She took a couple of deep breaths. Suddenly she felt as if a load had been lifted from her shoulders. She heaved a deep sigh, finally letting go of the pain. She knew that the past was finally where it belonged. With a new lightness in her step, she lifted her chin and walked quickly down the street.

She hailed a carriage and headed back for Petticoat Lane and the Hoop and Grape Inn, which she had chosen for its quaintness. It was a grand old house squeezed between two other buildings on the narrow street. It had four chimneys and a cupola. The interior sported a fire-place big enough to roast an elephant. Beyond the main room, people dined on succulent roasted meats, small red potatoes, and a variety of fresh vegetables, in a pleasant atmosphere. In this room one would discover a strange and rather crazy staircase, winding upward to the rooms.

The day Bridget received Chris's first letter, she had been lunching with Madame Adele. At the news that Rachel had disappeared from Plymouth Plantation, with no clue to her whereabouts, she immediately arranged passage on the fastest ship she could find. With bags in hand and an anxious heart, she sailed for Boston. Chris's second letter got to London a week after Bridget had left.

⌒◯

Rachel quietly entered Anne's meeting room. Most of the benches were filled with people still entering. Rachel slipped onto a bench farthest back against the wall and examined her surroundings.

A few people conversed quietly; most sat in contemplation awaiting Anne's entrance. Rachel counted seventy-five people, mostly women.

There was an audible sigh as Anne entered and took her place in a large chair at the front of the room. She was large with child now in her fifth month. She found breathing difficult at had to pause often. Her audience seemed intent upon hearing her message, as was Rachel. A hush fell on the room as Anne began to speak.

"Exactly what is the Covenant of Grace? Why do we feel this covenant is important enough to stand up and fight for?"

The room was silent except for some shuffling. Finally one man raised his hand. He appeared to Rachel to be in his early twenties. He wore a small goatee.

"We must always stand for the truth from God?" he offered.

"Thank you, Henry. As we know, the Calvinists fight to deny us the truth but truth is the bulwark of any faith. Some of us have been together for almost two years. Again and again they try to break up our meetings and challenge my right to meet with you. Why is this?" She stopped and looked around the room. "It is because a few clear minded ministers have discovered the real truth. We call it The Covenant of Grace."

"The Church fathers believe that only *they* have the right to teach, and can punish us if we break the rules written in the bible. We believe that there is an inner connection between our Father God and each person, and that the truth can be and is revealed to us personally by God, if we keep the faith. The Church feels it has the power to set rules for us, and punish us if we break those rules. I do not feel God gives that kind of power to any man or organization. God, and not the Church, allows us to decide wrong or right from the center of our own hearts. We are responsible for our actions. The covenant says that the Holy Spirit dwells in a justified person."

Henry Vane, who had spoken previously, was an ardent believer in Anne's covenant. However, he knew that Anne had attracted too many enemies in the Church, including Reverend John Wilson and now Governor John Winthrop. These two men fanatically opposed Anne's meetings and her following. Joseph Cotton, who had originated the Covenant of Grace, had recanted and turned against Anne, though she had been a faithful follower of his teachings. Because of this, Henry Vane feared they would expel Anne from the city as they had Roger Williams.

Vane, who had been the elected Governor of the Massachusetts Bay Colony for a year, knew that Anne's gender was the real reason for the hatred aimed at her. No woman should be leading discussions on religion. The story of Adam and Eve was of major importance to the church. They believed that women were tainted by original sin and were more susceptible to Satan and urged men to be wary of the seductive power of a woman.

Anne continued. "The Church has censured me, questioned me, spied on me, all to make me give up my absolute belief that the light within is our guide. Our trust is in God!"

Rachel was amazed that Anne had the strength and faith to stand up to the Church. Something in her heart sang. This type of love was what her mother had taught her.

Anne concluded with, "I tell you now; I will fight until the end of my life to be able to use the mind God gave me."

The audience stood up and applauded. The meeting broke up with both men and women assuring Anne that they stood with her.

That night Rachel had much to think about. Although she did not quite understand what Anne was fighting for, she knew what it felt like to be falsely accused; to be punished despite your appeals. But, she did fear for Anne. Rachel knew the power of the Puritan Church. How could one woman hold out against so many 'righteous' men?

Bridget's ship finally anchored in Boston harbor after having encountered bad weather.

Bridget was a bundle of nerves. She knew that worrying never does any good, but she was so frightened for Rachel. She had to know what Chris had found out. When she spied his tall figure and friendly smile she ran down the gangplank and rushed to him.

"Christopher! It is wonderful to see you again. I got here as fast as I could. Have you any news of Rachel?" Bridget blurted out.

"Rachel safe?

"Rachel is safe? But your letter said she ran away on her own?"

"You didn't get my last letter?"

"No. When I got your first letter, I took the first ship home I could find.

"She is not only safe, she is here in Boston."

"Here? Oh, thank God, thank God!" Bridget's trembling hand went to her heart, surprise and joy battling for prominence.

Chris led her toward his office. "I had some lunch brought to my office. There is so much to tell you, I felt it would be more private there."

An hour later, over the last remnants of a light lunch, Chris brought his story to a conclusion. "So, you see, you can relax now. You will see her tonight when she returns from work."

"Work? Did you say work?"

"Oh, yes, it was something she insisted upon. It seems you brought her up to be a hard-working, useful person. She was bored and needed something in which to be involved."

"But, she is only a child. What kind of work can she do? How could you take it upon yourself...?" Bridget huffed.

"Calm down, Bridget. It's not hard work. She working as a tutor to a good woman who really needed her help."

"Well, are you going to tell me who?"

"This woman has a large family and is with child. She is involved in some conflict with the Church, so she is away from home a lot."

"What have you done, Chris? Rachel is still a child. How could you let her take a position when you know how much I want her with me?"

"Please try to understand, Bridget. Rachel is very mature, and she was insistent that she be allowed to keep busy. Now that you are here, you can take her home."

Bridget's eyes narrowed.

"Are you going to tell me this woman's *name*, or is that a secret, too?"

"You won't recognize her name, but it is Anne Hutchinson. William and Anne are good Christian people. You don't have to worry about Rachel's welfare."

Bridget moved away, then turned and sighed. This man was a good friend.

"You know I trust you, Chris. I just wanted Rachel back."

"I'm sorry if I have upset you," Chris apologized. "I'll go get Rachel and bring her to the Cocks Crow Inn where I got you both a room."

"Whatever you think best, Christopher."

As Rachel and Chris entered the inn that evening, Rachel was nervous. An equally anxious Bridget could hardly believe this grown woman was her daughter.

"Rachel! Baby! I can hardly believe it's you." Bridget shouted as she flew down the inn stairs and grabbed her daughter in a bear hug.

Pulling away, Rachel recognized this woman to be her mother, but a woman very different from the one she remembered. This woman was beautiful and worldly. She was dressed in a blue silk gown and wore sparkling jewels. Despite the differences, she was finally with her mother again.

"Mama! Oh, mama, I was beginning to think you would never get here."

Bridget held her daughter at arms-length and examined her from head to toe.

"Honey, what are you wearing? I know this is still Puritan territory, but this dress is as bad as the ones we wore in Plymouth. I shall see to it that you have the best from now on. We are going to be so happy."

"I am very glad ye are home, Mama, but I have a position now and must dress appropriately."

Bridget turned to Christopher, expecting him to explain her daughter's stand. He shrugged.

Rachel couldn't help but compare her mother to Anne Hutchinson. Lost in thought, she hadn't realized that her mother was pulling her toward the stairs.

"We don't have much time before dinner. I had a hot tub brought up to our room. We will get you dressed for the trip home. I brought you several lovely gowns from London. I hope they will fit, you have grown so."

She stopped, noticing her daughter's lack of enthusiasm. "Oh, darling, I am sorry. You must be tired. I took a nap when I arrived. Are you sure you are up to a big dinner, dear?"

Rachel smiled at her mother. "Of course I am, mama. I am very excited about it, really. But, this is Boston, not London. I am afraid we might attract too much attention if we appear in clothes like yours." Rachel watched as the smile faded from Bridget's face. She did not want to hurt her mother, but she knew they would both have to make adjustments.

Bridget smiled and grabbed her daughter in a warm embrace. "Of course, darling, you are right. I will slip into something simple while we are in Boston. I am so excited having you with me again. I love you so much." Rachel was not quite able to say the words her mother wanted to hear.

That night as Bridget slept, Rachel sat on her bed at the inn mulling over what would be best for her life. She was unnerved to find that a gulf had grown between herself and her mother. Bridget was not the woman she remembered. That woman had been care worn, supportive, and loving. This woman gushed out her love, but it felt like it was coming from a stranger.

When morning finally arrived, Rachel rose and slipped into her clothing. Although she knew she had a duty to go with her mother, she also had to honor her duty to Anne. Perhaps there was a way to accomplish both.

Bridget was waiting for her in the inn's dining room downstairs. As soon as Bridget saw her daughter descending the stairs, she rushed to her.

"Come, Rachel, I have ordered a nice breakfast. Then we will send for your things. The ship leaves at seven o'clock tonight. I can't wait to get you out of this town." Bridget gushed.

She escorted Rachel to a trestle table covered with platters of eggs, ham and hot and freshly baked bread.

"Did you sleep well, darling?"

"Yes, mother. The bed was very comfortable."

"Good, now eat, darling. We have a long day ahead of us. I can't wait for you to see our house in New Amsterdam. I fixed your room with your favorite colors, and I have lots of pretty gowns for you. You will love it."

Rachel managed a smile as she toyed with her eggs. She finally managed to face her challenge. "Mother, I do not want ye to get the wrong idea. I am so happy to see ye again, but..."

Bridget stopped eating, her fork suspended, her heart growing cold. "Oh, darling, you are not still using the old 'ye'."

Rachel looked down at her plate. "Sorry. I will work on that. But, I really...I mean...I am afraid I cannot go with ye...you... right now, mother. I am committed to my work, and Mistress Hutchinson needs me so much. I cannot just walk away."

Bridget held her breath. She slowly laid down her fork. "Can't walk away?"

Rachel looked up. It was as if her mother had turned to stone. Bridget had gone white, her eyes full of pain.

"Mother, it will only be for a few months. Mistress Hutchinson has a house full of children. She is close to term with a new child and having a serious battle with the Church." She touched her mother's hand to bring her out of her silence. "Oh, dear, this is so hard. I do not want to hurt ye, Mother. I just need to stay here a while longer, then we will be together as we always planned. Please...try to understand," she pleaded.

Bridget sat immobile for a long moment, memories and dreams fighting a battle within her. Finally, she managed a small smile.

"Well, darling, though you are still a child to me, you are a now a young woman. You know what is best for you." Bridget held Rachel's cold hand. "I've waited this long, I guess I can wait a little longer."

"I knew ye...you... would understand. I promise to come home as soon as I can. We can write to each other...we can keep in touch."

"Of course, darling, you are right." Bridget hid behind a brave front. Her daughter was alive and well. That was all that mattered. "Now, eat your breakfast before it gets cold. I will hire a carriage to take you back to where you work. I will need the address, of course."

Rachel managed to hide her sigh of relief. Discovering that she was hungry after all, she enjoyed large array of food. She became so engrossed in her morning meal that she failed to notice that her mother's plate sat untouched.

∽◯

Life in the Hutchinson house was topsy-turvy as Anne's trial approached. Master Hutchinson and the children worried about Anne. At age forty-five, Anne was old to be bearing a child. She should be resting and taking better care of herself as the babe grew within her.

Anne was due to appear before the General Court during the sixth month of her child bearing. There was a heavy snowstorm the night of the trial, and Master Hutchinson dug out the carriage from the snow banks and hitched up the horses. By the time he finished, Anne had set off on her own to walk to the Court.

"It will give me time to think," she justified. Rachel tried her best to stop Anne from starting her long walk in the stinging wind. When Master Hutchinson came to drive her to the court, she was gone.

"We must go after her. She will catch the croup...and what about the baby...?" Rachel cried. Hutchinson put an arm around Rachel's shoulders. "Please do not worry, Rachel. Anne is a strong and determined woman. I trust her judgment in all things. She walks with God. We will go to the court and wait. We will pick her up when the trial is over."

Rachel and Hutchinson waited in the chilled foyer for hours, wondering what was going on behind the courtroom doors.

Anne stood inside the cold hall, her old bible clutched to her breast as she waited for the charges against her to be read. She was dressed in her usual long dark dress with white collar and cuffs. Her dark hair, which was graying slightly, was topped with a white coif.

The room was dark and forbidding. Before her on a dais Anne saw a large group of men waiting to condemn her. The facial features differed but all shared cold, haughty expressions.

Her nemesis, Governor Winthrop, rose. He was tall and thin, with a long nose that nearly obscured his upper lip. The expression in his eyes was cold and harsh, as it was with hatchet men from the beginning of time.

"The Court calls Mistress Anne Hutchinson!"

Anne took her place before the judges. Winthrop continued.

"Mistress Hutchinson, ye are called here as one of those that have troubled the peace of the commonwealth and its churches. Ye are known to be a woman who has had a great share in promoting opinions that cause trouble for the church. Ye have spoken many things which are prejudicial to the churches and its ministers. Ye have held meetings in your house that have been condemned by the General Assembly as things not tolerable, nor comely, in the sight of God, and not fitting for your sex. Notwithstanding that these meetings were cried down, you have continued the same."

Anne kept her peace.

"Therefore we have sent for ye so ye will understand how things are. If ye remain obstinate, the court will see to it that ye trouble us no further."

To this, Anne replied, "I am called here to answer before ye, but I hear no charges said against me."

"Mistress, I have already stated some charges, and will be glad to tell ye more."

"Name one of them then," Anne replied, "What *law* have I broken?"

"Ye have broken the Fifth Commandment, honor thy father and mother."

"How is that, sir?" Anne asked, surprised.

"The Church is father and mother to its constituents. You must obey the rules of this colony."

"But Sir, I do, in fact, honor ye."

Angry, Winthrop shouted, "We will not discourse with those of your sex...ye honor the faction against us, and in this way, ye do dishonor us."

"Sir, there is no law that I know of against private assembly. I only started these meetings for women, and I believe that the elder women shall instruct the younger."

"You deny that men come to your house for meetings?" Winthrop growled.

"I do, sir."

"What if a man should come and say, 'Mistress Hutchinson, I hear that ye are a woman who God has given his grace unto. Ye have knowledge in the word of God. I pray, instruct me a little.' Would ye not instruct this man?"

"I think I may. Ye tell me I may not teach women, and yet ye ask me to instruct the court."

The trial was as long and intricate as Anne had expected. In spite of chilblains and the growing pain in her low back, she stood her ground. This enraged Winthrop. He exploded and bellowed, "We did not call ye to teach the court but to reveal yourself!"

"How to answer that," Anne thought. A wave of exhaustion had washed over her. She was on the verge of fainting. Standing so long in one place had taken its toll.

She firmly refused to admit that she taught men, instead she quoted scripture which told of a woman and her husband who taught a man who came to them for instruction. After listening to Anne quoting this story and another bible passage, Governor Winthrop had enough.

"What rules do ye have to teach them?" he growled.

"Sir, I have quoted ye two verses from the bible that say I can teach. Must I show my name written in the bible passages?"

Winthrop, frustrated by his inability to extract a confession from Anne, turned to another charge. He attacked her for inciting religious disharmony and stirring up political dissent.

"We feel your teachings are greatly prejudicial to the State! Your opinions are known to differ from the word of God and ye have seduced many simple souls. Those who frequented your meeting no longer believe in their ministers and magistrates...we see no rule of God for this! We must therefore restrain ye from continuing your teachings."

Anne, now getting discouraged, went into many reasons why she felt her teachings were not in opposition to those of the Church, although in fact, they were. She wound up stating that Winthrop and the Court could only silence her if they could quote scripture to prove their charges. Winthrop again lost his temper.

"We are your judges, and not ye ours and we may accuse ye and judge ye!"

At this point, Winthrop decided to let another of the forty-nine members of the court take over the questioning. Deputy Governor Thomas Dudley took over. It was fifty men against one woman, but Anne still held her own. Dudley reread the charges against Anne and added one of his own.

"The Church believes that every person was born a sinner and is doomed to hell, except for the intervention of God, who bestows His grace *only* on the elect. The Church teaches that men should perform works of charity, live piously, work hard, and obey scriptural law. This is quite the opposite from this Covenant of Grace ye have taken up as your cause. Ye say that *any* person can be saved by a gift of forgiveness from the Holy Spirit that dwells in each individual."

Anne held her silence. Dudley faced Anne down. "I have also heard ye have said, that if the clergy do not teach a Covenant of Grace, they are automatically preaching a Covenant of Works."

Anne responded firmly, "No, Sir. What I said was that one person may be able to preach a covenant of grace more clearly than another."

Another of the judges angrily blurted out, "Ye are not a woman at all! Ye make a better husband than a wife, a better father than a mother! Ye are a disgrace to womanhood!" Anne bit her lower lip and offered no argument.

When the trial was into its fifth hour, Anne could hardly stand her back ached so. The room seemed to be getting colder, and the candles were burning down. Anne could no longer hide her disgust. She lashed out at the governor and the court; letting them know exactly how stupid and cruel they were being to an innocent woman. When she finished, there was silence in the room.

Governor Winthrop, after whispering to his panel, stood and announced that the court had decided to adjourn until the next day. Anne's case would be continued then and a decision made. This, he explained, would give Anne some time to consider her actions since coming to the colony and her unbecoming behavior before the court. The court finally closed.

When Master Hutchinson saw the state his wife was in, he lifted her in his arms and carried her to the buggy, a worried Rachel following them. That evening, tired as Anne was, she outlined her day in court to her family.

The family was incensed at the treatment Anne had been exposed to, and urged her into bed. Late into the night, her husband snoring beside her, Anne rethought her defense. The next morning Rachel watched as the Hutchinson's drove off to Court. Rachel and the children waited at home and prayed.

The second morning, as Anne stood before her accusers, her worst fears were realized. The trial ended in a sentence of banishment. Heartsick, Anne asked, "On what charge am I banished?" Governor Winthrop stated coldly, "Say no more. The court knows why and is satisfied."

Anne collapsed and was helped into a chair. Feeling she had let her family and followers down, she could not hold back the long overdue tears. Then she realized that Thomas Dudley was again speaking.

"However, in light of the harshness of the winter and Mistress Hutchinson's delicate condition, this banishment is delayed until spring. Mistress Hutchinson will be placed in the charge of Marshal, Joseph Weld of Roxbury."

Master Hutchinson helped a heart-broken Anne into their buggy and held her to him with one arm as he directed the horse home. His heart was heavy.

"Why, in God's name, could they not let ye stay in your own home with your family? Ye belong with us while awaiting the child, not with a bunch of hateful strangers. It is just too much! Oh, that I had the power to send them all to the devil!" he growled.

When they arrived home Rachel and the children gathered around Anne. Anne spoke. "My dears, we must be brave. I will not be alone.

The Holy Spirit will be with the baby and me. A month is not a lifetime, though it will seem like one without all of ye."

Rachel was as upset as the family. She had grown to love them all, and to see Anne suffer over some trumped up hypocrisy was too hard to face.

"Can we not ask the court to let me go with ye? Ye should not have to go alone," Rachel urged.

Anne started to speak, "Rachel is needed..." Her husband broke in, "No, Anne, Rachel is right. I think I can talk them into a maid to take care of your needs. It will give their good wives a break. I will feel better if one of us was watching over ye."

Anne finally relented. The next day Master Hutchinson spoke at length to the deputy, and was given permission for Rachel to accompany Anne.

The next few days were spent in packing Anne's belongings, and addressing the fears of the children. Hutchinson was so angry that he stormed around the place causing no end of delays. "I will curtail my business and stay with the children," he promised.

Subsequently, Anne and Rachel found themselves prisoners in the home of Anne's former mentor, Joseph Cotton, who now sat in judgment of her.

Anne and Rachel were installed in a small bedroom. There were thick pieces of unmatched fabric tacked over the one small window in an attempt to keep out the cold. There was one single bed with a straw mattress, and a sheepskin rug and a woolen blanket on the floor near the bed where Rachel slept, or tried to sleep.

Their everyday life followed a set routine. They were fed a breakfast of cold gruel every morning. Reverend Cotton's wife wanted no part of Anne or her help, and did not put herself out to make their stay easier. At noon, they were given some bread without jam, a small wedge of cheese and an occasional slice of ham. Rachel worried about Anne's baby, but Anne said that God would protect her child.

After lunch either Reverend Cotton or Reverend John Davenport labored to convince Anne of the errors in her thinking. This was the part of the day that Anne dreaded. She was careful not to say the wrong thing, but also not to betray her own beliefs. Anne still could not understand Cotton's change of heart. He had introduced her to the Covenant of Grace. How could he have gone back to the old way of thinking?

Twice during this stay Anne was brought before the Church of Boston. She was finally forced to recant in public. However, she later rallied and reaffirmed her beliefs. She was then accused of lying to the Church and the excommunication became formal.

Anne was ordered to withdraw herself from the congregation and leave the colony. The final words uttered by Cotton rang in Anne's head.

"The Church consenting to it, we will proceed with the excommunication. Forasmuch as ye, Mistress Hutchinson, have highly transgressed, offended, and troubled the Church with your errors, I cast ye up to Satan. I command ye in the name of Christ Jesus and Father God to withdraw yourself from the congregation." And so, it was accomplished.

In the spring of 1638, Anne and Rachel were returned to Anne's house in Cambridge so the family could make arrangements for moving their household. Master Hutchinson was at work at a neighbor's home, but the rest of the family greeted them. The children gathered around Anne and Rachel, the younger ones getting hugs from their mother. Anne pulled little Zuriel into her arms. "Mama's so glad to see her boy again, and all of ye children. Have ye been good for papa?" Anna clung to her mother's arm, tears for once replacing the perpetual smile. "Mama, why are those mean men doing this to us?"

The children found places on the floor around their mother to digest her wisdom. "They think they can stop me from being who I am, doing what I know God wants me to do. That will never happen. Ye children must be brave now. It will be hard, but we have each other." She smiled warmly at the children, and then looked into Anna's sad face. "Now, my Anna, let me see your wonderful smile."

Anna gave her mother a tentative smile, and received a hug in return. "Now, my darlings help mama to her bedroom. I think a few hours' sleep will make the baby and I feel much better." She turned to Rachel. "Rachel, take a nap. We will all get together this afternoon and make plans for the future."

The boys quickly carried logs into their parent's room and shortly a warm fire was burning in the fireplace. Rachel helped Anne into a warm nightgown and tucked her into bed, then headed for her own bed, where she collapsed fully dressed into a troubled sleep.

Early the next morning, after a quick breakfast, Francis approached Rachel.

"Rachel, how is mother, really?"

"I think she is holding her own, but this has been a horrible ordeal. She is not as strong as she thinks," Rachel explained.

"Do ye think she can make the trip to wherever we have to go?" Francis asked.

"She has no choice. Nor do ye," Rachel replied.

Anne slept until noon, and was hungry when she awoke. Rachel prepared a lunch of hot vegetable soup and fresh bread for Anne, and was pleased that she ate every bite.

When Anne finished eating and the trencher was scrubbed and stored, Rachel sent Francis to fetch his father from his work. As soon as Hutchinson arrived home he took his wife into his arms. He held her close for a long moment before he allowed the family to gather again.

Guilt lay heavy on Anne's heart that her family had to suffer for her convictions, but she knew they would do anything for her.

"We have been happy here," Anne started. "Now we must decide where we shall go."

"My dear," Hutchinson volunteered. "This problem has already been solved."

"Solved? But how...where?"

"As ye know, we still have a large number of staunch supporters. We held a meeting and they were all willing to fight to change the verdict against Mother. I talked them out of that for their own sakes.

Fortunately, Henry Vane came late to our meeting. Knowing our predicament, he told us that a man named William Coddington, along with Dr. John Clarke and others, has established a small colony on an island named Aquidneck. One of the men, a Roger Williams, has received permission from the local Indians for us to build a new home there."

Although their destination was distant, the news brought much relief. The next day found their belongings packed onto two large wagons. The buggy was filled to the brim with household goods and Hutchinson children.

Rachel was sad that she would be separated from the family she loved. After her long years of being a lonely child, to have a large, loving family was close to her heart.

She had packed her few belongings and was waiting to say goodbye. She took a last look around the house that had brought her so much security and peace. She could not halt a wayward tear. Christopher Johnson would take her to her mother. But her heart was torn because she felt so strongly that she belonged with the Hutchinson's. Finally, she approached Hutchinson, who had shown her that a father could be kind and loving.

"Sir, I know ye have enough problems of your own, but I wish ye might consider taking me with ye to your new home."

"But, my child, will your mother not want ye with her?" he asked. "She has waited a long time."

"I am sure she will want me home, sir, but I feel strongly that I should stay with Mistress Hutchinson. The baby is due at any time, and the traveling will be difficult. I could help. I know my mother will forgive another short delay."

"I guess we can squeeze in one more. You are sure now?"

"Oh, yes. I do so want to go with ye. Thank ye so very much, sir."

When the children heard Rachel was going with them, they whooped and hollered. Francis jumped down from the wagon and helped Rachel up onto the seat. Beaming, he squeezed her hand. Then he took her small bag and added it to the others.

"We are all mighty happy that ye will be coming with us, Rachel." Francis smiled.

Rachel blushed at Francis' attention. "I am very happy, too, Francis."

A beaming little Anna cuddled up next to Rachel. "Oh, Rachel, I am so glad ye are coming. I did not want to lose ye."

"I am glad too, Rachel dear," Anne smiled. The three shared a big hug.

The Hutchinson's were ready to depart when they heard a woman's voice. "Sister Anne!" Anne turned to see her neighbors making their way toward the wagons. "We wanted to say goodbye."

Rachel knew them as John and Mary Coggeshall and Atherton and Elizabeth Hough. The two men approached and John slapped Hutchinson on the back. "We are with ye, Brother William." As the men made their farewells, Mary and Elizabeth commiserated with Anne. "We will miss ye so very much."

"We will miss all of ye, too, but it is dangerous for ye to be seen with us." Anne warned.

"Oh, mercy sakes," Elizabeth smiled. "The worst they could do has already been done."

"Keep the faith, dear friends. God is with ye!" Anne smiled.

"God be with ye and your family. Take care, and do not forget us," Mary added.

Anne assured them that they would be in her prayers, as Hutchinson climbed back in the wagon and took up the reins.

As the wagons creaked into a roll the neighbors waved, both women fighting back tears.

Anne looked back at the empty house, allowing regret to flow freely through her.

Rachel pushed thoughts of her mother to the back of her mind. Anne needed her now. Bridget did not. She would go home when her job was done. Anne smiled, and all was well with Rachel.

When news reached Bridget that Rachel had decided to remain with the Hutchinson's she felt she had lost her daughter forever. What was there to live for now...an empty house? She grieved for days, and then decided she would do what she had to do...wait...somehow she would get Rachel back. She was not one to give up easily.

Part Two

AMANDA'S STORY
In the Southern States

Lineage chart:

The south covers Jamestown, Virginia and Maryland

Amanda McNeely (b.1606)

Hyrum Biggs, owner   **James MacDougal, I**   **James MacDougal II**

Melinda (Lindy) McNeely, (b.1625)

Cinnamon and Arthur (servants), Aggie Barrows, friend

Esther (b.1625

Historical Characters: Margaret Brent & Family

9

Jamestown Wilderness, 1623

Amanda could not believe what was happening. During the sea voyage she had been lulled by the close friendship of Bridget and Aggie. Somewhere in her heart hope had been born. Now she stood surrounded by a group of indentured candidates, most as dazed as she. She turned her gaze away from her fellow prisoners. These she would surely not miss. She patted her lumpy gown, seeking the comfort of her mother's mirror and brush set. Yes, they were safe...for now.

Amanda turned her attention to the large group of potential buyers. They were mostly men. No one held her interest except for a small group of people near a carriage. Amanda scrutinized the older woman who she assumed was the mother of the young brunette girl at her side. The delicate patrician had a sweet face, but appeared ill. The young girl was urging the woman to get back into the carriage. As Amanda watched, a tall handsome man, who appeared to be in his mid-fifties, returned to the carriage and took the older woman's arm. He assisted her into the carriage, and the young girl climbed in beside her.

As Amanda continued watching the tableau before her, she became aware that the handsome older man's eyes were resting on her. Their eyes met and held. His look of pity nearly made her knees buckle. He stared at her for a few moments longer, then turned and climbed into the carriage next to the older woman. He put his arm around he as the carriage pulled away. Amanda wished that he had stayed and bid on her. He looked like a kind family man who would not take advantage of her.

Minutes later Amanda was pushed up onto the bidding block. Her heart was beating so loudly she was sure everyone could hear it. She tried to be calm and appear brave, and ignore the loud, enthusiastic bidding. She couldn't help but notice one particularly vile character who was bidding at the top of his voice and using the language of London's back alleys. She was totally repelled by his thin, slightly misshapen body and his long black unkempt hair. He had bulging black eyes with bushy eyebrows lapping over a large wart at the bridge of his nose. Worst of all, his churlish mouth was filled with rotting teeth. Amanda's skin goose-bumped at the thought of being owned by such a man. She forced herself to turn and watch the auctioneer. As she watched she prayed that *any* other bidder would buy her. Her mind was filled with the memory of the Watch who had tried to rape her in London.

For Amanda this day was the beginning of a long nightmare. The ugly little man was jumping up and down, screaming that he had won! All off her dreams faded as she was pushed into the ugly man's arms. He tied her wrists together with a scratchy rope and pulled her away from the auction crowd. She couldn't resist one last yearning glance at the spot where the rich carriage had stood.

Not far from the bidding arena, Ugly, which would ever-after, be her name for him, pushed her up on to an old pack mule already loaded down with supplies. He mounted a shabby horse and attached the rope from Amanda's tied wrists to his saddle horn. They set off for God only knew where, headed for a life Amanda could not even imagine.

Amanda's whole world turned into forest. A large variety of trees, most of which she couldn't name, engulfed them in cool dampness. Amanda, unused to being on the back of an animal, was sore and aching all over, especially her bottom. When her mule occasionally broke into a trot, Amanda had to bite her lip to keep from crying out in pain. Ugly rode in silence.

They stopped long enough to chew on some hard strips of dried meat, which he called jerky. The trees grew denser as they moved farther into the forest. Amanda could make out no path, but her captor seemed to know where he was headed. By the second day, Amanda found that she was numbed by the hard ride. She lost interest in everything but her aching body. She spent her time in fervent prayers for an end to this nightmarish journey. At night, Ugly would make her lay down far back from the small fire. Wrapped in only a ragged wool blanket, she slept out of pure exhaustion.

On the morning of the fourth day, Ugly stopped in a small clearing. By this time, Amanda was blessedly asleep in the saddle. Ugly slid off his nag and began to loosen the pack on her saddle. Jarred awake by the hard tug on the ropes that bit into her wrists, Amanda watched him for a moment. "Can you help me down, please?" she asked, too tired to move.

"You can help yerself, lady. I ain't yer servant. Yer mine!"

Amanda struggled to get her leftt leg over the mule's back, fighting the pain in her muscles. She finally slid off the animal's back, letting out a yelp of pain as her feet jarred to the ground. She thanked God the journey was over, but the scene that met her eyes made her heart sink further.

The clearing was small, with no sign of a garden. There was a lean-to shelter for the horse and mule, and a small, roughly built cabin. Ugly pushed Amanda inside the cabin and closed the door, then went out to unsaddle his horse and mule. Inside the cabin and alone, Amanda looked around. The cabin confirmed her worst fears. There was filth everywhere, broken plates and empty sacks were stacked in the corners. The medium-sized fireplace was filled with a depth of ashes that spilled onto the splintery floorboards. There was one cupboard with no doors, and a pile of dirty wooden bowls and utensils lying on the floor in front of the fireplace. She felt the bundle containing her treasures and knew she would have to find a safe hiding place for them quickly. She knew she didn't have much time so she removed her bundle and pushed it under a pile of dirty clothing.

A moment later Ugly threw open the cabin door and dropped his belongings in an already crowded corner.

Amanda attempted a smile. "If you will tell me where your stores are, I will fix us something to eat," she offered, fatigue causing her shoulders to slump.

"There's only one thing I'm hungry for, little lady, and I been waitin' for it for four days," Ugly growled though his rotten teeth.

He moved toward her, the pure lust in his black eyes telling Amanda what he was hungry for. She backed away.

"You can't do this. I'm indentured to be a servant, not a whore!" she pleaded. He grabbed her by the shoulders, sending spikes of pain through her already aching body.

"I can do anything I damned well please, young lady. I hold your papers, and I say what you have to do. Besides, we're hundreds of miles from civilization. Who are you gonna complain to, huh?" he laughed.

Her struggles came to naught as Ugly ripped away her clothing. He threw her onto his filthy bed and held her hands above her head as he pressed his smelly body down upon hers. When the pain and horror became too great, she mercifully slipped into unconsciousness. It was sometime later that Amanda awakened to her life in purgatory. It hadn't been a bad dream after all.

Amanda had learned on the long, hard ride into the wilderness that her rapist's name was Hyrum Biggs, and he was a hunter by trade. He trapped animals which could be sold for food to the colonists. Ugly had grown tired of living alone in his own filth, so he had saved much of what he had earned, and had set off to civilization to get himself a housekeeper. Slave would have been a better word.

Amanda could have lived with the hard work, but she had no defense against his rapes. The first time had been the worst. She would never forget the sickening smell of his filthy body, and the odor of his rotting teeth. However, the physical pain was nothing compared with the shame she felt for losing her purity which she had guarded so diligently.

As time went by Amanda learned to turn herself off to his violence. This made living possible, but certainly not worthwhile. One of the worst things that Ugly forced her to do was help him in the bloody job of skinning his kills of the smaller animals and fowl he kept for them. She managed to cook them on a spit in the small fireplace. She wished it was larger as it was their only source of heat and light. She did find a few tallow candles but they smelled so bad that she settled for the hearth.

She asked Ugly to get her a book or two to fill her time. Instead he accused her of laziness and made her clean the larger animals and pack them for delivery to a butcher in Jamestown. This unpleasant job made her shoulders and arms ache, and the smell of blood nearly choked her. To her surprise, when Ugly came back from a trip to Jamestown he brought her some vegetable seeds for peas, carrots, parsnips and a couple of old potatoes with shoots. She immediately used his one shovel and dug a garden near the cabin.

She had to learn to cook meat and her small supply of vegetables in a large metal pot suspended over the glowing coals of the fireplace on a lug pole made of green wood.

She contemplated escape many times, but Ugly guarded her closely when he was there and kept her locked in the cabin when he was hunting. He was diligent in his 'protection' to the extent that he had built a privy attached to the backside of the cabin with a door in the wall so she would not need to go outside. The thick forests around them, and the miles of wilderness around the cabin, made escape an impossible dream.

Amanda spent her time keeping the cabin as clean as possible and devising ways to cover the stench of the attached outhouse. It had taken her a week to dig through the collection of garbage that Ugly had ignored for so long. The only dignity she had left was keeping herself clean and neat despite the worsening condition of her ragged clothing. Ugly told her there was a small stream about a mile from the cabin, and he brought a couple of wooden buckets of water to the cabin once a week. After a while he dug a well so they could have a good supply of water for butchering the kills.

She did her best to keep so busy so that thoughts of the past and her present pain were forced to the back of her mind. If only she could be with Bridget and Aggie again. They were often in her thoughts.

At least her dresser set was safe. It had been well hidden beneath the piles of dirty cloths, so she had left the cleaning of that pile for last. On Ugly's first hunting trip, she had loosened two short planks from the floor and after hours of digging and hiding the dirt, she had managed to make a small space beneath the floor. Here she secured the wrapped mirror and brush. She knew that if Ugly found it he would surely sell or destroy it.

After three months of being subjected to the pain of Ugly's attacks, a new fear gripped Amanda. She feared that she was with child. She had many days of being sick to her stomach, which she did her best to hide from Ugly. She tried to get rid of the unwanted child by eating spoiled food and dust, but the child persisted.

Day after day she cooked and cleaned. She knew she should tell Ugly about his child, but she feared his reaction. Fortunately she was thin, so the babe did not yet show beneath her full skirt and dirty apron.

She diligently worked to keep her heart from becoming attached to this coming child. To her, it would be another monster. She cringed when she pictured a child who would look like its father.

However, as the months flew by she found it impossible to hide her stomach. She finally had to tell Ugly. Surprisingly, he was not as upset as she expected. He even asked her if she was doing all right, which amazed her.

As the birth drew nearer, she couldn't help wondering about him. There was always hope that he might not look like his father. She prayed she could learn to accept the child, and as the days fell away her good sense finally took hold. As she felt the babe moving within her, she had to admit that it was an innocent. If she could only get the child away from Ugly, she could bring it up to be a decent person. That healing thought took root and gave her a reason to live. She would have something to love, and she *must* learn to love again.

As she contemplated motherhood, she often thought about Bridget and Aggie and wondered where and how they were. She prayed that their lives were turning out better than hers.

As the days shortened for her birthing time, a tremendous fear came upon her. Memories of the birthing of Mistress Chester's son on the voyage returned to her, and she was not sure she could remember what she had to do. What if something went wrong? How was she going to manage the birthing by herself?

She also worried if she could nurse the baby as she was still very thin thanks to meager meals of cornmeal cakes, beans and occasional meat. Her breasts were not as round with milk as she hoped to keep her child properly nourished. She dug out vegetables from the garden when Ugly wasn't around, but she needed milk for herself for strength.

When Ugly finally accused her of eating too much of his precious food, he added two years to her indenture. His reaction to the coming child was lackadaisical; his only comment being it would be hell to provide for another mouth. In spite of Ugly's lack of interest, Amanda suspected that he might be looking forward to a strapping son to help him with his hunting. As her time came close, Amada told him she was afraid she didn't know what to do. Surprisingly, he set off to Jamestown a week later to find a midwife.

Jon Webster watched as Hyrum Biggs spoke quietly to Tom Munk at Tom's St. James trading post. He wondered what the disreputable hunter was hatching now. He waited until Biggs left, and then approached Munk, who was a small, wiry man with a shiny baldpate and a mustache, curled up at both ends. "What's that asshole up to now,

Tom?" Jonathan queried. Munk laughed. "Not what you'd ever guess, Jon."

Jon smiled. "I need a little entertainment. Tell me."

"It seems he has a woman out at his cabin; indentured, so he says. Only problem is, he's gone and got a babe in her."

"God damn that pig! He has no business having a female indenture. He's obviously used force on the woman. Things like this make me madder than hell!" Jon banged his fist onto the bar. "Isn't there anything we can do to help her?"

Tom's usually merry face lost its smile as he realized the seriousness of the situation. "Knowing Biggs, I don't imagine she's had a healthy diet for a woman in the family way. He did ask for a midwife. Maybe I can go into Jamestown and get one. And, I got an old cow that the MacDougal family sent out for Molly. She still has some milk. The woman will need some nourishment so she can feed her babe. I'll send the cow along with the midwife."

"Oh, no you don't, papa. I'm as good a midwife as any in Jamestown," a jolly middle-aged woman said as she joined them at the bar. She had reddish brown short hair, a rosy complexion, and her rounded figure rested on short legs. At this moment, her hands were fisted at her hips, her brown eyes twinkling. "I heard what that animal wanted."

"You got enough to take care of here, Molly mine." Tom quipped.

"The kids are big enough to care for themselves. It sounds like that little lady needs me more than they do right now," Molly stated adamantly.

Tom looked into his wife's face and knew he had no say in the matter. "Guess that's settled then. I know better than to argue with my Molly."

"Well, Molly dear, Biggs did make one condition. He will pay us a fine deer, but you must not tell the lady about our place. He's gonna tell her you came from Jamestown."

"Why ever would he insist on that?" Molly frowned.

"He's afraid that if she knows how close she is to Jamestown she will try to escape. You gotta promise me you won't tell her."

"I would love to see her escape," Molly affirmed.

"He would only catch her and beat or kill her. Are you gonna promise?"

"All right, I promise. But it will kill me to see her suffering."

The two men nodded and Jon rubbed his bearded chin with a large, callused hand. "One of these days, I'll take a ride out there and check out the lay of the land. I can't go now as Hank and I will be going deeper into the forest for deer." Jon's face mirrored his concern. "I'll make sure I go check on the woman when we get back."

To Amanda's great surprise Ugly came back in four days, not only with a midwife, but with a sagging old cow with udders still filled with milk. Having done what he considered his duty, Ugly set off on a hunting trip, leaving the two women alone. He promised to be back in two weeks.

Three days later Amanda lay on Ugly's wooden bed and watched as Molly washed her firstborn child with warm water from the kettle hanging in the fireplace. Molly wrapped the baby in clean fabric, and handed the child to her mother. She then went about cleaning up the afterbirth.

Amanda gently held her tiny swaddled son in her arms, she was almost afraid to look at him for fear he would have his father's homely features. Finally she pulled back the edge of the sacking and beheld the most beautiful little creature she had ever hoped to see.

"Oh, he's beautiful!" she sighed.

"Beautiful, yes, my dear, but not a 'he'," Molly smiled. "You have a fine, healthy daughter."

"Daughter? But, I never even *thought* of a girl. I just assumed it would be a son. How strange, a little girl." Then she remembered Ugly's wish for a son. How would he take this? She opened her gown and directed the baby's mouth to her swollen nipple, where the wee one quickly grasped on to her lifeline and began to suckle.

Amanda, watching as her daughter took her first nourishment, felt a light go on in her soul. Love began to pour into her. She caressed the soft fringe of dark hair on her daughter's head. "I don't care what I have to do, I will take care of you always. Somehow I will make a good life for you. I shall name you Melinda, 'my beauty' and we'll be all right. Don't you worry, my sweet one...we'll be fine now that we're together!"

Amanda was very grateful for Molly's help, and the much desired news of the outside world, but right now her mind was filled thoughts about the beautiful new being that God had given her.

Molly, knowing that Biggs would provide nothing for Amanda's needs, had brought some of her daughter-in-law's work clothes for the new mother. Feeling better and happier than she had in many months, Amanda proudly wore her new underpinnings and a cotton print dress which had small yellow and pink flowers on it. It had a white collar and sported white cuffs on the long sleeves.

Molly's heart went out to the girl, but she knew she could not help her as long as Biggs held the indentures. She could not even give the girl hope. That would be too cruel.

Molly took good care of both mother and child, but Amanda was afraid of what the woman must think of her birthing a child out of wedlock. One day she looked up while nursing the baby and was embarrassed at the look of pity she saw in Molly's eyes. Shame filled Amanda. She knew she could not stay with Ugly for the length of her indenture, that he continued to increase. She owed it to her daughter to make a better life for her. Somehow they would have to get away.

Molly filled the girl's lonely hours with tales of her husband, her son and his young wife who she claimed lived far away in Jamestown. Molly stretched her visit for another week until Ugly finally arrived back at the cabin from his hunting trip. Amanda was heartbroken when Molly had to say goodbye, knowing she would never see her again.

As Amanda feared, Ugly was angry with her for not giving him a son. He warned her that he would have her more often to assure she would give him the son he wanted. She dared remind him that since they were not married, any children she had would not legally be his. She received a black eye in response.

Amanda was grateful that Ugly had left her alone when he found out she was with child, but now she paid the price. She had thought his rapes bad before, but now he took out all his hate on her young body. Whenever he saw the baby, he glared at her, so Amanda kept Melinda hidden in the corner near the fireplace when Ugly was in the cabin. She was grateful that Melinda was a quiet child. Unfortunately her milk dried up after a month, but with the sweet milk from Bossy that Amanda spooned into Melinda's mouth, the baby seemed to be thriving.

Amanda thanked God every night for her precious daughter. Now having Melinda to work for she survived from day to day, suffering silently the physical abuse and guarding her daughter from harm, always planning and praying. She vowed that she and Melinda would one day be free, even if she had to kill Ugly to make it happen.

10

The fear of an Indian attack was never far from mind when living at the edge of the vast wilderness to the west. In the five years Amanda had been out there, the only relief she found from the fear of Indians was when Ugly was present. He was well armed and diligent to protect what was his. Now at age twenty two, she often wondered how much worse it could be to be a slave of a red man than to be one for Ugly.

To Amanda's great surprise and pleasure, Melinda was thriving. She and Melinda had celebrated the child's third birthday two weeks before. Amanda marveled that Melinda's beauty increased as she grew. Her hair was now a dark auburn; her sparkling light brown eyes were specked with gold. Her face was round and usually wreathed in smiles that expressed her merry personality.

Amanda had not given up hope of escape, but being with Melinda somehow dulled the ache and the longing for companionship. Ugly was gone most of the time now, and she was grateful for every moment free from his presence.

Fortunately, he had lost interest in her body since it once again harbored a child and his hopes for a boy grew. Amanda determined that she must get away before this child was born. To this length, she had stored whatever she could for the escape in the hiding place that held her mother's brush and mirror. Any kind of food that was not quickly perishable she carefully wrapped in sacking and buried in the crawl space beneath the cabin.

Ugly, to protect what he hoped was his son, also dug a crawl-space beneath the cabin floor. He had heard that a band of hostile Narragansett were in the area. He told Amanda to take her child and crawl into this space if Indians ever came to the cabin. When Ugly had first told Amanda of his plan to dig a crawl-place, she had been terrified that he would find her own hiding place under the floorboard by the bed. But he dug his crawl space on the other side of the cabin, near the front door.

On this day, as she was wrapping some cornbread in sacking to add to her escape cache when she heard the sharp sound of a musket shot. Her already taut nerves caused her to jump. She put her hand to her heart as fear began to fill her body. She looked around to find Melinda who was playing with a wooden ball near the fireplace. She grabbed the baby into her arms, and ran to the door. She could see nothing unusual, but heard a commotion in the woods to the right of the cabin.

Suddenly, a figure broke from the edge of the woods. It took a moment before she recognized Ugly running toward the cabin, musket in hand. He started to yell, but she could barely make out what he was saying. "Get in the crawl! Ugly screamed. Indians coming! Get in..."

At that moment, he stopped, his head jerking backwards. He dropped forward to the ground about twenty yards from the cabin, a quivering arrow sticking up from his back.

Amanda was torn between going after the musket or hiding, but one look at Melinda, whose face was screwed up in alarm, made her quickly close the door and rush to the crawl-space's trap door. It took her a minute to find the latch, as Ugly had hidden it well under a small woven rug. She lowered herself and her child down into the narrow space and closed the lid, praying the rug would still hide the trap door.

It had never occurred to her that she would ever have to use the crawl space, so it was a shock to her that the space was so tight and afforded so little air to breathe. She knew she must not panic, that somehow she must keep Melinda quiet or their fates would be sealed. If the Indians took them, she knew that even if they were not killed, they would suffer torture.

She could hear her heart wildly beating. It sounded so loud, she was sure the Indians would hear it. She was having a hard time breathing. Melinda was frightened.

"Oh, please do not cry now, baby. Please!" Amanda whispered.

The closeness of the privy added a horrible stench to the already fetid air. She tried to hold her breath and take only small whiffs of air through her mouth. Fortunately, the thin air was making Melinda sleepy, and Amanda rocked her gently back and forth.

The silence was broken by the crash of the cabin door as the Indians broke in. She could hear their voices and laughter. It sounded like at least three men. The language was foreign to her ears, and very strident. It sounded more like grunts and yelps.

Amanda did not know how long she lay there; rubbing her baby's back and praying that she would not wake up. She could hear wood splitting as the men above tore the small cabin apart looking for she knew not what. She remembered the half-dozen bottles of liquor Ugly kept in the cupboard and knew they must have found that. After a while they seemed to have settled down, laughing and enjoying themselves. "Would they never leave?" she screamed inwardly.

It seemed like hours before she heard them stumble out the open door. She could hear their hoots of pleasure fade as they left the clearing. By this time, her back was aching. She was gasping for air, but afraid they might not be gone. Suddenly she smelled smoke, and noticed tendrils of it coming down between the cracks in the floor.

"Oh, my God!" she gasped. "They have set the cabin on fire!" She pushed frantically at the trap door only to find it stuck fast. Melinda, awakened by the sudden movements of her mother's body and feeling her mother's fear, began whimpering. Something must have been placed or fallen on the floor above the trap door. Amanda tried not to panic, but fear rose in her throat like bile. She held tightly to the squirming child, as she pushed upward with all her might against the door. She managed to sit up enough to position her shoulder against the door. She gave one mighty heave and the door gave. The broken pieces of shelving atop it fell away.

Struggling to get her stiff muscles to move, Amanda worked herself up through the trap door, pulling Melinda up behind her. She grabbed the old blanket that Ugly had placed on the floor of the crawl-space and wrapped it around Melinda. The room was quickly filling with smoke, and flames were licking at the walls. The whole fireplace wall was in flames. She could not tell if the doorway was aflame due to the thickness of the smoke, but she pulled her skirt up over the baby and ran headlong through the open doorway and out into the yard.

Amanda placed her now crying toddler on a mound of grass at a safe distance from the house where she knew Melinda would be safe. Her thoughts turned to her treasure and cache of food and supplies hidden beneath the floorboard in the flaming cabin.

She must go back. She and Melinda could not survive without food, and her mother's mirror and brush were the child's only inheritance.

Finding the well untouched, she dipped a bucket of water out and doused herself with it. Then she pulled her dampened skirt over her head, and covering her nose and mouth, she forced her way back through the smoke-filled doorway. It was hard to see in the smoke, but she knew exactly where the loose boards were.

Fortunately, the flames had not yet reached that area of the cabin. She quickly pried up the boards, and emptied the contents of the hole into her apron. She shoved as much of the food supplies as she could into her apron pushing them down over the treasured dresser set. Just as she began to get up, a flaming board fell from the wall and narrowly missed her. The extreme heat was making breathing and movement very difficult. Amanda could see the flames begin to singe the fabric of her skirt and batted them with her free hand. Flames were flicking up around the doorway, but thinking of her helpless child spurred her on. She steeled herself and, head down, ran as quickly as possible through the open doorway and out into the fresh air. Just as she reached the spot where her baby sat crying, a large portion of the cabin's wattle and daub roof collapsed with an eerie wail.

Amanda sank to the ground near Melinda, totally exhausted and close to tears. She felt something warm and wet sliding down the inside of her legs. She lifted her petticoat and saw that blood was streaming down as the life of her second child came to a premature end.

A while later, Amanda sat with Melinda in her lap, and surveyed the black charcoal and gray ashes, that had housed her for nearly five years. She knew they had to move on, find a place where they could live. She mourned the loss of the little infant who would not be there to share their lives. She tore fabric from her petticoat and wrapped the tiny infant in it. There was just enough growth for her to see it was a boy.

She rose and cleaned herself with cold well water, and then slumped beside the well crying her heart out. She was grateful now to old Ugly for finally digging the well. Melinda toddled up to her and held out her chubby hands.

"Mama sick?" the baby crooned. "Lindy loves Mama." Amanda grabbed her daughter and pressed her to her breast, thanking God they had both been saved. She vowed to put the memory of her lost son in the far reaches of her mind, and swore to make the best life she could for the trusting little girl in her arms.

What was she to do now? Ugly was dead. She knew she must bury his body, though heart urged her to let the buzzards have him. Unfortunately neither Ugly's horse nor his mule had made it back. She assumed the Indians had stolen them.

Amanda found her old basket behind the burned cabin. It had somehow survived the fire. She packed her supplies and treasures in the basket, and as the air was getting cool, she made sure that the blanket was wrapped tightly around Melinda. She wished that Old Spotty, the cow had lived long enough to provide them with milk but she had died a year earlier of old age. Ugly had threatened to butcher her, but for once she had been able to prevail upon him. The cow had become a beloved pet so Amanda had buried Old Spotty in the soft earth near the edge of the woods.

Now it was time to bury Ugly. In her weakened condition, it had taken nearly an hour to drag his corpse to a place behind the wood pile where the earth was soft enough for her to dig a shallow grave using a broken piece of charred wood. The day was waning and she did not want to stay another night in this hated place.

Amanda's hands were blistered by the time the hole was deep enough. She rolled Ugly's body into the grave and then placed the tiny stillborn infant beside his father. She covered them with the loose soil and piled on logs from the log pile to discourage scavengers. In spite of everything he had done to her, Amanda knew she must place his name on the grave. She found a scorched board and scratched Ugly's real name, and that of Hyrum Junior, and propped the board among a small pile of gathered rocks.

Then Amanda dug around in the vegetable garden, and was blessed with a few carrots and about a dozen potatoes, which she added to her small store of supplies. She took one last look around the small clearing. So it was finally over, she thought. This part of her life was now behind her, and for the first time in nearly five years, a feeling of hope blossomed.

She was alive. She was young and strong, and her little girl was healthy and beautiful. She looked up at the clear, blue sky with its fluffy white clouds and gave thanks. She was free at last from the domination of a cruel man.

While the years behind her had been filled with grief and revulsion, they had given her a strength of spirit and a determination hitherto un-recognized.

Lifting Melinda and positioning her securely under her left arm, she propped the supply basket on her right hip and headed into the stretch of trees that edged the forest.

Travel was rough as there were no paths Amanda could find. Ugly had been careful to enter and leave his clearing by different routes so that there would be no clear path of escape worn in the forest floor.

Amanda often had to stop and rest. Her groin ached from the miscarriage, and made walking difficult. She had to carry Melinda over the rough terrain. When she found places where the trees were thin and the forest floor was covered only with leaves and pine needles, the baby toddled along happily beside her. Fortunately, the weather was still warm, summer surrendering slowly to autumn. To Melinda, this was all a great adventure.

The sky was darkening above the treetops, and Amanda knew she needed to find a place for the night. Fortunately she had added a flint to her supplies, and when she found what looked like a safe haven beneath a giant, red barked tree, she set about making a small fire to keep them warm and to frighten away wild animals. When the fire was burning, she slipped off her skirt and placed it on the soft pine needles. She then placed the exhausted youngster atop the skirt and covered her with their one blanket.

It took only a few minutes of Amanda's softly singing her favorite lullaby before Melinda was fast asleep. Amanda sat for a long time gazing at her child. As the firelight played on her daughter's sleeping face, Amanda's heart was filled with love and pride. She sat quietly contemplating her next move. Finally giving up this energy-wasting pastime, she set about preparing a meager meal for the two them.

Amanda woke Melinda and they ate silently. The child had hardly finished her hard biscuit when she lay back on the blanket and was again fast asleep. Amanda repacked the supply basket, and settled down next to Melinda on the cold ground. She pulled the edge of the blanket over her slim body. Hugging Melinda close to her to share their warmth, Amanda soon fell into a deep, restful sleep, the animal sounds soothing rather than frightening her.

Amanda opened her eyes to a bright new morning. As she blinked her eyes to accustom them to the sunlight dappling through the tree branches, they flew open in surprise. There before her eyes were two large booted feet.

Her first thought was that Ugly had followed them, and then she remembered he was dead. Her eyes followed the boots upward, past sturdy leather leggings, and a heavy dark green doublet to a smiling, bearded face.

"Do not be afraid, little lady. I will not hurt you or your child," a deep bass voice assured her.

"Wh...who are you?" Amanda managed.

"My name is Jonathan Webster, but most folks call me Jon. I have been searching the woods for you," he answered.

"For me?" Amanda stammered. "But how could you know anything about me?" she asked, sitting up and pulling the blanket tight under her chin. "Oh, we have known about you since Biggs brought you out here, Ma'am."

Amanda was mystified. "But, how could you? We are hundreds of miles from any people."

"Hundreds of miles? Is that what Biggs told you? He musta been afraid you would try to escape if you knew where you were."

"You mean....?"

"There is a trading post about two miles from here. The owner's wife, Molly, was the woman who helped you birth your child," he revealed. "Molly did not tell you about it?"

Seeing Amanda's shocked expression, he continued. "I guess Biggs made her promise to keep her mouth shut! He was quite a bastard. Pardon my language."

Amanda sat up quickly, upset. "You mean to tell me there were others who knew where I was, and no one ever came to help me?" she cried.

"There was not much we could do. Biggs held legal indenture papers on you. But me, or my other trapper, kept an eye on you from time to time, knowing what type of man Biggs was. That is how I come to be lookin' fer you. We saw the smoke from over at the trading post, and I lit out for yer place. That's when I saw what was left of yer cabin. What was it, Injuns?"

Amanda sighed. "Yes, they killed Hyrum and set fire to the cabin after they took what they wanted."

"I found Bigg's grave but no sign of you or the child. That's when I came lookin' for ya. Ya musta been goin' in circles, cause I tracked you until dark and then started again at daybreak. Mighty glad to find you. I found Bigg's horse dead in the woods near the cabin. No sign of the mule. How'd you survive them Injuns?"

"Hyrum built a hiding place under the floor. We hid there until they left." Amanda explained. "We got out of the burning cabin just in time. I had to get Melinda away from there in case the Indians returned."

"Well, better get your things ready and I'll get you to the trading post where Molly can take care of the both of you. I imagine you are right hungry."

Amanda gathered her little girl in her arms as Melinda slowly awakened, rubbing her eyes. "Yes, we could both use a decent meal, and then perhaps you can set me on the path to Jamestown."

"No problem. Here, let me carry that basket. Jamestown is only ten miles from the trading post. I'll let you get dressed and we will go."

Webster picked up the supply basket and walked a few feet away. He stood with his back to Amanda as she shook the twigs and pine needles from her skirt and pulled it on over her petticoat. When she and Melinda were ready, she followed the huge trapper to the trading post. As they walked, Amanda became more and more confused. "But, I do not understand. It took us three days to get to Ug...Hyrum's cabin. He told me we were very many miles from any civilization."

"Probably rode you round-and-round so's you would think you could not find yer way back, Ma'am," Jon offered. Amanda shook her head. Why should this surprise her?

Amanda was amazed at the warm greetings they received at the trading post. It was nice to see Molly. She enjoyed Molly's warmth and hugs. Molly could not get over how big and beautiful Melinda was.

"Proud it is that I helped bring this lovely child into the world," Molly cooed. She then set about fixing a big breakfast of eggs, milk, and fresh baked bread covered with honey. Melinda was thrilled with all the attention she was receiving, and drank two large mugs of warm cider.

As they ate, Amanda surveyed the inside of the post. It was a large building with heavy wooden beams in the ceiling. There was a bar along one wall and tables and chairs around a big black wood-burning stove. Shelves held all types of supplies.

Amanda liked Molly's husband, Tom Munk. He was kind and thoughtful, and he and Jonathan Webster kept the breakfast alive with funny stories of their adventures in the wilderness. Melinda's merry laughter filled the room and Amanda felt genuinely happy for the first time in years. Upon finishing his meal, Jon grabbed up his supplies and excused himself. "Got to get back to work. Please excuse me ladies." At that he tipped his hat and trudged out the front door.

"What kind of work does Jon do?" Amanda asked.

"He's a hunter. We work with two of them, Jon and Hank. Biggs used to come in once in a while with an animal. We support our men with ammunition and supplies. They bring their carcasses to us and Tom sells them to the butchers in Jamestown," Molly explained.

When Amanda and Melinda had eaten their fill, Tom provided Amanda with an old wooden tub filled to the brim with warm water. Amanda bathed Melinda, accompanied by the youngster's screaming and giggling. Amanda then took her place in the tub as Molly added some steaming water. Years of washing in a large pot with a rag had left Amanda feeling soiled. Now she luxuriated in the tub as she scrubbed away what seemed like five years of dirt. She had saved the best for last as she ducked her head in the water and scrubbed her raven hair. Molly poured clear, warm rinse water from her pitcher over Amanda's head. Amanda stepped from the tub and quickly dried her body and hair. How wonderful it felt to be really clean again. When she was dry, she slipped into one of Molly's warm flannel nightgowns, as Molly insisted that she and the baby needed naps. Molly refused to discuss the future until her wishes were obeyed, so Amanda nestled down into the softest bed she had ever experienced, cuddled Melinda to her breast, and they both drifted into deep, dreamless slumber.

Upon awaking, Amanda looked around for her print dress but it was nowhere to be found. Molly entered carrying a dress over her arm. "Oh, you are awake, dearie. I brought you my favorite dress. I will never get down to this size again, so you might as well have it."

"Oh, Molly, how kind you are." As Molly held up the dress, Amanda caught her breath. It was of a dark blue woolen fabric trimmed with light blue satin at collar and cuffs. It was the finest dress Amanda had ever seen. Fabric died with Indigo was much desired.

"It is just sitting there in the trunk going to waste. I want you to have it, dearie. You cannot go to Jamestown in that old cotton dress I gave you. Here, try this on and we will see if it needs taking in." Molly helped Amanda into the dress, after supplying fresh linen underwear and a full petticoat to her guest. The dress fit perfectly. Molly fastened the small buttons up the back of the dress and turned Amanda to face her.

"Well, if it doesn't look like it was made fer you. Wish you could see how elegant you look, dearie," Molly smiled happily.

"It is beautiful, Molly. I do not know how I can ever thank you."

"I worried myself sick about you and that little one, but Tom said we had no right to interfere. I am glad that monster is dead! Everyone hated him. He was a cheat and a liar. I know your life must have been hell, but you are free of him. Now, let us see what kind of a dress we can come up with for this beautiful baby."

Molly found an old cotton print dress made of a sturdy material, and the two women cut it down for Melinda.

"Do you have any idea what you are going to do when you get to Jamestown Colony, dearie?" Molly queried.

"No, none at all. I guess I will try to find work at an inn or as a maid in some household. I can read and write, so that should help."

"I used to be a lady's maid before I married Tom and came out here. The folks I worked for were real nice people. I'll write you a letter telling them how special you are. I bet they might give you a place."

"Oh, Molly, would you? That would be wonderful! You, Tom and Jon have been so kind to me. I do not know how I can thank you."

"Just seeing you and the youngster started on a decent life is thanks enough for us, dearie. We are expecting Jon back from his hunting trip in a day or two. He will take the two of you into Jamestown on his mule if you are up to it," Molly promised.

"Oh, Molly, that will be wonderful, not that I won't miss you, but I have to get situated for Melinda's sake."

Three days later, Jon Webster loaded his restless mule with Amanda's belongings and a large bundle of food that Molly had prepared. Jon enjoyed some of Tom's beer while Molly said her goodbyes to Amanda and Melinda. She barraged them with good advice.

"I am sure as heck gonna miss you two," Molly said, tucking a new woolen cloak under the baby's chin. "This here youngun' is a smart little lass, and she sure has her mama's good looks."

"I am not looking too good now, as thin as I am," Amanda complained.

"That makes no difference, young lady. The kind of beauty you have comes from within, and shines around you like a candle."

Amanda smiled shyly. "Thank you, Molly. My self-respect needs a lot of healing, but I am starting to feel human again. I know that Melinda and I are going to be fine, thanks to you."

"And do not forget where we are, Amanda. You know if you ever need us, we are here for you," Molly assured.

Amanda bent down to pick up Melinda and was promptly included in a game of toss the ball. Jon heard the wonderful sound of their laughter, and joined them at play. Then he lifted the child into his huge arms and carried her out to the waiting mule. Amanda followed and climbed onto the mule's broad back. Jon set Melinda down on the mule in front of her mother.

Amanda waved her last goodbyes. They left the trading post behind with Jon walking beside the mule.

"How you doin, young lady?" Jon asked Melinda.

"Me doing fine, papa," the baby replied.

Amanda laughed gaily. "Oh, Melinda, Jon is not your papa."

"Yes, papa! my papa...I want!" Melinda insisted, eliciting laughter from both of her adult companions.

Jon took great joy in being with the two young females, enjoying their appreciation of the world around them and the lush beauty of the forest. They were surrounded by trees of all sizes and shapes, and shrubs. Some of the trees were sporting leaves of red and yellow as Autumn was upon them. Occasionally they passed berry bushes and Jonathan picked the remaining berries to the delight of Amanda and

Melinda. Jon pointed out which berries were safe to eat, and Melinda's face was soon purple around her mouth from the colorful fruit.

Jon, a bachelor of forty-five, felt a small ache in his heart for never having a wife and child of his own. He knew nothing could come of the feeling he had developed for the young raven-haired beauty he traveled with, but somewhere in his heart he wished he were twenty years younger. He knew that Amanda deserved a better life than he could offer her. She belonged to the light and she deserved the very best.

As the sky started to darken, Amanda spied a small house in the distance. As they moved closer, the settlement of Jamestown came into view.

"We can get supper at the Settler's Inn, then my cousin is gonna put you up for the night in her home. It is not far from here. In the morning you can check on that job," Jon smiled.

"Are you staying there, too?" Amanda asked.

"No, I'll see you two get to Hannah's place, but I have to get back to the woods. I got lots of work to do tomorrow. This is our best hunting weather."

As they shared generous bowls of delicious stew in the public room at the small inn near the harbor, Amanda wondered what the morrow would hold. The stew was full of meat and fresh vegetables and was accompanied by fresh bread and honey. She washed the food down with a mild ale while Melinda enjoyed a mug of apple cider.

Amanda could not know that in the kitchen of this very inn, her old friend Aggie was taking a dessert of hot plum pudding from the huge oven. As Aggie carried the hot pudding out to the public room, Jon led Amanda and Melinda out the front door of the inn and set off in the direction of his cousin's home.

The next morning, having been fed a large breakfast by Webster's cousin, Hannah, who was a small gray-haired spinster woman of a friendly nature, drove Amanda and Melinda to the entrance of the MacDougal mansion. Amanda was scared, but stopped to say a small prayer that she and Melinda would find a position and a home.

11

Jamestown Colony, 1628

Jonathan Webster had arranged for his cousin, Hannah, to take Amanda and Melinda to the entrance to MacDougal property in her small carriage. As Hannah's carriage drove away, Amanda stood at the entrance to a long drive leading to a huge house. She held Melinda's tiny hand in hers. As she stood gazing at the house her knees felt week and her heart advised her to take flight.

"What if they turned her down? Where could they go from here?" she wondered.

She straightened her shoulders and they started up the drive, passing beautifully landscaped areas of grass and flowering plants. The mansion seemed like a castle and had an overlarge carved wooden front door.

Making sure she had Molly's note in the pocket of her cloak, she helped Melinda up onto the veranda. Taking a deep breath, and holding it for an agonizing moment, she reached up and lifted the large bronze doorknocker. She breathed a quick prayer, and then let it drop.

A few moments later, the large doors opened and a tall, elegantly dressed man stared down his haughty nose at her. His skin was a deep mahogany, his eyes large, his mouth full. His hair was black, shiny and tightly curled. Amanda remembered seeing a few men of similar complexion at the auction. Finally, he spoke. "Yes?" Amanda swallowed hard and showed him Molly's folded missive. Clearing her throat, she spoke. "I am here seeking employment. I have this letter..."

"Around to the back, mistress. This door is for family and guests only." He moved to close the door.

"Around...?" Amanda stammered.

Pointing to the left side of the building, he explained, "Around that way and left again. You will see the servants' entrance. Good day!" He closed the door on his final word.

As the door closed, Amanda lifted Melinda into her arms and started around the house. The door of the servant's entrance was standing open, but Amanda stepped up and tapped lightly. After a few moments, she tapped again.

The woman who came to the door was of indeterminate age. She wore a black gown enhanced at collar and cuffs with cream colored lace. Her long face made Amanda think of their pet cow, and she would have laughed had she not been so frightened. The woman looked her up, and down with narrowed, dark eyes. When the woman looked at Melinda, her thin mouth became tighter.

"How can I help you?" her cold voice queried.

"I...I am a friend of Molly Worth, who is now Mistress Thomas Munk. She used to work here. I have a letter..." She held the folded note out to the woman who took it and scanned it. The woman then scrutinized Amanda. She finally motioned them in and indicated a chair by the door.

"Wait here while I talk to the mistress," she said. She then turned and headed for a stairway near the fireplace. As she disappeared up the stairs with a haughty air, Amanda sat in the chair, lifting Melinda onto her lap and placing her bag on the floor.

She then surveyed the kitchen. She had never seen anything like it. It was tremendous. The room was constructed of dark, polished wood. There were shelves stacked with food goods. Amanda was entranced with the massive fireplace and its brick hearth. It was almost as wide as the wall and had a chimney which was wide at the bottom and narrowed as it reached the ceiling. There were kettles and pots of all sizes hanging from it. At the top of the hearth there was a long pole. Suspended from this pole was an arm that held a huge cooking pot. Amanda watched entranced as a woman stoked the dying flames beneath until all that remained were red coals. What the woman was stirring smelled delicious. Amanda's mouth was watering in spite of the breakfast Hannah had provided.

"Lindy wants food, mama." The child's tiny hand tugged at her bodice.

"Not right now, sweetie."

A maid, who was arranging a tray, noticed the child's gesture. She spoke a few words to a plump woman, who was probably the head cook. The woman nodded her head. Her round chin sat on two rolls of fat but she had a merry smile.

The young maid ladled some porridge into two bowls and placed one before Melinda.

"Here, honey gal. You looks like you could use somethin' tasty. I will get ya some honey to put on it. "Straight from the bees, honey," she smiled. She placed the second bowl before Amanda. Dig in, ladies." The girl's smile was warm and welcoming, and did a lot to help Amanda relax. The maid got the honey and Melinda gobbled down the porridge.

Amanda could not help staring at the young maid as she went about her business. Amanda had heard about dark skinned women but had never seen one. This girl looked about sixteen or seventeen, and she was lovely. She had a softly rounded face with large brown eyes. Her complexion was that of a cup of cocoa, and her brown hair was cut short and curled softly. A good linen print dress covered by a huge white apron completed the picture.

As the girl cleared away Melinda's dish, she smiled up at Amanda. "I got myself a youngun, too, Missy. She about the same age as this 'un. She about three ain't she?"

"Yes, she just turned three." Amanda looked down at Melinda who was watching the maid intently.

"Thank you so much for the porridge. It seems Melinda's always hungry. Part of growing up, I guess."

"Melinda," the girl repeated. "My, that shur is a purty name. My baby named Esther. You know, fer thet lady in the bible. They calls me Cinnamon, cause my skin so light. My real name Uganya, but we ain't 'lowed to use that name no more. I ain't no slave though, I'ze a paid housegirl. Well, I better finish this tray before Mizz Curtin get back."

Amanda dipped her own spoon into the thick porridge and took a bite. She could not remember when anything had tasted so good. She looked up in time to see the cook smiling at her. She returned the smile, nodding her thanks.

Moments later, the woman in the black dress returned, and asked Amanda to bring the child and follow her. They made their way through some swinging doors and found themselves in a short hallway. The walls were paneled, and were covered by beautiful tapestries. There were huge ceramic vases set at intervals on the long table in the center of the hall. These were filled with fresh flowers. The floors were almost too beautiful to walk on, being highly polished inlaid wood. Above the center of the foyer hung a huge chandelier which held hundreds of candles. Amanda thought that it must have taken weeks to make all of those candles. They came to a wide stairway leading to a floor above.

They slowly ascended the staircase with its highly polished banisters, and upon reaching a landing, turned down a hallway. The walls on each side of the hallway were covered with large oil paintings of proud, stern-faced men wearing strange outfits with skirts. They came to a halt in front of a tall door elegantly carved with patterns.

The woman in black tapped lightly on the door and a soft feminine voice bid them enter. As Amanda stepped into the room, her jaw slackened and her startled eyes took in the most magnificent bedchamber she could have imagined. "This must be a palace," she whispered. "No one but a queen could have a room like this."

The woman in black almost let a smile reach her stern lips, but thought better of it. She watched as Amanda's amazed eyes scanned her surroundings. It was indeed a beautiful room. It had many tall windows. Soft sunlight swept past fine yellow lace curtains that moved with the breeze from the open panes. The beams of sunlight set the gold trim on the walls afire. The walls were also pale yellow trimmed with ivory, and the floor was covered with thick carpeting with patterns of pastel spring flowers.

However, the thing that dominated the room was the draped four poster bed made up with ivory satin pillows and comforter.

"I spend so much time here; I wanted it ta be cheery," a sweet voice met her ears. Her attention was drawn to the woman propped up against satin pillows in the center of the bed. The woman spoke with a soft accent unfamiliar to Amanda. "The ceiling is ma pride and joy."

Amanda's eyes were drawn upward and her breath caught in her throat as she stared at the ceiling in awe. The whole ceiling was delicately painted with sky, clouds, and flying cherubim, with many gold highlights.

"Ma old husband had it painted fer me when he built this house. It was completed in 1625. Ma husband designed the house as close as possible to our castle in Scotland. We were forced to give our home and lands in Scotland over t'the English, before escaping to the colonies. Come over here, lassie, so I can get a better look at ya."

Amanda took Melinda in hand and moved to the side of the bed. This also gave her a better look at the sweet-voiced invalid. Propped cozily among the large down pillows was a small delicate woman who was probably younger than she looked. She was very thin, and there were small dark pouches under her bright gray eyes. Amanda imagined that she must have been a beauty when she was younger.

Amanda stood gazing at the bed's occupant. It was almost as if she had seen this woman someplace before, but of course, she could not have.

While Amanda stood contemplating, Melinda had used the time to climb onto the bed- stool and pull herself up onto the comforter close to the old woman.

"Oh, Melinda, shame on you." Amanda started to pull back the child. "I am so sorry, She is a curious child."

"Nay. let the bairn stay. It has been a long time since I have had a young lassie around." At that, the invalid opened her arms and Melinda flopped into them, a smile wreathing her little face.

Amanda looked on in amazement. The woman and child were hugging and laughing as if they had always known each other.

"Well lass, do not be standin' there with yer mouth open."

Amanda could not hide a smile as Melinda cuddled into the woman's arms, looking up happily at her confused mother.

"So, ye're a friend of Molly's, are ye? Is she still wastin' her life out there at that old trading post?"

"Yes...yes, mistress," Amanda managed to stammer.

"Molly's note says ya are a good lass and ya even know how to read and write. I can always use someone with a wee bit a learnin'."

"I am a good worker, mistress. I helped my mother with the laundry and mending she took in to support us. I also kept her books. I want to make a decent home for my little girl."

"My old husband, The MacDougal, is the former Laird of Clan MacDougal in our homeland, Scotland. He is away right now, but I expect him home any time. I am sure he will go along with my wishes."

"Do you mean...?" Amanda questioned.

"I will be happy to have you here, Amanda, is it?" Amanda smiled, "Yes, mistress."

"I think this old house is too gloomy for this wee lassie. I will have the foreman make a few repairs t'the wee cottage behind the buttery. Like I say, 'tis small, but should be comfortable enough fer ye and the bairn."

She indicated the woman in black. "This is Bertha Curtin. She is my housekeeper, and is in charge of all household activities. She came over from Scotland with us." Amanda nodded and Martha MacDougal turned again to Mistress Curtin. "Bertha, will ye please see that the cottage is cleaned and supplied with linens, food, and whatever else Mistress McNeely and her bairn might need. And have Addie fix something for them to eat at lunchtime."

"I will take care of it right away, mistress," Bertha replied, looking none too pleased.

Mistress MacDougal turned again to Amanda. "Ya and the lassie must be tired, now. Ya can stay in the guestroom down the hall 'til the cottage is ready. Tomorrow we will decide on yer duties."

"We must not tire the mistress," Mistress Curtin warned. Amanda nodded.

"I cannot thank you enough, Mistress MacDougal. What time would you like to see me in the morning?"

"Nine o'clock is the witchin' hour, lass. And, please, call me Martha; since we seem ta be sharin' a bairn." She laughed happily and relinquished Melinda to her mother.

And so it was that Amanda and Melinda became part of the MacDougal household.

As time went by, Bertha Curtin became a close friend and confidant, and Amanda was pleased to see the tight mouth soften until the long face lit up with recurrent smiles. Bertha visited Amanda and Melinda often in their tiny cottage. The rooms were small, but charmingly decorated and furnished. There was a kitchen and sitting room, plus, to Amanda's great delight, two bedrooms. For the first time in her life, Melinda had a bedroom of her own.

Amanda placed her other pride and joy, mother's mirror and brush set, on the mahogany dressing table in her airy bedroom. She polished the hand-worked pattern to a rich glow. Loving the feel of it, she often ran her hand over the back of the mirror as she passed the dresser. This was so far above what she had ever known that she felt a sense thanksgiving for the first time in her life.

Martha and Bertha Curtin had agreed that Amada would take over Martha's care, relieving Bertha to her household duties. After a time, Amanda also took over the posting of the household accounts.

Amanda learned much about the family from the young housemaid, Cinnamon, who she discovered was married to Arthur, the man who had answered the door when she and Melinda first arrived. Arthur served as both butler and valet when the master was present. Amanda was intrigued to learn that both Arthur and Cinnamon had been purchased by The MacDougal.

The story Cinnamon confided to her was like something from a book. It seemed that she and Arthur had been taken from different villages in a place called Africa. They had been brought to the New World on a Dutch ship. Since 1619, African men and women had been transported to the colonies for sale as workers.

Their trip over had been worse than Amanda's. The future slaves in large numbers had been crowded together in the ship's hold with little food or water. Arthur, whose real name was Mowanga, had spotted Cinnamon and his heart had gone out to her. He had kept his eye on her to protect her, but chained and weak as he was, he was unable to prevent one of the sailors from dragging her up on deck and having his way with her.

In her grief and shame, the girl, Uganya, had accepted Mowanga's comforting words. He had begged a guard to let her stay near him until the landing in Jamestown. On the day the two Africans were put on the auction block in Jamestown, an older man in the crowd had heard an indignant cry from a young female. He had turned to see a burly sailor shaking a young dark skinned girl. She was holding her ragged dress closed over her bosom. At that moment a tall chained black man broke away from his captors and pulled the sailor away from the girl.

The auctioneer signaled his men, and they dragged Mowanga away, as he struggled to get at the offending sailor.

Without a second thought, the tall, gray haired man immediately put up his hand and signaled the auctioneer to his side saying that whatever they were asking for that girl, and the man who tried to rescue her, he would double it. He instructed them to bring the pair to him right away. He warned them to handle them gently. The auctioneer had nodded, checked with the Dutch captain, and come back with a large monetary figure. He was paid on the spot by the older man, and then the man directed the pair to his buggy.

"So, you became part of MacDougal life," Amanda noted.

"Thet right, Mizz," Arthur spoke as he entered the kitchen. "The MacDougal brought us here to this great house, let us choose new names, and bought us some decent clothes. Addie March, the cook, who had originally been indentured, trained Cinnamon and me in the household arts, and Mistress MacDougal gave us lessons in both English and Scottish," he explained.

"So you two are slaves? That is hard to believe. I know how horrible slavery must be. You were blessed to belong to a good man," Amanda sympathized.

Oh, no. We is not slaves! The MacDougal had his people make out papers for us. We is free, paid servants."

"Oh yes, I remember Cinnamon saying that. It is extraordinary! But, if you are free, why do you stay here?" Amanda queried.

"There ain't no place for us to go, Mistress. If we was to leave here, even with our papers, we would be picked up by slave dealers and forced to go into bondage. We gots to stay here where we is taken care of and is safe." Cinnamon explained.

Arthur took up their story again. He explained that before another month had elapsed Cinnamon had discovered that she was with child. Since she had been a virgin when taken from her village, there was no doubt that the sailor who had raped her was the father.

It was at that point that Arthur had made his love for Cinnamon known. The two servants had subsequently been allowed to marry. Arthur's love and devotion soon sparked a mutual love in Cinnamon's heart.

Cinnamon liked to care for Melinda when she was not on duty. She enjoyed having a companion for her Esther who was three months older than Melinda. The two children became fast friends and playmates. Amanda was happy to see both girls growing chubby, more talkative, and fun loving. She thanked God daily for their new life.

Amanda also learned that the MacDougal's had two children who had survived to adulthood. There was a daughter, Fiona, who had married into a wealthy family that was gambling on a new produce called tobacco. They lived in a European style house just outside of Jamestown. There was also a son, but Amanda was given no information about him.

It was not until their first Christmas at MacDougal House that Amanda would meet the daughter. Fiona's first visit was not a happy occasion, as she was anything but pleased that her mother had taken in this young woman and her chubby child. Worst of all they were being treated like members of the family.

Fiona was an attractive young woman, with warm chestnut brown hair and brown eyes that were, unfortunately, bereft of emotion. She stood five feet tall and was slim of figure. Her face was diamond shaped and her forehead was high over a patrician nose. Her mouth was thin. She might have been considered a beauty, except for the hard lines that were beginning to form at the sides of her mouth.

"How are we supposed to maintain our standing in the community if you take in riff-raff off the road?" she demanded of her mother.

"I have no intention of arguing w'ye, Fiona. This is my home, and who I invite into it is my business," Martha countered.

"It is father's house, too! What is he going to say when he comes home and finds this woman and her bastard living here?" Fiona demanded.

"Yer father is a kind and generous mon. Ya dinna have to worry about what he thinks. I have never seen him turn from anyone in need."

The argument went on through Christmas dinner, which Amanda and Melinda enjoyed in the kitchen with the servants. Obviously Martha had won the day as Fiona had stalked off after Christmas breakfast and had not been heard from since.

If Martha was unhappy about Fiona's cold departure, she did not show it. She was aware that her daughter had become a snob. "She will coom back when she is needin' something," the old woman muttered.

As time went by Amanda got a picture of the missing son. She heard nothing but good about him. The offspring that Martha was most proud of was a man of twenty-five named James the Second. The missing son was the reason the master of the house was absent. James Junior had remained in Scotland to try and reclaim the family's ancestral holdings. However, when the dust of battle settled, and their holdings had gone to an English lord, James had not followed his family to the New World. He had stayed in Scotland to fight with the rebels in the Highlands. When the MacDougal's had not heard from their son for two years they feared he was either a prisoner or dead.

The old MacDougal refused to give up on his son and heir so about eight months before Amanda and Melinda arrived at MacDougal House, he had set off for the old world to trace his missing son. He determined to bring James or his body back to Jamestown.

Amanda also learned that the MacDougal's made their living off a herd of cattle, which had sprung from the six head of cattle, and one bull they had transported to the colonies from the Highlands.

The cattle were being raised and marketed by a very able man named Angus Breen, a Scotsman who had accompanied his employer to the New World. Since the family's arrival, they had acquired two bondsmen to assist in raising the cattle.

One of the bondsmen was Mathew Fergus, a Scotsman, who had fought with the MacDougal in the wars against the English. He had followed his clan leader to the colonies by signing as an indenture. When his indentures were fulfilled, he had sought out the MacDougal and had immediately been employed.

The second hireling was a Swedish man named Swen Larson. His family had immigrated to England when they had lost their land in Sweden. Unhappy with their life in England, they had taken ship to the New World. They purchased a small piece of farmland and raised enough food to survive. In time Swen had acquired ten head of cattle, and was fascinated by animal husbandry.

However, in Swen's second season raising his own cattle, a disease had hit his animals and he found himself and his family so deeply in debt that he had to sell his property. With no home, his family, a wife and two sons, had gone back to Sweden to stay with Swen's parents until he could afford to send for them. The MacDougal was happy to hire Swen, who proved to be a good worker and also showed an interest in the gardens. He happily took over the extra job of tending the vegetables and the flowers.

As time went by, Martha became more worried about her husband. She blamed herself for sending the aging man on a search that was probably hopeless, and was afraid that he had come to harm. She had no communication from him in many months.

Amanda was concerned about the toll it was taking on the old woman. Martha seemed to be getting weaker every day, and occasionally coughed up blood, which was a sign of the dreaded lung fever. Amanda realized that she had become very attached to this kindly woman. Melinda loved her dearly, and called her grandma.

The times when Martha blossomed were when the two young girls plopped themselves on her bed and questioned her on her life in Scotland.

"You really lived in a castle?" Melinda queried, "A real castle with a big river around it? Mama told me you did."

"Yes, I guess ye could call it a castle. It had water around it, which we called a moat. It had a big gate, called a portcullis. It kept bad people out. We also had two high towers so we could see a long way and could tell when bad people were coming," Martha explained.

"Is this house anything like it?" Esther asked.

"Oh, yes, except we did not need the portcullis, the moat and the towers. The rest of the house is much the same."

"Oh, I like this house. I shall call it our castle anyway," Melinda chirped.

"Me, too," echoed Esther. I am gonna be a princess!"

"Me, too!" Melinda squealed, as both girls bounced up and down on the bed.

Fortunately, Bertha Curtin came into the room and rescued a tousled Martha.

When Amanda's daily chores were completed, she was left with a great deal of free time. Amanda often assisted Addie March, the head cook, in the kitchen, but Addie was so competent that this did not fill much of Amanda's time.

She and Melinda enjoyed their cottage. Amanda's bedroom was fairly large, and contained a comfortable bed and a rocking chair. She loved cuddling Melinda while telling her bedtime stories.

Amanda often took the little girls for walks on the property. They loved the cows and stopped to talk to them. Slowly Amanda started taking an interest in the cattle business. She liked Angus, who was a crusty old fellow. He knew cattle. She was amazed how much work the little man could handle so she offered to take care of the bookkeeping for the cattle business as well as the household books. This offer was greeted with a grateful smile.

It was now 1630, and Amanda was amazed that two years had slipped by since she and Melinda arrived at MacDougal House. Amanda's life had assumed a pattern that had given her a feeling of wellbeing. Nightmares of her early years in the wilderness became less frequent, and she was thankful she was no longer subject to a man's hands on her body. Although she enjoyed no social life outside her home, she was satisfied at the ease of her days and the way Melinda was blossoming.

Aside from Martha's failing health, life was serene for the occupants of the mansion. But this peace and quiet was shattered on that fateful day when the master returned to MacDougal House. Amanda and Cinnamon had been cleaning up after a small birthday party for Melinda in Martha's room. Esther was included because her birthday was so close. The two little girls were very proud of their five-year-old status.

The sounds of a carriage coming up the drive caught Amanda's attention. Her first thought was that Fiona was going to descend upon them again. Amanda looked out a front window to see what was happening. Her eyes widened as she saw a large, gilded coach pull to a halt in front. A groom dropped from his spot on the rear of the coach and opened the carriage door. He pulled down a step to accommodate the passenger. A tall, white-haired man stepped down and stood gazing at the mansion. He looked in his early sixties, but was still handsome. His features were even and strong, his posture proud.

He stood there long enough for her to take note of his fashionable attire, European in style, all gray with a touch of silver threading in the vest. His coat was long and fitted and his jabot was starched and elegantly tied. His high boots were black and highly polished. A dark blue cape was slung over one shoulder, and a black top hat was clutched in his long, graceful fingers.

As Amanda watched, Arthur ran out to greet the man, his usual dignified air vanishing in his joy to see his master again.

Arthur nodded to the groom, who immediately unloaded the luggage from atop the coach. Arthur ushered the white-haired man into the entryway of the house. By now Amanda knew he must be The MacDougal. She could hear much excited talking and laughter as the servants greeted their beloved master.

Amanda stepped back from the window, her heart beating faster, her feelings mixed. She did not know whether to go down and join the others, or go back to her cottage and wait to be summoned. She settled on the later and, taking Melinda by the hand, scurried down the back stairs and out onto the path to her cottage.

A few minutes later, Cinnamon sneaked out of the big house and went of Amanda's cottage. She was very excited and described the master's welcoming. "Right after Masta James give his cloak and hat to my Arthur, he went straight up to Mizz Martha's room." Cinnamon shook her head. "He was shocked to find out she was so sick," she frowned.

"Thanks for telling me, Cinnamon," Amanda said. Cinnamon then hurried back to the big house, leaving Amanda even more worried.

Twilight had dipped its cool colors on the landscape and dulled the hues of the roses by the time Amanda received her summons. She was singing a lullaby to Melinda. Just in case, Amanda had slipped into her best dress and redressed her chignon after tucking Melinda in bed. Cinnamon again knocked on the cottage door. Amanda followed Cinnamon through the back door of the mansion and down the hall to the library. Trepidation filled her as she prepared to meet the master of the house. She stood at the carved wooden door for a moment, gathering her courage, then lifted her chin and tapped lightly.

Amanda did not see him when she first entered, but as her eyes became accustomed to the candlelight, she made out the form of a tall man standing at one of the dormer windows. He dropped the drape back into place, and as he turned she experienced the full impact of the man's character. It was at that moment that the memory of that compassionate face came back to her. He looked much older, very tired and discouraged, but she could never forget those gray eyes. They had caught and held her attention from across the auction impound seven years ago.

Amanda realized she had been staring, and lowered her gaze.

"Will ya take a chair, young lass?" the deep resonant voice offered.

"Forgive me, sir. It is just that...it is just such a surprise, and a happy one that you have returned. Hope almost failed us many times."

"Ma wife told me all about ya, lass...and about the bairn. I went up ta see her as soon as I got home," he offered. "Sit down, ma dear." Amanda settled into a chair in front of the desk.

"Mistress Curtin tells me you and the wee one have been here for about two years, and that ya have been like a family t'her. I didnae know how t'express ma thanks ta'ya for yer care and services ta ma Martha. I hear she's grown to love ye both verra much. It eases ma guilt at ma own neglect a wee bit t' know she was nay alone, as I had pictured her," He explained.

"I know she is overjoyed at your return. We have been praying for this day."

"I have much ta discuss with ya. but I find that exhaustion has caught up wi' me. Not as young as I used to be, ma dear. If ye will fergive me, I will go up ta the encin' hot bath tha' Arthur's prepared fer me and retire for the night. We shall talk again i' the mornin.'"

"Of course," Amanda smiled.

He returned her smile and led her out to the hallway. As he turned away from her to climb the stairs, he stopped and gazed intently into her violet eyes. Then he shook his head as if he had given up placing her, and bid her good night.

The next morning after Melinda and Esther were settled with Martha. Amanda, fortified with a good hot breakfast, slipped into the library to do the household accounts. Startled, she stepped back as she saw the master of the house going over the books.

"Oh, I am...I am sorry, sir. I thought you were still in bed," she stammered.

"Quite all right, Martha and I had a wonderful reunion early this morning, lassie. Jest goin' over tha accounts to see how the place has fared in ma absence."

"We are in good shape. The livestock's healthy and bringing good prices."

"So I see. Martha tells me ya have been doin' the books fer the past year."

"Yes, sir."

"Verra good, ma dear. They look in fine order. I must thank ya fer your efforts on our behalf."

"I guess you will be taking over now, sir."

"Do ya mind doing this type a' work, lassie?" he asked.

"No, sir, not at all. I enjoy the books and working with the foreman."

"Verra glad to hear it, my dear as I have a lotta catchin' up ta do. It will help me verra much if ya be willin' ta continue yer excellent work."

Amanda realized she had been holding her breath, and released it in a fast rush of air. She and Melinda could stay! She smiled brightly.

"Oh, sir, I will be more than happy to continue doing the books."

"Fine, fine, ma dear. And how are yer livin' arrangements? We could find a place for ye in the house if ye'd prefer."

"Oh, no, sir, Melinda and I love our cottage. We are fine there."

"Then I had better let ye get to yer work. I'm goin' up t'visit wi' Martha for a while, and I understand the wee ones will be there. A good chance ta meet yer bairn," he smiled. "Thank ya again, ma dear, for all ya've done fer Martha n'me."

As the door closed quietly behind the MacDougal, Amanda heaved a great sigh. She looked at this room which she had worked in every day for so long, and realized how much she had learned to love it. It was a warm room, made so by the walnut wood of the desk, chairs and book cases, and the glow of the many colored books that lined the shelves.

She and Melinda were now secure.

Life soon slipped back into its normal pattern. Most of the business was left to Amanda and Angus, with the help of the two bondsmen. The master spent his time visiting with Martha, playing with Melinda and Esther, or reading in his huge leather chair in front of the library fireplace.

It took some time for the story of MacDougal's search for his oldest son to trickle down to Amanda and the servants. The MacDougal had taken ship to London, and then headed for Scotland, where he had looked up old friends still living in the Highlands. Most had been slain, imprisoned or evicted to be replaced by English noblemen. He had to keep his search quiet, and friends had hidden him while he searched records of those lost in battle. Nothing had been found to assure the safety or expose the whereabouts of young James Jr. The rebel bands had broken up, and the men dispersed throughout Scotland.

James had returned to London, where he hired men to search for his son among mercenary armies. When eight months had passed with no word of Jamie, he realized he could no longer neglect his home and family and purchased passage to the colonies.

Fate intervened. There was an outbreak of the Pox. He boarded himself up inside his rented house, and sat out the worst of the dread disease. Though he was spared, he was unable to get passage home. No ships were allowed to leave the harbor until the contagion was controlled, and with no ships, there were no letters carried. When the disease posed no further danger, James again made arrangements to take ship back to Jamestown.

The loss of his only son hung on the MacDougal like a pall, and he was worried about Martha. He had counted on the return of young

Jamie to lift his mother's spirits and aid in her recovery, but this was not to be.

Amanda's sympathy went out to him. He had tried so hard to find his son, but Amanda was pleased that the one bright spot in the lives of both Martha and James was Melinda. The child was growing more beautiful every day. Her brown hair was beginning to darken, and take on a chestnut hue. Amanda doubted it would become the jet black of her own locks. Melinda's dark blue eyes were large, and Amanda was sure Melinda's mouth had been turned up a birth, as it her face was always wreathed in smiles. Amanda marveled that the cheery little spirit had survived so much squalor and violence.

The MacDougal's appointed themselves godparents to both little girls, and as a result, Melinda was showered with gifts and beautiful dresses. Amanda made sure that Esther got her share of Melinda's dresses, and both little girls were always picture-book perfect, except when romping in the garden, or playing in the fields. The two girls could easily been mistaken for sisters, as Esther's skin was that of a white person with a light tan. Her hair was light brown, and softly waved. The two girls were inseparable, in mischief as well as duty. Their laughter echoed through the halls, filling everyone with joy. Both children loved the old couple with all their hearts and Amanda had learned to love the old man, too. She worried about both oldsters.

From time to time, Amanda would catch the old MacDougal looking at her as if trying to place a memory. One afternoon, as she was working on the household books, he joined her in the library. After making a show of looking on the shelves for an appropriate book, he took a seat in front of the desk and sat staring at her until she finally felt his stare and looked up.

"I am sorry, sir. Is there something I can do for you?" she queried.

"Yey, ma dear, there is. I have been plagued wi' a feelin' of havin' seen ya before ever since I returned home. I know 'tis highly improbable that we've ever met, but I can't rid maself a this feelin'. I have asked Martha about ya, but she feels it is not up ta her to reveal what ya have confided to her about yer past."

"I have no reason to keep it secret, but it was considerate of Martha to do so." She set her pen down, folded her hands on the desk, and proceeded to tell her story to the MacDougal. When she got to the part about the auction, he immediately interrupted her, sitting up straight and looking amazed.

"Of course! The ragamuffin at the auction in twenty-three! We were lookin' fer a bondservant to care fer Martha, when I spotted ya. Ya were so fragile in those rags, but those amazin' violet eyes caught ma attention. I was about ta suggest ya to Martha, when she had one a her spells and we had'da return home. I often thought about ya in the followin' years, wonderin' what had been yer fate." He lowered his head on his shaking hands. "Had I known what ya were to suffer, I would ha' moved mountains to save ya. I am so sorry, ma dear."

Amanda's heart went out to this caring man who had added her welfare to his many responsibilities. She rose and went around the desk to put her hand on the old man's shoulder.

"Please, sir, do not grieve for me. As you can see, the good Lord has made up for the past, making my daughter and I a part of this loving household. You and Martha are the grandparents Melinda would never have had. We are so happy here that the past has faded like a bad dream," she comforted.

"Ya know, ma dear, that Martha and I have become verra fond of ya and Melinda. There is no question that ya will ever be wi'out a good home from now on. I shall see ta that."

It was a promise he kept. As the next few years rolled by, Amanda and Melinda grew in health and happiness, and their roots grew deep into the soil of MacDougal lands.

12

Amanda, even lovelier at twenty-eight than as a young girl, sat embroidering in front of a huge gilded fireplace at MacDougal House. Dropping her embroidery on her lap, she sat staring into the leaping flames, hypnotized by their flickering movements. She relaxed in the warmth of the flames. Having leisure time was a luxury she relished.

She pulled her focus from the bright flames and examined the small parlor that was now her private hideaway. She marveled at the beauty of the pale green walls trimmed at top and wall seams in gold Rococo. The floor-to-wall drapes were ivory velvet with golden tassels. The chandelier was of multifaceted crystal drops attached with gold filigree findings and boasted ten candles. Delicate Chippendale furniture sat upon soft carpeting of a rose and leaf pattern on an ivory background. The seat coverings on the gracefully carved chairs were made of the same ivory velvet as the drapes. All of these luxuries had been imported from the motherland.

As Amanda stood to add a log to the fire, the folds of her teal blue gown swayed gracefully. The dress was the latest mode from Paris, with beige lace at collar and cuffs. Her figure had matured and the dress closely fit her small waist and flattered her now generous bust-line.

Amanda sighed as she returned to her chair and picked up her sewing. She was a different person now. She was fashionable and content, a beautiful woman in the prime of her life. Her heart shaped face had regained its porcelain smoothness and her raven tresses were pinned up in fashionable curls that fell to below her shoulders. Her wide-set violet eyes had lost their hunted look. Amanda could not help but compare her present luxurious quarters with her mother's small attic room in London, and the dilapidated wilderness cabin where she had borne her beautiful Melinda. Here she sat, a whole lifetime away from the day she had applied for a position as maid.

Happy now, she often wondered about Bridget and Aggie. She prayed that they were alive and well. Would the ever meet again?

As the pleasant aroma of cedar logs wafted up from the fireplace, she let her mind drift. Her life had taken a drastic change two years before when her dear Martha had finally found peace. James had been inconsolable, and had retired more and more into himself, taking his meals in his room and secluding himself from everyone.

Bertha Curtin stayed on after Martha's death and continued to run the household. Together she and Amanda had decided to reduce the household help to Addie, Arthur and Cinnamon. Addie took the rear cottage that Amanda and Melinda had shared, and her husband and two children joined her there.

Melinda, now eleven, was a precocious young girl. When she was six years old, James had hired a tutor and her lessons had begun. Due to Amanda's request and Martha's urging, little Esther had been allowed to join in Amanda's studies and was becoming quite a refined young lady.

At eleven and a half, Esther was pretty and even lighter skinned than Cinnamon. Her features were refined, giving no hint of her African heritage. Melinda and Esther were closer than ever. Esther's speech had also lost the rhythm of her forbears, although she reverted when speaking with her parents.

Little disturbed the quiet of the MacDougal residence after Martha's death. The cattle business was running smoothly under the guardianship of Angus and his two bondsmen. There was now a new gardener named Lazar Epstein. Lazar had been a horticulturist in his native country. Lazar had left Russia due to over-taxation and starvation earnings for Jewish people. As a result, Lazar, upon the death of his wife and separation from his children, had signed on as an indenture to make a new life in a world which he hoped would be less prejudiced.

Due to the tireless efforts of Lazar Epstein, the landscape around the mansion was beautifully redesigned and maintained. The gardens were filled with the fragrance and colors of roses, periwinkles, asters, and several varieties of lilies.

The only dark spot in the lives of the MacDougal House occupants was the absence of the master in their daily activities. The two young girls missed him terribly, and had urged Amanda to talk him into rejoining them.

Amanda rose, laying her embroidery on the end table near her chair. She went to the large kitchen and picked up the tray that Cinnamon had prepared for the MacDougal. "I will take this up this afternoon, Cinnamon." Cinnamon smiled. "I understand, Missy."

Amanda climbed the long stairway to the second floor. She knocked gently on the door of James' room and was rewarded with a soft "Come in."

"Set the tray where it usually goes, please, Cinnamon." James' ordered.

He sat in a high back chair facing the window to the garden, his usually straight back bent, his thinning shoulders drooping. Arthur had draped a shawl around his master's shoulders when he helped him out of bed. Had he not insisted, James would have remained in bed, which would have weakened his aging body.

Amanda put the tray down on the table and stood waiting.

"Well, what're ye waitin' fer Cinnamon? Ye may go!"

"It is not Cinnamon, sir. It is Amanda."

The old man turned around slowly, and looked at her with displeasure. "I thought I made it clear I was not ta be disturbed," he growled.

Amanda moved slowly to stand beside his chair. As she stood watching him, he turned his face away.

"No use looking away, old man. You cannot sit here forever, and you cannot die just because you want to."

James looked up, surprised at the firmness in her tone.

Amanda continued. "Hiding away from life and from all of us who love you will not bring back either James Jr. or Martha. You were not responsible for either of their deaths, and wallowing in guilt will only destroy the years you have left."

"Please go away now, lass. There's nothin' ya can do fer me," he begged.

"No. I will not go away. I am not leaving this room until you decide to come down and join your family for lunch. Those girls miss you so much. Not a day goes by that they do not beg me to get you out of this room," she asserted.

"Ya are all better off wi'out me," he sighed.

"That is where you are wrong. We all need you. You are the cornerstone of this household, and grandfather to the two girls. The staff is at odds without your guidance." This was not quite true, but she thought she could be forgiven a little white lie.

"What good would I be ta them, as heartbroken as I am?"

"The best way to get out of these doldrums is for you to come down and join the living. It will take time for you to heal, but being with all of us is your best hope. Do not let your heart and mind die until your body can no longer sustain them."

James looked up at Amanda, gratitude glowing in his gray eyes.

"If ya want it, my dear, I will try. But, I didnae promise anything."

"You just join us downstairs for lunch and we will take it from there."

The old man nodded and turned back to the window. Amanda stood by his side for a moment, then turned and left the room.

That day, at lunch, the table was graced once more by the master of the house.

Two days later Fiona once again invaded. She had been at the house for her mother's funeral. She now came bustling in with the news that she was in the family way.

James was delighted. He hoped for the grandson who would inherit MacDougal House and properties.

Amanda and Melinda judiciously retired to their rooms. They still missed the cottage, that Melinda had named Hollyhock House for the tall colorful stalked flowers that fronted the small veranda.

Fiona was there for three days, in which Amanda caught up on her reading and started work on a bedspread for Melinda's new brass bed. She was glad she now had a room far from the sounds of angry arguments between Fiona and her father.

After Fiona had departed, James was more himself, spending time with his adopted family and reading to the girls.

One day, six months later, James called Amanda into the library. She looked especially lovely that day wearing a dress she had just finished making. The pattern had come in the mail from London for Martha, as they had done regularly in the past. One pattern had caught Amanda's eye, and she had purchased enough fabric out of her savings to make matching dresses for herself and Melinda. Amanda felt especially stylish in her new garment. It was soft wool in a warm rose color. It was trimmed with rose satin and tiny roses that Amanda had fashioned from small pieces of the same satin. The neckline was high, with ivory lace trim, and the same trim was at the wrists. It fit her figure perfectly. Her jet-black hair was parted in the center and pulled back in its usual soft bun.

When she was comfortably seated in front of his large oak desk, James stood. He paced a while in front of the large dormer windows, and then sat again at his desk. She could tell that he had something on his mind that he was loath to discuss, and was afraid she might have displeased him in some way. She waited until he finally spoke.

"Ma dear, ya've been here fer most eight years now." Seeing a worried look come into Amanda's eyes, he quickly added. "Nay is wrong. In all that time, ye've served ma dear departed Martha and myself in an exemplary manner."

Amanda relaxed a little, still in suspense.

"You know how dearly I loved Martha." Amanda nodded.

James continued. "Ye are also aware of my inability to come to terms wi' her death. I want ya ta understand what was behind that. When I married Martha Forbes, she was eighteen. She was chosen fer me by ma father. She was the oldest daughter of the neighboring Forbes clan, and the marriage served to cement a peace with her clan."

"Martha was a pretty young thing, and verra amenable. I shaped her into the kinda wife I thought I should have. She gave me two livin' bairns, and was saddened ta have lost four others. She was a dutiful wife, and I learned ta care for her, though not the type a love that set's ones heart a-flutter," he smiled.

"Nonetheless, I endeavored ta be a good husband ta her, and when we lost our estates i' Scotland, moved her and our family ta safety in Virginia. Ya've heard the story a how we managed ta bring enough cattle wi' us to get us started."

"Yes, I have," Amanda smiled. James continued.

"However, after a time when Jamie didnae follow us, I left Martha alone and went ta find him. I cannae let go of the guilt I feel fer desertin' my wife when she was ailin', and getting trapped i' London fer so long. I feel ma not being here took too much of a toll on her."

"None of that was your fault," Amanda countered. "I know what guilt can do to a person, sir. Because I could not earn a decent living in London, my mother died. She was only thirty-four. But guilt is a destructive emotion and not to be courted."

"Y're right, lass, and I have come ta grips wi' much a ma guilt. However, I fear I wronged ma lovely wife in another way that I find hard ta forgive. Y'see, from the moment I first saw those violet eyes of yours, I knew I could nae love another woman, not even ma Martha, in the same way."

Amanda sat transfixed, her breathing halted.

"I do nae want to frighten ya, ma dear, but I feel I do nae have too much more time and I want ya t'know the truth. No, do not say anythin' yet!" he implored as she opened her mouth to speak.

"I would be a stupid mon had I supposed one sa young and beautiful could return that love, but I reveled in your presence and that of Melinda. The time ya two have been here has been the happiest in ma life. But, when Martha died, I felt the full weight of my unfairness ta her."

"In what way unfair?"

"She should have had the love I feel for you. Don't look so shocked, ma dear. I swore I would never burden ya with this love. I am concerned wi' what will happen to ya and the bairn once I am gone. As things stand, I would have t'leave everythin' to Fiona as ma only livin' heir, but I fear she has turned out ta be a selfish and cruel person. This mornin', I received a note from her. I am afeered there will nay be a grandson to inherit MacDougal House. Fiona lost her bairn, and we almost lost her. Fiona'll naer be able to bring forth bairns."

Amanda bit her lower lip to keep from interrupting him. The old man let his head droop for a moment. Then, pulling himself together, he continued. "She has become bitterer than ever, and, true ta her character, or lack of it, she has decided that the stress due to my having given sanctuary ta ya and Melinda, caused her miscarriage. Her letter was very angry and vindictive. She hates ya and Melinda so. If I don't make some arrangements fer the both of ya, I know she will put ya out when I am gone, and I cannae allow that."

"Oh, James, you have given us both so much already. We would not want to be a burden to your family. You saved our lives and we both love you," Amanda persisted.

"I know, lassie, and 'tis a love I cherish greatly. However, I want ya ta know that I have thought long and hard on this, and feel the only solution would be for ya ta become my wife."

Amanda's mouth fell open, and her heart started pounding loudly.

James spoke again. "I know this is a shock ta ya, and I wish I could'a spared ya that, but this needs ta be taken care'a as soon as possible. Fiona has a verra rich husband, and no need fer MacDougal House or this property. She would only sell them off, or bankrupt the place. Ya care about the property, and though I am an old, ailing man, I feel ya do care some for me."

"You are the kindest, wisest man I have ever known, and both Melinda and I love you like a parent. But, what would people think if you gave your name to an ex-bondservant? We would never be accepted into your society."

"Ya have seen how much my 'society' means ta me, my dear. Who I marry is nobody's affair but ma own. And I want'a assure ya, I will make no conjugal demands on ya. Ya will continue your life much as it is, except ya'll be the lady of the house and, a'course, choose the best suite in the house fer yourself. Melinda's old enough now ta have a suite a' her own. And feel free ta redecorate in whatever manner ya each desire; money's nay a consideration."

James finished and sat looking at the surprised girl as she twisted the fabric of her skirt in her lap, trying to make all he said come together in her head. Finally, she looked up at him.

He spoke softly, "Well, my dear, will ya be sa kind as ta do me the honor a becomin' ma wife?"

Amanda searched his eyes for the truth of what he was asking, and finally came to the realization that he was totally sincere. "I would be greatly honored, James," she whispered.

James rose from his chair, his happiness and love shining in his gray eyes. He took her slim hands into his aging ones, and lifted her hands to his lips. "Ye've made me the happiest mon alive, dear lass. Please tell Bertha ta have the chapel readied. I will make arrangements wi' Pastor MacFarland in the local parish. On this comin' Sunday, ye'll take your place as the lady of MacDougal House."

James was a good husband, and true to his word the relationship was platonic. It was a happy house, and everyone benefited by the old man's kindness.

The tutor, Peter Foster, who had been hired to see to Melinda's education, was also a good musician. He played the harpsichord in the parlor on many evenings. The one most fascinated with his playing was young Esther, who finally talked Peter into giving her lessons on the harpsichord.

James' health was failing. He did his best to hide his pain, but they were all worried. Amanda's heart sank when James called in his attorney and re-written his last will and testament. He confided that he was leaving all of his earthly possessions to Amanda, except for a painting of Martha, which he willed to Fiona. Arthur Cinnamon and Esther were free to make new lives for themselves, but they asked to stay on at MacDougal House. James willed the couple funds enough to be on their own in case it was ever necessary.

James died in his sleep four days after his sixty-eighth birthday. Arthur had tried to wake him for his morning ablutions to discover the loss of his beloved master.

Pastor MacFarlane presided at a touching memorial service and James was buried next to Martha in the family plot to the rear of the mansion. Fresh flowers were kept on their graves.

Amanda grieved his loss for many months. She hid the true depth of her grief from the girls, not wanting to worry them. Life with the MacDougal had been happy and fulfilling and the security of the marriage had lightened her heart.

It was 1638. At thirteen, Melinda had blossomed into a pretty, well-educated young woman, and left in the spring for a very elite school for young ladies in New Amsterdam, a new colony established by the Dutch. Such a school was very unusual in the New World so it was small and very exclusive.

Amanda, who had retired to her sitting room after lunch, checked the imported mantle clock, and quickly rose and went to the kitchen to remind Addie to make some pudding that the girls loved, for dinner. When the bell above the front door rang, she called out to Arthur but he had heard the bell too. Amanda watched him as he went to the door.

Arthur opened the huge carved door, and standing there was a solemn, but decidedly good-looking young man. He was about six feet tall, and was dressed in a dark blue long-coat with a light blue brocade vest. His jabot was sparkling white and neatly arranged. His short trousers displayed long muscled legs and his feet were encased in short, well-polished boots.

The two men stood in silence for a moment, and then Arthur spoke.

"Are you expected, sir?" Arthur asked, knowing this was not the case.

"I am afraid I was expected too many years ago to be remembered," the young man said in a deep, pleasant voice. He smiled at Arthur's confusion.

"I am sorry, my man. I guess I should come right to the point. I am here to see my father and mother. I am James MacDougal, the younger."

Amanda, who had come up behind Arthur out of curiosity, slid gently to the floor in a faint.

⁓⊙

The whirlpool in which Amanda was swirling began to take on different shades of green and blue. Finally daylight began to retake its place in front of her eyes. As she slowly opened them, she recognized the parlor. She was laying on the lounge and someone was putting something cool and wet on her forehead.

"Take it easy Missy. You be all right now," Arthur comforted.

"Oh, Missy Mandy. Is you gonna be okay?" Cinnamon worried.

"Wha...what happened. I remember....oh!" Amanda looked past Arthur and her worst fears were realized. The tall stranger who claimed to be Jamie MacDougal was really standing there. He looked far too substantial to be a spirit. She slowly pulled herself up, straightening her skirt.

"You are truly Jamie MacDougal?" she asked.

The young man moved past Arthur, his dark gray eyes examining her from head to toe. "There is no question of who *I* am, Madam. More important is who are *you*, and what are you doing in my parent's home?" James MacDougal the second asked in a decidedly unfriendly voice.

Amanda turned to Arthur, trying to regain her dignity. "Arthur, please see Master MacDougal settled in his father's suite. And have Mistress Curtin see that a hot bath is sent up."

Turning to their guest, Amanda continued, "I know you would like to get settled, sir. Dinner will be at seven, and we can meet after dinner in the library where we can both get some questions answered. Is this acceptable to you?"

"I prefer to see my parents before dinner. It has been a long time."

"I am so very sorry to have to give you such sad news, but your dear mother died in 1634. James passed away in his sleep."

Except for a small muscle jumping in his tightened jaws, Jamie MacDougal, showed no sign of the shock he must be experiencing.

"Is a Mistress Curtin still among the living?" he asked coldly. "I believe she came to the New World with my parents."

"Yes sir, I will send her to you later, if you wish, after you have had a chance to refresh yourself. You must be exhausted," Amanda soothed.

"I would like to speak to Mistress Curtin in the library right now, and then I will get cleaned up for dinner. He paused significantly. "And I am very curious to hear *your* story." With these curt words, Jamie turned and left the room. Arthur followed him, sending Amanda a supportive look over his shoulder.

Amanda's thoughts were in pandemonium. Not only had James MacDougal Junior returned miraculously from the dead, but it was obvious he was going to challenge her position in this household. Fiona had tried to break James' Last Will and Testament after he passed, but all her efforts failed. It had been an extremely difficult time for everyone in the household, and the thought of having to go through all of it again made Amanda's stomach turn.

"Are you all right, Missy Amanda? You is white as a sheet." Cinnamon hovered over her protectively.

"Wha...oh, yes, Cinnamon. I am fine. It is a shock, but I know everyone is happy to see young James." She rose shakily and headed toward the door. "I will be in my room if you need me."

As she headed for the stairs, she was surprised to realize that she had been very impressed by young Jamie's imposing figure and handsome face. It was spoiled only by the uncompromising expression and the tight jaw. His features resembled those of his father, but the resemblance stopped there. She had never seen such ferocity on the face of her late husband.

Amanda entered her dream room, which had once been Martha's. She remembered the first time she saw this magnificent room on the day she had arrived at MacDougal House. She sank onto the edge of the satin comforter which covered the huge four-poster bed, her heart thumping madly. What did life hold in store for her now? She rose after a few minutes and headed for her armoire. Amanda felt that she must look especially good at dinner so she chose her favorite gown, a soft pink silk, which flattered her creamy skin.

She could have been dressed in a flour sack for all the impression it made on young Jamie. He sat at the head of the table eating in silence, and did not once glance her way.

She tried to make conversation several times, but the lack of response left her feeling rejected and uncomfortable. She toyed with her food, until Cinnamon finally retrieved the plate and returned it to the kitchen. She replaced it with a light pudding dessert.

Finally, James touched his linen napkin to his lips, and rose from the table. "I think now is the time for that little talk, Mistress."

Amanda followed him into the library and sat in front of the desk with what dignity she could muster. Somehow this man had the power to make her feel like the fifteen-year-old bondservant she had once been, invoking feelings she had relegated to the past.

"Mistress Curtin tells me my father married you and left everything he owned to you and your daughter." His piercing look made her feel he was inspecting some sort of many-legged insect.

"That is true, but only because he had given up hope that you were still alive. I cared for your parents in their last years and loved them both dearly. James felt marriage was the only way Melinda and I would be protected financially. Both he and Martha..."

Cutting her off abruptly, he continued "Your sob stories do not influence me in the least. You will find that I am not as easy to fool as were my good parents."

"I do not know what you mean...I...," she stammered, cut by the insinuation.

"Women like you find easy victims in lonely old men. I admit, you do have an air of innocence about you, but I am sure you worked hard to perfect that. Beauty can be a powerful weapon when it comes to seducing an unsuspecting man."

Amanda just stared at him. How does one justify themselves in the face of such a horrible accusation? The woman he was describing was so far from what she knew herself to be that she was appalled.

"Master MacDougal, I am afraid you have a very wrong impression of me. My relationship with your father was..."

"I am not interested in the sordid details. You wangled your way into the hearts and pockets of my family. Mistress Curtin told me how much my parents cared for you, a caring I feel was built on deceit and greed. My sister was right in trying to break my father's Will. But, where she failed, I will not! I think you will find me a more formidable opponent. I mean to have my inheritance."

Amanda tried to talk past the lump in her throat. "I do not know how to convince you that you are wrong about this whole thing. We all thought you were dead, or James would have left everything to you as his legitimate heir. If it were not for Melinda, I would give it all back to you right now, but she..."

Once more, he cut her off mid-sentence. "Yes, the young lady who is now going to finishing school in New Amsterdam on estate money? We will see about that, too."

"The money for her education was set aside for her while your father was still alive. It is not part of the estate," she defended.

"We will see about *that*, also. In the meantime, the girl must be sent for. The two of you will be allowed to remain in this house only until my barristers get this mess straightened out. Until that time, I want to see as little of you as possible. Understood?"

Amanda felt totally beaten and defenseless, startled that he could be so mean. "What about the accounts? I have been in charge of both household and field accounts since shortly after I arrived here."

"I'll go over them this week. If I find any mishandling of funds, I will call you in. With that, he dismissed her as one would a servant. She left the library feeling like she had been run over by a coach and four. How on earth was she going to defend herself against a man who would not even listen to her side of the story?

She had felt blessed, and justified in accepting the love and protection of the MacDougal's. For the first time, she realized how it must look to others.

As she threw herself across her large feather bed she wondered if she was the type of woman Jamie described. She wanted a nice home and pretty clothes, and most of all she desired a good education for Melinda. Had she been wrong in accepting what James had offered her?

Tears began to roll down her cheeks seeping into her satin pillow. Whatever happened in the weeks to come, Amanda knew that she would need all the strength she could muster. She sobbed as if her heart would break, finally falling into an exhausted sleep atop the covers.

The next morning, she was awakened by a light knock on her door. It was Bertha Curtin's, special knock. She called out "Come in, Bertha."

Bertha entered, juggling a tray. "I am sorry to wake you so early, dear, but I have to talk to you. This is unbelievable."

Amanda slipped a warm robe over her rumpled gown as Bertha placed the tray on the end table. "Those are your favorites, dear. Are you able to eat?"

"I am still in a state of shock," Amanda admitted. "How did your meeting with him go?"

"Somehow he has the idea that because I came here with his folks, I will naturally be his ally."

"But, he never met you before, did he?" Amanda queried.

"No, and I asked him how he knew my name. He told me that one of this father's letters reached him in Scotland with news of the family, but he had no way of letting his father know he was alive. When he got back to London, his father had taken ship for Virginia. Whatever he thinks, Amanda, I am on your side. I loved the old couple, but I am not bound to their son. You do know that, don't you?"

"Of course, Bertha, you are my dearest friend."

"I love Melinda like she was my own. I do not want to see you two forced from your home."

"This is your home, too, Bertha, so do not do anything to turn him against you. You can be a valuable ally if you play along with him."

"Exactly what I was thinking, my dear. I wanted you to know that whatever happens, I am on your side. I will do my best to make him see the truth, but, I have some advice for you. Let him think you are going along with all of his demands. Don't let him know that we are smarter than he is."

Amanda gave Bertha a big hug. "Good advice. Go now, in case he is looking for you. And, Bertha, knowing you are with me makes all the difference. I feel much better about the whole affair. I am not defeated yet."

Later that morning, Amanda wrote a letter to Mistress Wharton at her school telling her Melinda was needed at home. She enclosed a draft to cover the trip. She knew she would have to write to Melinda, too, but her heart was not in it. Melinda was doing well at school, and had another year and a half to go.

When dressed, Amanda pulled the bell cord. In a few minutes Cinnamon appeared in the doorway. She hung back, knowing how upset her Mistress must be.

"It is all right, Cinny. Come in," Amanda invited.

"Oh, Missy Mandy. How could this happen? Arthur n' me always thought how wonderful it'd be if'n the young Masta come back. We hear how he treatin' you. We'z awful sorry, Missy Mandy."

"I know, Cinny. Do not worry about it. It will all work out. Please make up Melinda's room."

Cinnamon nodded. "Oh, Missy," she sighed. With drooping shoulders, Cinnamon turned and left the room.

Amanda headed for the door. "This is not the worst thing that has happened to us." she encouraged herself.

⤽౦

While Amanda faced an uncertain future, Cinnamon and Arthur discussed their own plans.

"What we gonna do, honey man. How we gonna take care our child if we got to leave this house, with no job, no place to live?

Arthur, hearing the fear in his wife's voice felt the same fears, but dared not show it. Their inheritance would not last long if they had no income.

"I don't know, Cinny. I just know God has the answer. We gotta trust in Him." He put his arm around Cinnamon's shoulders and gave her a squeeze.

"You sure we gonna have to leave?" Cinnamon asked.

"We have not been told to leave, but we can't stay when he is doin' these bad things to Mizz Mandy. Just don't seem right"

"We don't know nobody else Arthur. We gotta think 'bout our Esther."

"Honey girl, when I was taken from Africa, I thought it was the end of the world, but, see what good care God took.

"I know I should have more faith, honey man, but I gets scared at times."

"Esther, she got an education. She could pass for white. She be all right."

"Arthur, why's the new MacDougal so hard on Missy Amanda? She ain't done nothin' wrong!"

"Missy Manda and her girl bein here is eatin' at his craw. He don't want to lose his inheritance to a woman. Maybe he will change when he gits ta know her."

"If he stay mean, we in a lot of trouble, ain't we? What we gonna do, honey?"

Arthur patted her hand. "We gonna talk to Mizz Mandy. See what she thinks."

"That the thing to do, Arthur." Cinnamon agreed.

Arthur watched his wife pick up her mending, a deep frown marring her face. He hated to see her unhappy. She had had enough grief in her life.

Arthur vowed to do everything he could to heal the rift between Master Jamie and Amanda.

13

New Amsterdam, 1638

We find Melinda in school in New Amsterdam, a new adventure about to begin. Her friend, Penny, stuck her head in her doorway. "Are you writing letters, again, Melinda? Put that down and come out in the garden with us."

Melinda smiled, "I am almost finished. I have to keep Esther up to date." Penny entered the small room, which housed three close friends. She plopped down on her bed. "Knowing you, I will just take a long nap while I am waiting."

"Where is Willa?" Melinda queried.

"She is working in the rose garden. She wants us to see her latest rose."

Melinda finished her letter, capped the inkbottle, wiped off the tip of her quill, and straightened her small writing table. "Let us go, lazy."

The two girls traversed the dark halls of Mistress Wharton's School for Young Ladies in New Amsterdam, exiting into a bright well landscaped garden. The school was loosely called 'the academy', though it was a small school, one of the first schools for girls in the colonies.

Willa was on her knees loosening the dirt under a large rose bush which sported one beautiful coral rose. Looking up as the two girls approached, she smiled. "I finally have a blossom. What do you think?"

Melinda leaned over and buried her nose in the fragrant bloom. "Oh, Willa, it is heavenly. The perfume is like nothing I have ever inhaled!"

Melinda, at thirteen, was no raving beauty, but her features were even and pleasing. She had always been a merry child, and had retained her happy smile. Her hazel eyes were large, her long lashes being her pride and joy. Her dark brown hair curled softly around her oval face and was tied back with a navy ribbon matching her school uniform. The uniform consisted of a white blouse and a navy pinafore. The other two girls were also dressed in the uniforms.

It was obvious they were a close trio. Penny was a year older than Melinda. Her full name was Penelope Winslow. She was the daughter of a wealthy merchant in Jamestown. She was not blessed with physical beauty, being quite plump with a round rosy face, brown eyes, freckles, and straight brown hair. However, her personality more than made up for her lack of beauty. She was a warm and giving girl.

The third girl, Wilhelmina Hart, was the daughter of a lesser noble from England. She was intelligent and studious, and when not with her two friends, tended toward introversion. Willa was the real beauty of the trio, having a delicate face, a small, sweet mouth, large ice blue eyes fringed with dark lashes, and hair like pure spun silver. At sixteen, she was the most mature of the trio. Her slight figure belied the strength which allowed her to work for hours in her off-time to keep the garden, and especially the roses, in good health.

The first few months had been hard on the three girls. Then they found each other.

As the weeks went by, they formed a close alliance against the academy elites, who were primarily Dutch. The Dutch girls looked down their noses at girls from other colonies, and enjoyed speaking Dutch in their presence, but the bond between Melinda and her friends would see them through their stay at the academy.

The three girls settled themselves in the vine-covered gazebo. Willa begged Melinda to tell them again about her trip from Jamestown and her first day at Mistress Wharton's school. As they sat quietly, Melinda relived that day for them.

"My mother and my friend, Esther, traveled with me by ship from Jamestown to the port of New Amsterdam. Esther and I were ecstatic to see a northern city for the first time. New Amsterdam was very different than Jamestown, in spite of the fact they are both large seaports.

"The three of us had two days to enjoy ourselves before being enrolled in Mistress Wharton's Academy where the higher education and the training in the social graces would turn us into proper young ladies. Since Esther had shared a tutor with me, Grandpa James had decided that she should also go to Wharton's. He had put it in his will," Melinda explained.

"We went shopping, and purchased several bundles of beautiful fabric, plus trims, laces, threads and the like. But best of all, mother took us to see a puppet show. We stayed at a large, crowded inn not far from the academy. As we ate supper that night, we ogled the local inhabitants. We could not contain our excitement. Esther and I looked forward to the academy.

Mother reminded us to behave ourselves and not get carried away. I laughed, assuring her that we would be perfect angels. Mother made a face. Our response to this was smiles and giggles."

"You were so brave. I was totally paralyzed with fear," Penny confided.

Melinda continued. "The next morning, dressed in our best gowns, we arrived at the academy. However our smiles were wiped away in no uncertain terms when Esther was refused entrance to the school. My mother was incensed, but no matter how she argued, Mistress Wharton stood firm."

"Tell us why she was refused. I love that part." Penny urged.

"Well, my mother demanded an explanation. Why could I be enrolled and not Esther? Mistress Wharton explained that they had done their usual background check and found that, in spite of her appearance, Mistress Esther was not considered to be of the proper bloodline. Mother demanded to know what that meant."

"I can just see Mistress Wharton's face," Willa offered.

"Mistress Wharton asked mother to keep her voice down. She explained that it was not her personal feeling, but she had a business to run. Her wealthy patrons did not wish their daughters to be subjected to the lower classes. She urged us to try and understand. Mother countered that Esther was only one quarter colored and had been educated in the same manner me."

"What happened then?" Penny asked.

"Mistress Wharton folded her hands on her desk. She apologized, but would not take the chance. One slip of Esther's speech could give her away and the school could be closed on the spot. Mother was incensed. She told Mistress Wharton that she thought that kind of thinking was left on the continent. She snapped that this is supposed to be a New World, a world of opportunity for everyone. Mistress Wharton countered that this was wishful thinking, and that it was people who nurtured prejudice, not lands. However, she promised that *I* would have the finest education available."

"That poor girl. Do go on," Willa said.

"I could not believe it, and mother's heart ached for Esther who sat with her chin high, her eyes focused out the nearest window. I looked at her in awe. One might imagine she was the belle of the ball at a high tea. I was angry, but Esther was brave. Esther finally told mother not to worry. She rose and said they had a long trip ahead of them. I was thunder struck. I couldn't understand what was happening. Mother tried to calm me, but I told her I could not stay at school without Esther. Mother looked at Mistress Wharton, who had the good graces to look embarrassed. Mistress Wharton took my arm and told me she would show me to my room. She told me my mother expected me to make the best of things, that it was a sign of good breeding. I looked at mother's face and knew Mistress Wharton was right. I had no choice but to go with her."

"So you had to stay here. We are so glad you did, Melinda," Penny sighed

"Mother promised to have me back at MacDougal House for the holidays, and keep me posted on everything at home. I was crying as I was pulled away, but mother said she was counting on me. I realized how my struggling was upsetting her, so I pulled away from Mistress Wharton and stood firm. "I am fine, Mother. I will do what I must.""

"Then I turned to Esther, who stood looking at me with sad eyes. We fell into each other's arms, promising to write every day. I assured her that I would be all right and stood frozen watching them leave."

"That is such a sad story," Penny offered. "Thank you so much for telling it to us again," Willa gave Melinda a quick hug. "But, we are so lucky Melinda remained."

Melinda jumped up. "Oh, we better hurry. English class is about to start."

There was a part of the story that Melinda did not know. On the trip home, Esther had handled herself with utmost dignity. Not until Amanda and she had arrived in Jamestown, did she break down. They were gathering their belongings to debark, when Esther's shoulders drooped. She sank down on the bunk. Amanda quickly dropped her bag and sat beside her. At this sign of sympathy, Esther finally let the tears flow.

"That's right, honey, let it all out. Tears are wonderful medicine," Amanda crooned.

"I...I do not understand, Aunt Amanda. What did I do wrong?"

"Oh, darling, you did nothing wrong."

"Then why could I not go to school with Melinda? And what did that woman mean about bloodlines. Was it because my family is not rich?"

"No, honey, it is...well; it has to do with something much more foolish. Some people feel that if your skin is not the same color as theirs it makes you inferior to them."

"What do you mean? My skin is the same color as Lindy's?"

"You see, Esther, if you have even a little bit of the blood that made your folk's skin dark, you are considered 'colored'," Amanda explained.

Esther's eyes opened wide. "You mean because my parents have darker skin than you and Melinda, we are not as good as you?"

"Heavens no! I am saying that there are many stupid people who believe that. It is a lot of hogwash. Esther, we know you are a lovely intelligent girl. But, you are going to have to learn to ignore the unkindness of people who are bound by prejudice. We can hope that someday this kind of thinking will be revealed for the evil it is. In the meantime, you have to know how wonderful you are, and how much we all love you."

Esther sat silent for a moment, then wiping her eyes; she put on a brave smile. "You are right, Aunt Amanda. Let us go home."

That first day at Mistress Wharton's school would remain with Melinda always. Her life at Wharton had not improved greatly in the first three months. Most of the Dutch girls tended to ignore girls who did not belong in their society. The fact that Melinda had a wealthy Scottish father made no difference. Rich or not, Melinda just did not come from the right stock.

So Melinda had applied herself to her studies, determined to make her mother proud. It was not until she received an award for poetry that she became acquainted with Penny Winslow, another outcast in the academy. When Willa was enrolled shortly after the holidays, she had quickly been awarded the friendship of Melinda and Penny.

Willa's new rose was a success with everyone at the academy. She named the rose the Brent Rose, in honor of a guest speaker at the academy. They had been looking forward to her visit because she had elevated the status of women by studying law. Willa planned to present her rose to Mistress Margaret Brent at the luncheon following her lecture.

Melinda was chosen to read a poem at the luncheon. Mistress Wharton picked a flowery poem about the sea. However, when the moment arrived, Melinda switched poems and read, with great emotion, her own poem extolling womanhood and urging young women to believe in themselves.

Mistress Wharton was mortified, apologizing profusely to Margaret Brent. However, Mistress Brent's reaction was not the expected one. She clapped loudly, and asked for a private meeting with Melinda. That meeting started a great and lasting friendship and a profound change in Melinda's future.

Two weeks later, the girls were still extolling Margaret Brent when Mistress Opal, the math instructor, joined them, slightly out of breath, "You are wanted in Mistress Wharton's office right now, Melinda."

"What about, Mistress Opal?" Melinda inquired.

"It is not for me to say, Mistress. You had better hurry!"

"Have I done something wrong again?" Melinda moaned. At the door, she stopped, took a big breath, and knocked. Ten minutes later, she walked out, totally dazed, and headed for her room to pack her belongings. It seemed she was going home.

༄

At home, Amanda was having a fit. "Who does he think he is, anyway?" she fumed as she paced her room. "Until otherwise informed, I am still the lady of this house, the legal heir to my husband's estate! He is welcome to stay here if he wishes, but it's *my* home. I am staying where I belong!"

She realized she sounded more confident than she was. She was aware that James Jr. had a good chance of breaking the will. Women had little legal standing in 1638. Her hopes of retaining the inheritance were slim.

In spite of her fears, Amanda dressed plainly to play down her youth and beauty. She wore a violet wool gown with soft beige lace at the throat and cuffs. Her raven hair was pulled back in her usual bun, but no curls were allowed soften her pale face. She headed down the hall.

Arthur exited the library carrying an empty brandy bottle.

"Is he in there?" she asked, eyeing the bottle. "Yes, Ma'am, he goin' over that number book you use. Shall I announce you?"

"No thank you, Arthur. I will announce myself." Arthur walked away, muttering under his breath.

Amanda held her copy of her husband's will and their marriage papers. She lifted her chin and stomped to the library door, pushing it open.

"I will not require anything but the brandy until dinner, Arthur." Jamie said.

"It is not Arthur, Master James. It is me, Amanda."

James didn't bother to look up when she spoke. "What do you want?" His voice was cold and matter of fact.

In spite of the weeks of being ignored, Amanda was taken aback. She was still not used to being spoken to in such a manner. No man since Ugly had used that tone of voice with her.

"I beg your pardon, but this is still *my* home, and I am not accustomed to such rudeness."

This made James lift his head and examine her more closely. What he saw surprised him. This was not the same insecure young woman who had fainted at his mere appearance. There stood before him now a serenely confident woman, dressed elegantly, but simply and tastefully. Her expression was steely. Her amazing violet eyes gazed at him void of fear. He had to grudgingly admit that she was an extremely lovely and intelligent woman. Perhaps he had judged her too quickly. Finally, he spoke. "Do sit down, Mistress MacDougal."

"So you finally admit that my marriage to your father was legal," Amanda said.

"We will accede to that."

She decided not to sit, giving herself the advantage of height. He took note of this, but decided to ignore it. Placing his fingertips together and resting his elbows on the ledgers, he looked her in the eyes. "What can I do for you?"

She held her copy of the will and marriage papers out toward him. "I have here your father's Will and my marriage papers. You can see that all is in order."

He took the papers and laid them on the desk beside the ledgers. "I have my own copies. Is that all?"

Amanda's small chin lifted. "No. That is not all! Until I am otherwise informed, this is still my home, and I will remain where I am!" He just stared at her, so she continued.

"I will also continue running the estate and maintain the lifestyle to which we are accustomed. You will be our honored guest and relative. You are free to inspect all aspects of your father's property, and I will assist you in any way I can, but... I am here to stay until all legal matters have been satisfactorily settled."

When finished, she stood waiting for his reaction. She hoped her fear and nervousness were not apparent. She was rewarded by a nod of his head.

"That will be satisfactory. Is there anything else?" His lack of expression nearly did her in. How could anyone be so cool and unfeeling? However, she accepted her victory with a modicum of grace, and sank into the chair he offered her.

"One more thing, I have written to my daughter's school and Melinda will be put on the first ship leaving New Amsterdam. I will meet her ship and bring her back here. Her room is adjacent to mine in the West Wing. She will stay here until the matter of the Will has been settled."

"If that is all, I would like to get back to my work. I have a lot of years to catch up on. Good day, Mistress."

Amanda's bile rose again at this summary dismissal from her own library, but decided she had enough confrontation for one morning.

Once back in her study, she flopped weak-kneed into her chair by the hearth. Arthur had anticipated her use of the study, and a cheery fire crackled in the fireplace. He had also provided a tray of tea and crumpets.

"How could any man be so hardhearted?" she pondered. How different he was from his father. In spite of her experience with Ugly, Amanda had no prejudice against men. Ugly had bad enough to set him apart from the male sex. The MacDougal's were upper class, and she expected more from them. James Jr. had her stymied.

At least, she and Melinda would have a home for a while longer. How Melinda must have been shocked and disappointed to be recalled from school. But it would be wonderful to have her daughter home again.

Amanda finally calmed down, closed her eyes, and took some deep breaths. Her body began to relax. She was on the verge of drifting off to sleep when she heard a carriage in the drive, and a loud commotion. She rose and pushed the curtains aside in time to see Fiona being helped down from an ornate carriage by a footman. She watched, crestfallen, as James Jr. exited the front door and rushed to greet his sister. He lifted her and swung her around. Amanda watched as the first smile she had ever seen wreathed Fiona's face.

As distressed as Amanda was, she noted the warm smile on Jamie's lips. The smile changed his face completely. He was really quite attractive. As he set his sister down, Fiona's usual sour expression returned. Amanda could hear her strident voice railing against their father's "so-called" wife.

"I am in for it now," Amanda groaned. "One of them was bad enough!"

She sighed, then rang for Bertha Curtin, who entered her room in a state of agitation.

"How are we to deal with both of them, Amanda?"

"Unfortunately, we have no choice. Please ready the guestroom for Mistress Fiona."

"You know she is going to complain about everything we do," Bertha grumbled.

"I know, dear friend, but we must deal with her. Just do the best you can."

Amanda straightened her dress, smoothed her hair, and headed for the front of the house to greet her unwelcomed guest.

While Amanda was welcoming Fiona, Melinda was answering a knock on her door at the Wharton Academy. She called out permission to enter.

"Melinda, my dear, I came at once."

"Oh, Mistress Brent, I am so happy to see you again. But, what are you doing here?"

"Mistress Wharton is aware of my concern for you. She sent a note to the inn to tell me that you were leaving school. What happened, my dear?" Margaret Brent inquired.

Melinda, who had been fighting to keep her emotions under control, totally lost the battle. She threw herself into the open arms of Mistress Brent. The tears welled up and out. Margaret held her, patting her and murmuring soothing sounds.

When the tears dried up, Margaret pulled Melinda down next to her on the cot. "Now, tell me what happened."

"That is just it, Mistress Brent. I don't know. All I was told is that my mother wrote a letter to Mistress Wharton telling her I must come home immediately and that I would not be coming back. I cannot imagine what is wrong. I hope my mother is not ill."

"Well, this sort of ruins my plans." Mistress Brent sighed.

"Plans? What plans, Mistress Brent?"

"I think it only right that you should know. I had spoken to Mistress Wharton in regard to obtaining your mother's permission to take over your education upon graduation."

"You mean...?"

"I mean that I would like to take you to my home in a new colony in Maryland, and provide you with tutors who will further your studies in writing and poetry. I feel you have an exceptional talent, and we women need someone to further our independence and self-authority. Your poems on this subject are powerful. I value your opinions and your zeal."

"I cannot believe it. I would love that so much. But, now I will not be graduating."

"That is not the problem. The problem is convincing your mother to let you go. When are you leaving for Jamestown?"

"I am booked on the *Goodfellow*. It leaves at ten o'clock tomorrow morning."

"Then I can see no help for it. I will go with you. My business here is concluded. If your mother agrees, we can then take ship for Maryland."

"Oh, Mistress Brent, this is so exciting. I was thinking my life was over and now..." Melinda's excitement spread to her mentor.

"Good! I will arrange my passage on the *Goodfellow*, and have a carriage pick you up first thing in the morning. We will to leave the rest to fate."

⌒○

Amanda felt sick about having to take Melinda out of school. She knew how much Melinda loved it.

Esther was happy that she would have her best friend back. Arthur and Cinnamon had cried together when Esther had run into her first taste of prejudice. They had talked to her for hours to reinstall in her a love for herself. In the end Esther had come to her own realization that she was all she needed to be. God had made her parents the color they were and she took pride in being their daughter. She quickly settled into her life at MacDougal House. She was happy to be back to her music. Because of her deep love of music, she was able to create some commendable compositions on the harpsichord.

Amanda now lived in constant emotional turmoil. She tried to be friendly with Fiona, her unwelcomed houseguest, but had found it impossible. Fortunately, James stayed out of their frays, for his own protection.

When Amanda finally had enough of Fiona, she garnered her courage and sent her packing. It had been a real shouting match. Amanda had finally let out a loud, ear-shattering scream. James poked his head out of the library then prudently ducked back to safety. Fiona had stopped dead in her tracks, her ordinarily tight mouth wide open in astonishment.

Amanda spoke softly but strongly.

"For the sake of your beloved parents, I have put up with your ranting for years. That is all that could be expected of anyone. Now, I must ask you to leave my house. No, do not say a word. Until this mess is cleared up, this is *my* house, and I want you out of here...now! Cinnamon

214

will pack your things, and I will ask Arthur to take you to the inn where you can get a carriage to take you home!"

For once, Fiona was speechless. She let out a 'harrumph and stalked out of the room. Fiona complained loudly as she stomped down the hall. Amanda watched as Fiona stopped in front of the library door, stood there for a moment, then she lifted her chin, crossed to the entryway and started up the staircase to her room. After Fiona left, the house was blessedly silent.

Amanda was going to the port to bring Melinda home. She smoothed the skirts of her blue velvet traveling gown, and checked her image in the armoire mirror. Approving her appearance, she picked up her matching bonnet from the end of the bed and settled it atop her raven hair. She took in the total picture, and made a small moue with her mouth. She was satisfied.

She did not like leaving James Jr. in charge at MacDougal House, so she had talked to Angus, Mathew and Swen, telling them to take good care of the estate. "Placate him and stall any changes until I return," she advised. The three workers smiled agreement.

Amanda took a deep breath. Grabbing her handbag, she rushed into the upper hallway, calling to Arthur. "Hurry, Arthur. I do not want to be late for Melinda's ship." Arthur met her at the foot of the staircase. "Angus has the carriage ready, Mistress MacDougal. Do not worry, you got plenty of time. That boat don't dock 'til late this afternoon."

Seeing the door to the library slightly open, Amanda tapped on the door. "What do you want?" came Jamie's voice.

"May I?" Amanda queried.

"Oh, Amanda, come in." Jamie put down the papers he was working on.

"I am leaving now to pick up my daughter. I may be staying in town for a few days."

"Perhaps you will be fortunate enough to find a new place to live," Jamie suggested.

"I hardly think so, Master MacDougal. This is our home, and you can rest assured that we will both be back."

Jamie stared at her for a moment, and then sighed. "Have a good time."

Amanda turned and exited the room, seething inside. Angus helped her up into the rig, checked her luggage, and then headed toward town.

The day was warming up. Amanda had to cool her face with her fan. When the carriage pulled into Jamestown, there were still three hours before the *Goodfellow* was to arrive.

"Oh, dear, I guess I was a little over anxious. It is going to be a long wait, and the day is heating up."

"There is a fine inn near the docks. Angus offered. While I tend to the horses, you could get yerself a class of ale. It will be cooler inside, mistress."

"An excellent suggestion," Amanda agreed. "I will check on a room for tonight, in case Melinda wants to stay in town. There is no reason for you to wait around here, Angus. Just be back in time to get me to the ship."

"Well, if yer sure, mistress. I guess you will be safe at the inn."

When they arrived at Settler's Inn, Angus helped Amanda down from the carriage, and doffed his cap. Taking up the reins, he set off down the lane.

Inside the inn, Amanda lowered herself onto a bench, enjoying the cool sea breeze blowing through the windows.

"What can I be gettin' for ya, young lady?" Amanda looked up into the smiling face of a chunky, red-haired woman. She couldn't speak she was so engrossed in the woman before her. Then the woman let out a loud laugh. "You okay, honey?" the woman asked. Amanda's memory sparked as she looked at her dear friend.

"Aggie? Aren't you Aggie?"

"That's my name, honey. Now how could you know that?"

"Oh, Aggie, Aggie." Amanda leaped to her feet. "It's me! Don't you know me? It's Amanda McNeely...from the ship...remember?"

Aggie stood stock-still and stared at the young woman in front of her. She had a difficult time connecting this richly dressed, voluptuous young woman with the starving waif who had traveled with her to the New World.

"Amanda? Is it truly you? I can't believe it."

"It's me, Aggie. I never thought I would see you again, and here you are right here in Jamestown." The two women flew into each other arms, hugging and crying at the same time.

Finally settling down, the two sat at a table and brought each other up to date.

"I'm happy you are so close, Aggie."

"The good man who purchased my indentures wound up marrying me. He made my dream come true. I own this inn. I've been working to improve my English, but I still got a way to go." Aggie refilled Amanda's glass. "You say you have a daughter?" Aggie asked.

"Yes. Her name is Melinda, and she is very special. That's where I'm going now, to meet the *Goodfellow*. Melinda is on her way back from school in New Amsterdam."

"That sounds exciting." Aggie's face brightened. "But I have something more exciting to tell you. Bridget is alive and well, too. She stopped here on her way to London. She is a successful milliner in New Amsterdam. Can you believe it?"

Amanda was thrilled to know Bridget was doing well. New Amsterdam was not that far away. Perhaps one day they could all get together again.

The two women talked for an hour, and then Aggie noticed her husband looking her way.

"I better get back to business before John has a fit," Aggie sighed. "It's been so wonderful seeing you again. Bring your daughter back here this afternoon. I'll feed you dinner and John will save you a nice room."

"Thanks Aggie. Heavens, you're right, it is late. I cannot miss that ship. Angus will be waiting for me," Amanda replied. "We'll be back. I'm so glad you are here and all right."

Aggie walked Amanda out to the courtyard and they hugged goodbye. Angus was waiting, and helped Amanda into the carriage.

A half-hour later, the *Goodfellow* let down its gangplank, and the passengers began to disembark. Amanda saw Melinda and waved. A beaming Melinda rushed up and fell into Amanda's welcoming arms. As Amanda held her daughter, she noticed a plainly dressed woman who had followed Melinda down the gangplank and was now standing close to her. Remembering her manners, Melinda pulled away and presented Margaret to a surprised Amanda.

"Oh, mother, I want you to meet Mistress Margaret Brent."

"I am happy to meet you Mistress Brent," Amanda smiled to hide her confusion.

Margaret returned her smile. "Now I know where Lindy gets her good looks. I'm very happy to meet you too, my dear."

"I'm sorry. Did you two meet on the ship? Melinda is incurably friendly."

Margaret started to speak but Melinda touched her arm. Margaret allowed Melinda to explain her presence in Jamestown.

"Mother. Mistress Brent is with me. I've known her for quite a while. We met at school. I wrote you about her. She's very important in the fight for more opportunities for women."

More confused than ever, Amanda looked at Margaret. "And you have business here in Jamestown, Mistress Brent?"

"Well..." Margaret started.

"Mother, can we all go someplace where we can talk?"

"That can be arranged. An explanation is definitely in order." Amanda replied. Amanda spotted Angus waiting in the carriage and waved for him to pick them up. Angus was surprised to see a strange woman climb into the carriage with Amanda and Melinda, but held any questions for a later time.

The three women took seats at a corner table at the Settler's Inn. After Aggie was introduced to Melinda and Mistress Brent, she supplied them with a pitcher of ale and freshly baked muffins.

Margaret began to tell Amanda of her interest in Melinda's future.

"I know it is a lot to ask, but I would like to take Melinda to my new home in St. Mary's, Maryland, where I can provide her with many opportunities."

"You want my daughter to live with you?" Amanda was astonished. "Did you think I could not provide for my only child?"

"Please, Mistress MacDougal, try and understand. This as no insult to you. I have no children of my own, nor do I ever hope to have any. When I saw this spectacular girl, all my instincts urged me to help her grow, to introduce her to the world of education, law, literature." Margaret sighed. "I am quite wealthy, and I have much to offer her, and now..." She paused. "Now that there is trouble at home with your husband's family, I feel it would be nice for Melinda if she were not put in the middle. It would be wonderful if she could come with me until we can get your inheritance settled. You would be free to put all of your energy into that endeavor. What happens after that will be up to the two of you, of course."

Amanda turned to her daughter. "Melinda, you should not have discussed our business with a stranger."

"Oh, mother, Mistress Brent, is not a stranger to me. She has been my friend and wants to help us. Mistress Brent has studied the law. She can help us to protect ourselves from that horrible MacDougal monster." Melinda cried. "And she wants to..."

Margaret noted Amanda's confusion and concern. "Melinda only told me about your problems because she knew I would do my best to help you win your case."

Amanda watched Melinda's face as Margaret spoke, then turned to her. "Is this what you wish, Melinda?"

"You know how much I love you, mother, but now that I have had a taste of learning, I long for more. It's not like I would be leaving you forever. We can all travel to see each other, and...and, if Mistress Brent can help us get our home back, that would be a good thing, wouldn't it?"

In the end, Amanda reluctantly agreed that Melinda could travel to Maryland with Margaret Brent, whose warmth and sincerity had struck a chord with her. Margaret wrote down her address in St. Mary's on a slip of paper.

"Any letter will find us at Sister's Freehold. The colony is small." Then Margaret requested that Amanda make a hand written copy of all of her inheritance papers and any other pertinent materials and send them to her in Maryland.

"I promised Lindy that we would help you fight this outrageous injustice, and we will." Mistress Brent promised.

"Why are you calling my daughter Lindy?" Amanda asked.

"Oh, I am sorry. The name just seemed to fit her. I hope you do not mind."

"If it is all right with Melinda, I guess it is all right with me. You are welcome to stay at MacDougal house, until you can arrange passage to St. Mary's." Amanda offered.

"Well..." Margaret started.

"Mother, I know this is hard, but we have already made plans to leave with the *Goodfellow* which is sailing tomorrow afternoon. We will then take a smaller ship up river and go by coach to St. Mary's Colony."

"You think this is easy? I come to retrieve my daughter and I find she's not coming home, and she even has a different name."

"I'm sorry, mother, it's not that I don't want to come home with you, but if we don't go tomorrow we will be stuck here in Jamestown for another month. Mistress Brent has to get back to watch over the building of her new home."

Amanda was silent for a long time then her normal good sense kicked in. Realizing that the situation at MacDougal House was disruptive, she finally accepted Mistress Brent's offer.

Feeling better once the decision was made, the three women talked and talked about Margaret's plans. As it neared twilight, Aggie provided a hearty meal. Mistress Brent arranged for rooms for herself and Melinda.

"Oh, what about your clothes, Melinda?" Amanda remembered.

"We are going shopping in the morning. She'll have everything she needs for her stay in St. Mary's," Margaret explained.

"Let me give you some money to help with her shopping." Amanda offered.

"I appreciate your offer, Mistress MacDougal, but that won't be necessary. The clothes are part of our bargain. I will be more than repaid when you and Lindy legally own your home."

Amanda decided to go back to MacDougal house. She did not want Melinda to see that she was still upset.

"Mother, please give my love to everyone at home. Tell Esther I'll write to her as soon as I get settled in Maryland. Oh, mother, I will miss you so much!"

Melinda grabbed her mother and hugged her tightly. "I love you, mother. I'll write soon, I promise. And thank you for trusting me."

"I know you, Melinda, and I do trust you. Take care, darling."

As Amanda watched Melinda and Mistress Brent go up to their rooms, she wanted to quickly return home. She climbed into her carriage and started the long trip back to what would again be a very lonely house.

The next morning, after a fun shopping spree, Melinda and Margaret Brent once more boarded the *Goodfellow* and started on their journey of personal discovery.

14

Melinda, free of the tension of convincing her mother that what she was doing was right, felt more relaxed than she had in years. She was excited, and the trip took on new delights.

After Mistress Brent and her ward dined with the ship's master and were ensconced in their small stateroom, they settled down for the night. It had been a long day and they were both exhausted.

Tired as she was, Melinda could not fall asleep. As the excitement of the trip calmed, she wondered if she had done the right thing going to Maryland with Margaret Brent. Perhaps she was letting her mother down. Melinda loved MacDougal House. She did not remember much of her life with Biggs. Her mother told her about him, and their escape from the wilderness but it seemed like a fairy tale to her.

Life with the MacDougal's and her friendship with Esther were uppermost in her mind. She wondered what Esther would think when she did not return with Amanda. She would write to Esther as soon as they reached St Mary's.

In spite of her feelings of guilt, Melinda realized that she was excited by the thought of her stay with Mistress Brent.

Margaret Brent was an enigma. She was a woman who devoted her life to proving that women could manage their affairs without a husband. As a result, the feminine areas of her own private life had been sadly neglected. She saw to it that her slim figure was always appropriately adorned, but clothes were a necessity rather than an indulgence. Although not a beautiful woman, her features were even and her gray eyes warm. She wore her light brown hair pulled back in a chignon, and her caps were simple and unadorned. Her best feature was her smile, which transformed her plain face and lent her a serene beauty. Despite her small build, she had a will of iron.

Margaret was also having trouble falling to sleep, so as they relaxed in their bunks, she revealed some facts about herself. She had come to the New World from Gloucester, England, in this year of 1638, and was getting settled in the small colony of St. Mary's, Maryland. Margaret had already attracted a considerable amount of hard feelings for establishing herself and her sister, Mary, in a large land holding in St. Mary's. Although women were not allowed to own land in the New World, the Brent sisters, being daughters of an aristocrat, had money and connections which had enabled them to purchase their property in Maryland. Lord Baltimore in London had encouraged the Brent family to establish themselves in the New World, and being tired of the hardships of being Catholic in a Protestant country, they had finally agreed to relocate in Maryland. Margaret was the New World's first female landowner.

Margaret Brent prided herself on her mind for business and her knowledge of law. Her emotions were held rigidly under control... except for the feelings she had for Melinda. She had a strong desire to protect the girl and help her grow into an independent, useful woman.

Their arrival in St. Mary's was more exciting than Melinda expected. When they disembarked they were taken up the Potomac River by a sailing boat that traversed the river carrying colonists. They were met at the small boat dock by Margaret's sister, Mary. She was accompanied by two good looking young men who were introduced to Melinda as Margaret's brothers, Giles and Fulke. There was much hugging and laughing, as the young men stowed the luggage in a large carriage, and helped the three women up to their seats.

"We arranged a nice room for you two at the Maryland Inn that was just built." Mary explained. "Our house is nearly finished, but they are still working on the interior. When they have finished, we will need to go to the warehouse at the harbor where our furniture is stored and pick out what we need. I'm already in my room at the house, but I waited to finish furnishing the rest of the house until you could choose what you wanted in your suite. Oh, I am so excited to have you home!" Mary bubbled. The two young men chose to sit with the carriage driver, so the women had the interior of the coach to themselves. Melinda watched as the two sisters conversed and was surprised to see how very different they were.

Mary was a little taller than Margaret, with a rounder figure and honey blond hair. She had a warm, outgoing personality, and gave the impression that she liked everybody. The one thing the two women shared was the beautiful smile, but it was obvious from Mary's pretty face that she wore her smile more often than Margaret.

Mary turned to Melinda. "So you are Lindy. I have heard so much about you. Welcome to our family."

The newly named Lindy felt suddenly shy. "I am glad to be here, Mistress Brent."

"Oh, for heaven's sake, call me Mary. You are going to be our new little sister."

Further conversation was cut short as the party arrived at the inn. There was more laughter and joking as their luggage was delivered to the large room which they would inhabit for the next few weeks. Lindy was surprised to see a trunk sitting in a corner. There were two cots.

"We had one of your trunks brought over from port storage, Margaret, so you won't feel so strange while you're waiting to get into the house," Mary smiled.

"That was very thoughtful of you, Mary. I will unpack a few things after I have had a short nap."

"I will let you settle in and get some rest. We will all meet downstairs for dinner around seven." Mary suggested.

"Sounds wonderful," Margaret agreed.

"Giles and Fulke are coming. They are anxious to hear about your business in Boston. Tomorrow they will pick us up and take us to the house. I hope the workmen followed your directions properly."

"We will soon see about that. Thank you, Mary dear, for all you have done. We will see you this evening."

As Mary took her leave, some of Lindy's doubts went with her. Maybe this adventure was not going to be so bad after all.

Margaret had her nap and, as planned, they all met for dinner. The food was delicious, but Lindy ate little. She was engrossed in the conversations. There was much laughter as the brothers told of the mishaps in the building of Margaret and Mary's new home that the sisters had named Sister's Freehold.

"Margaret, you will be pleased to know that a Jesuit priest has joined the colony, so we will not have to worry about missing Mass." Giles explained in a quiet moment.

"You can hardly call it a colony yet, Giles. We have to do our part to bring settlers here." Mary corrected.

Turning to Lindy, who was finally starting to empty her plate, Mary asked, "Are you Catholic, my dear?"

"Catholic? I don't know. What is it?"

"Why, it is our religion. You never heard of it?" asked Margaret.

"No, I guess not," Lindy answered, a little nonplussed.

"I guess I never thought to ask. What religion are you, Lindy?" Margaret asked.

"Well, I don't think I am any religion, Mistress Brent. Mother and I believe in God, but we do not go to any church," Lindy explained, worriedly. "Is that bad?"

Margaret reached over and put an arm around Lindy's shoulder. "No, dear, of course it is not. We will take you with us to Mass. You can see if you like it."

When they had finished their meal, a dessert of custard pudding and had a small glass of wine was provided. After more conversation, Margaret and Lindy excused themselves. The brothers and Mary made their farewells.

Margaret and Melinda washed in the large basin provided. The water was cold, but it felt good to be clean.

As they settled into their cots, Lindy voiced some of her questions about the Brent's property. She wondered how these women could build a home of their own.

Stimulated by Lindy's curiosity, Margaret felt the fatigue fall away. They talked long into the night, as Margaret continued her story of her earlier life, and explained how she came to be in the small colony of St. Mary's.

"As I was telling you, my family lived in Gloucestershire, England. My mother, Elizabeth married my father, Richard, when she was seventeen. I was born in 1601, one of thirteen siblings. Fortunately, my parents were wealthy landowners. I was educated by a tutor, so it bored me to live in the country spending my time embroidering and wasting my brain.

"A family friend, Lord Baltimore, was starting this colony in the New World where Catholics could worship without censure. He persuaded my two younger brothers, who you met today, into taking ship for Maryland. Mary and I begged join them, and we agreed to entice settlers to colonize on Lord Baltimore's land."

"You were very brave," Lindy said.

"Not brave. My family wanted me to marry and start a family. Marriage is not for me. I want to use my energies making this colony grow and thrive; to devote myself to building a Catholic community and managing my own life."

"It is amazing that your parents allowed you to go." Lindy voiced.

"I guess they thought I would be relying on my brothers for support, and that I would eventually marry. The fact that I am a thirty-eight-year-old spinster might have influenced them, too. But they are in for a big disappointment."

"So, you will all be living in your new house?" Lindy queried.

"Oh, no dear, you Mary and I are going to live there. Giles has a freehold of his own near a place called Chancellor's Point. Fulke will probably live with him until he marries." Margaret yawned, so Lindy stopped questioning her. Finally, they drifted off to sleep.

The same comfortable carriage picked the two women up the next morning. Margaret's family chatted about their new lives in St. Mary's, and their plans for the future.

So much had been going on the day before that Lindy had not had much of a chance to study Margaret's two brothers. Fulke, who she assumed was the younger of the two, was a little shorter in stature and of stockier build. His hair was rather unruly and a dark shade of brown and his eyes were large and brown. He was an attractive young man but of a quiet nature. He let his brother do most of the talking.

Giles was amazingly handsome. He was tall, over six feet, slender and well built. His hair was a golden blond that glinted when the light touched it. His eyes were a dark shade of blue, his nose straight and his mouth full. His personality was open and positive, and he smiled often. For a girl who had spent her life among old men, he was a God. Lindy knew that this handsome man was way out of her reach, but that did not stop her heart from pounding a little faster when she looked at him.

The carriage wended it way down a fairly new path made by wagon wheels. The land around them was green and lush, with many small copses of trees, and an occasional pond. As they progressed, Lindy noticed how much flat land lay around them. Maryland was obviously blessed with very rich farmland.

A short time later, Giles announced they were on Margaret's property. Lindy was amazed as the miles slipped by. The MacDougal estates were large, but nothing like Margaret's estate. Between them, the two sisters had been granted more than seventy acres of land.

As they emerged from a small wooded area, Lindy's mouth dropped open. Ahead of them, standing back from at least an acre of well-groomed green lawn, stood the most beautiful house she had ever seen. Its design was plain and tended to be four square, but it had graceful dower windows, and was made of wooden planking, whitewashed so that when the sun hit it, it emanated a golden glow.

"Of course, there is still much to do on the house," Mary explained. "We have negotiated with a farmer who has a small land holding about three miles down the river. He and his sons are going to help us with the landscaping. I think it will be quite acceptable."

"It looks wonderful, Mary, just like I had imagined it." Margaret complimented.

"Fulke and I will be over to help, too, Maggie. Our place at Chancellor Point is finished. We used some of the furniture in storage at the dock, but you girls can have rest of it," Giles offered.

A circular drive curved around the front of the house, and the carriage trundled down it and stopped at the front door. Even the door was beautiful to Lindy. It was carved and had a large, shiny doorknocker in the shape of an angel. A small diamond shaped window would reveal the identity of visitors.

Melinda discovered there was a cook, a butler and two maids already installed in the house. They had come over on the ship from England with the Brent's. The cook prepared a cold lunch. They gathered in the kitchen, which boasted a large wooden table, to enjoy cold chicken, fruit and apple cider, which quickly became Melinda's favorite drink.

The remainder of the afternoon was spent going from room to room and planning what furniture would go where. Lindy, not being involved in this, soon became bored and decided to go for a walk in the yard around the house. Being used to the MacDougal's well-manicured landscape, her mind was soon intent on planning a flower garden, a potting shed, and shrubbery which would complement the front facade of the house.

For the next two weeks everyone concentrated on getting the house furnished and decorated. Drapery was hung in all the windows and the beds were made, each having a warm comforter. In no time the place was transformed from a house into a home. Lindy worked with the landscapers as new plants and shrubs were planted.

Margaret and Lindy finally moved in. Mary had a suite of her own on the East Side of the house. Margaret chose the West Side, and installed Lindy in a large airy room next to hers. Margaret also had an office built on the main floor, which contained shelves for her library.

As soon as the office was finished, Margaret retreated to its confines, and Lindy found it hard to fill her time. Finally noticing Lindy's restlessness, Margaret called her into the office.

"What's the matter, my dear? You seem a little depressed." She offered Lindy a chair beside her desk.

"Oh, everything is wonderful, but...I guess I'm a little homesick. I wish I knew how things were going at home."

"Lord, child, you have written to you mother, haven't you?"

"Well, I do not seem to have anything to write with, and do not know how we would get a letter to her anyway," Lindy explained. "I promised to write to Esther, too."

"Forgive me, child. I have been very shortsighted. I am going to have a small desk put there in the corner just for you. There is plenty of paper, ink and quills. Not only should you be corresponding with you mother, but I know you will feel better when you get back to your poetry."

"That will be wonderful. Thank you so much. I was wondering if there is anything I can do to assist you? You seem to have a lot of work."

"That is a possibility, Lindy. Are you getting used to your new name?" Margaret inquired. Lindy thought a moment and decided she liked the nickname. "Yes, I have begun to like it. A new life deserves a new name."

"Then you are officially Lindy. But right now we need to discuss your mother's legal problem. I've gone through the copies of all her papers she sent me, and I am writing her with some suggestions. I also offered to be with her when the case is brought before the Jamestown Assembly."

Upon seeing Lindy's face light up, she laughed, "Of course, you would go with me for a visit."

"Oh, Mistress Brent, that will be wonderful."

"Now let us see what work you can do."

"I can store some of these papers for you, Mistress Brent." Lindy offered.

"Lindy, we are family now. Please feel free to call me Aunt Margaret."

"That will be wonderful, Mis...Aunt Margaret."

"I'll tell you what I'm working on right now, Lindy. I told you, I made a promise to Lord Baltimore to induce families to colonize this area. So, I am writing letters to people we know in Europe, and to groups that may be interested. I am also working on a project with a gentleman in London to send over as many Catholic indentured people as possible to work for those colonists who take freehold land to farm."

On hearing this, Lindy's heart started thumping. Indentured servants! She knew the hell her mother had gone through as an indenture. In her heart she felt that no one should ever have to be indentured. A fear also grew as to how Margaret Brent would react if she knew her own sordid beginnings. In that moment, Lindy vowed never to let Margaret know of her true background, or how she hated the thought of any person being a slave to another.

"Why, Lindy, dear, you are positively white. Did I say something to alarm you?" Margaret asked.

"Oh, no, Mis...Aunt Margaret. I guess my stomach is a little upset. I ate my breakfast too fast."

"Well, go and lay down a while. I will have Hector bring that little desk in the den for you. As soon as it is installed and is supplied, we will set about finding a good tutor for you. Tomorrow you can write your letters and we will get them off to your mother and Esther. Hector drives the mail to the port at Chesapeake Bay where it is put on ships going to different destinations. It is such a nice harbor. I just know that one day there will be a great city built around it."

Amanda did her best to deal with the loss of her daughter. She settled into her normal routine, and worked with Bertha Curtin to maintain a smoothly run household. Cinnamon and Arthur went about their work with little joy. They worried about their sweet Esther who seemed lost without Melinda. Amanda, Cinnamon and Arthur spent many an evening discussing Esther's future.

One evening, while Amanda sat before the fireplace in her special room, there was a knock on the door. She gave permission to enter and Esther entered tentatively.

"Why, Esther, darling, come in," Amanda smiled.

"I don't want to bother you, Aunt Amanda."

"You know you could never be a bother to me. Come, sit here near the fire. This big house is rather cold."

Esther sat, her hands folded on her lap. She gazed into the flames. She was quiet. Amanda gently cleared her throat. "How can I help you, dear?"

"Well...I know you and my parents have been wondering what to do with me. I just wanted you to know that I have some money of my own hidden away from what Ma and Pa saved for my school tuition. I have also earned a few pounds for doing odd jobs around the property."

"Why, that was very clever of you, Esther," Amanda smiled. "You'll have some spending money for the holidays."

"Oh, no, Aunt Amanda, I didn't save it for anything foolish. As you know, our tutor has been teaching me to play the harpsichord. I've been practicing a lot. However, Master Patrick only knows the basics so I want to hire a real harpsichord instructor. There is one in Jamestown. I know that sounds frivolous, but, music is my great love and the only thing I have in my life right now."

Amanda was taken aback. "Why child, I know you spend time on the harpsichord, but I had no idea you were so serious about it."

"I get so lonely without Melinda. With the harpsichord I can forget everything else and feel my soul being filled. I could play for the Sunday services in the chapel, too, so it won't be a waste of money."

Amanda looked long and hard at Esther. She had turned out to be beautiful, as well as poised and intelligent. Her light skin was smooth over sculptured features. Her dark brown hair was wavy but not tightly curled. Her velvet brown eyes were large and heavily lashed and her mouth generous and nicely formed.

After a few moments of contemplation, Amanda took Esther's hand and held it between her own. "You are right, Esther. We have that lovely old harpsichord and it should be used. This house needs something to cheer it up."

"Then you will let me hire a teacher?"

"No. I think not," Amanda replied.

Esther's face paled and her body slumped. Amanda patted the girl's cold hand.

"What I mean is that *I* will hire a teacher for you. I, too, have some funds put away which I was saving for Melinda's school needs, but now Mistress Brent is taking care of her. I know Melinda would want you to have it."

Tears welled up in Esther's eyes then overflowed. "Oh, Aunt Amanda, I don't know how to thank you."

"Just enjoy your lessons and play some beautiful music for us."

Esther squeezed Amanda's hands and jumped up, now full of joyous energy.

"I have to go tell Ma and Pa. They will be so happy!" She started to the door, then ran back and kissed Amanda on the cheek. "Thank you, so much. Now I can get something nice for my parents for the holidays."

For a long moment after Esther left the room, Amanda sat in silence thinking of the two young girls in her life and wondering what their fates would be.

James Jr. was disgruntled when he heard of Amanda's plan to hire a music tutor for the daughter of his hired servants. He didn't mind so much the thought of having music around the house, but he couldn't figure why that much money should be spent on a maid.

"I hope you are not using any of the estate money on this fiasco, Amanda," he said as he leaned against the fireplace mantle in the library. "You know it is in holding until our case is settled."

Amanda drew herself up, lifted her chin, and explained. "Her parents and I are funding this. I would not presume to use what you consider 'your' money," Amanda asserted, her violet eyes sparkling in defiance.

James stood silent for a few moments looking at Amanda. He was fighting his genuine admiration for his father's widow. He wanted to hate her but the more he observed Amanda, the harder it was to be angry with her.

He could certainly understand why his father, in his dotage, would be taken. She was undoubtedly the loveliest woman he had ever seen. She reminded him of the princesses in his childhood fairytales. Her skin was so satiny that he could hardly keep from reaching out to touch her cheek. All her features were even and perfectly proportioned in her heart shaped face. Her hair was soft and shiny and as black as midnight. It had blue highlights. He longed to see it set free of its bonds and flowing over her creamy shoulders.

James pulled his thoughts back to the present. He knew he could not afford to think such treasonous thoughts. This woman was his enemy and he must not trust her. He owed it to his parents to regain his inheritance. He could not let this temptress get under his skin.

"Well, then, I guess it will be all right and...I will be sharing the dinner table with you from now on. There are things we need to discuss, and it seems a more civilized way to come to terms."

Amanda tried not to show her surprise. "Of course, you are always welcome. I have been having my dinner in the kitchen with Bertha and the staff, but, I will have them set a place for me at the other end of the dining room table...if that is all right with you."

"That will suit me fine." He moved away from the fireplace as Amanda headed toward the door. Jamie called to Amanda, "However, I think it will be too hard to talk across that long table. Your place should be on my right."

Amanda could not believe this change in attitude from James. "That will be arranged. Do you want to start this evening?"

"That will be fine. Thank you." Jamie watched Amanda move gracefully out the door. As the door closed quietly behind her, he attempted to resume his paper work. But his traitorous mind kept returning to his father's widow. How could he have imagined that while fighting for his country in Scotland, he would one day have to fight a beautiful woman for his own home?

When Jamie's coach had first arrived at MacDougal house, he had been excited to see that the house was almost an exact replica of their home in Scotland. He had even had the coachman stop so he could feast his eyes on his new home. His thoughts drifted back to his homeland, and its troubles.

As the fighting had lulled in Scotland, he had slipped secretly into London for a much-deserved rest and to let heal a bad back wound. He used the time to work on training himself to speak English without his Scottish brogue. He was staying with a friend when he heard that his father had been in Scotland and London searching for him. He had then arranged passage on the first ship headed for Jamestown. However, his wound had become infected and his physician would not let him go until the infection was under control. So, like his father, Jamie was stuck in London. As soon and his wound was healed Jamie had once again arranged passage to the New World only to be delayed again when he heard that his best friend, Thomas Forbes, had been captured by the English in the highlands. Forbes was being held in a confiscated castle.

Jamie had decided that Tom was the priority, so he had crept out of London in the dead of night headed for the Scottish boarder. Unfortunately by the time he managed to reach the castle, Thomas' head was displayed on a pole.

Heartbroken, Jamie had managed to return to London, not without several close scrapes. Finally free, he had bid his fellow Scots farewell and finally managed to take ship for Jamestown. He felt guilty that the fighting with England would continue without him, but he knew his aging parents were missing him and needed him home.

As he thought back on the years of fighting, he wondered if he would ever feel human again. In all those years he had not been able to forge a relationship with any decent woman. Camp followers had assuaged his physical needs, but his heart had grown cold with a loss of hope. Until he had come home he had no longer thought of himself as a man, just a fighting machine. The death of both of his parents, and the unbelievable marriage of his father to a young girl tore away at his heart. Why should an old man be blessed with what Jamie would have given his life for?

When Fiona was at the house she had built a picture of Amanda's role at MacDougal House that roused Jamie's anger to the breaking point. The thought of his poor old father being used by Amanda made him ill. But he was convinced that Fiona was right. No matter how beautiful Amanda was, he had no choice but to rid himself of her.

However, he could no longer deny that he felt a strong physical desire for her. He could understand how an old man could be taken in by such an enticing woman, but he fought to convince himself that he was too wise to follow in his father's footsteps. So, until now, he had stayed to himself, avoiding contact with Amanda and leaving the running of the household to Bertha Curtin.

Pulling himself out of his reverie, he reached for parchment and quill. He jotted a quick note to his barrister to see if anything could be done to speed up the adjudication in the Jamestown Assembly. Ringing for Arthur, he sighed deeply. "There's no point in tempting fate any longer than necessary."

As surprised as Jamie was at his decision to have his meals with Amanda, she had been stunned. She knew she must avoid being taken in by this seeming change of heart, but she was definitely intrigued. She could not help feeling some trepidation about spending so much time with Jamie. She must remember what he was trying to do to her and put his striking good looks in the back of her mind. He was the enemy, and she must be wary.

That night as she descended the stairs, she repeated to herself all the warnings she had listed in dealing with her stepson. Somehow she managed to get through the evening. However, both individuals were fighting two battles now...the inheritance and their attraction to each other.

"As long as we will be dinner partners until the adjudication, I suggest that we make a truce," Jamie announced.

Amanda looked at him for a long moment, then smiled and replied. "That will be fine."

She watched Jamie as he toyed with the food on his plate. "I've been wondering, how is it that you do not have the Scottish accent your parents had? You speak good English."

Jamie smiled. "While I was hiding in London, I felt it prudent to rid myself of the accent that could so easily identify me. It was hard, but I had a lot of free time. I still slip back into the accent when my emotions are embroiled."

"Well, it was worthwhile. Your speech is excellent." Amanda again slipped into silence.

Jamie ate little that evening. He found Amanda's presence unsettling. He could not keep his eyes off her. His mind struggled with the thought of his old father making love to her. Was money really so important to her that she would seduce an old man?"

He had almost decided that dining with Amanda would be too difficult when Amanda spoke. "It seems strange to eat in here; I've been eating with the rest of the household for so long. But, it will be nice to talk to someone who has been involved in so many adventures. I would love to hear more about Scotland. What is Scotland like, anyway?"

Amanda had hit the right chord, for Jamie loved his native home with all his heart. He soon found himself telling Amanda things that he had not shared with anyone else.

"It is a country of many different landscapes, each as interesting as the other. The MacDougal clan was a small one. We lived in the southern part of the Highlands. Father did a wonderful job replicating our ancestral home here in Jamestown. Of course, he could not transport the lineage and spirit of our home." As Jamie spoke he dug into his dinner with enthusiasm.

"I do love this house. I have lived the best years of my life here." Amanda confessed. "You must miss your old home in Scotland."

"I do. The Highlands are beautiful in a very craggy way. They are wild and challenging, and it seems like we Scots have been fighting for her freedom since the beginning of time. It was the hardest thing for me to desert my homeland and come to the New World, but I felt I owed it to my parents to keep the MacDougal legacy alive."

With her gentle questions, Amanda drew from Jamie the story of his youth and his years as a freedom fighter. Somehow she found it harder and harder to keep him in the role of villain. She knew that she would have wanted her inheritance too, that is, if she had one. But, wait a minute! She did have one and he was trying to take it away from her. Suddenly, she could no longer sit and talk with this man.

"I'm sorry, but I have a bad headache. Please excuse me. Do continue your meal. I will see you tomorrow."

"Yes, of course." Jamie rose as she quickly pushed her chair back and walked silently toward the door. For some reason, he felt an acute loss. He hoped he had not caused her headache. He found that he could not eat another bite of the food that had tasted so good when she was with him.

Jamie rang the hand bell on the table and Cinnamon entered, wondering at the premature call.

"Can I help you, master?"

"Yes, Cinnamon, Mistress Amanda does not feel good so would you please clean up. I am turning in for the night." He started to go, and then turned back. "You might check in on her later. Have Addie fix her some warm milk." He turned and left the room, leaving an open-mouthed Cinnamon staring after him.

"Now what ya figger got into him?" She commenced to clean the table noticing that both parties had not cleaned their plates. "That should mean something." she thought.

Two weeks later, James Jr. informed Amanda that they would be going before the Assembly in a month. "So, you should start thinking about where you will be going after you leave here," James stated coldly, unable to look directly into her face.

Amanda stayed cool though fear made her stomach seethe. She wondered again how this man could be so officious and cruel. How could two such kind and loving parents have sired two such hateful siblings? She had thought Ugly the worst man in the world, but Ugly had not hidden who he was. Jamie hid his malice behind a hard, cold exterior. In moments like this, her gentle nature failed her. He was so pleasant during their evening meals. But now she felt like hitting him in the face.

It took all the strength she could muster not to turn around a run from the room. Jamie turned his attention to his work, leaving Amanda standing there. Finally she walked sedately out of the library and headed for her room. Jamie could not hold back a feeling of admiration for her inner strength and single mindedness. He knew she would soon be gone, and Arthur, Cinnamon and their daughter might chose to leave with her. But he would once again be heir to MacDougal House.

As the days for the adjudication drew closer James grew more confused. He was used to the whole staff now and his home was functioning well. Shaking his head, he decided to go for a walk in the garden. Fresh air should clear his head. However, since Amanda had worked with the gardener to design the colorful landscaping, thoughts of her could not be so easily squelched. Amanda's essence was in the bright petals of the roses that surrounded him, but the perfume of the roses could not compete with the scent of her hair.

The more time he spent with Amanda, the harder it became to credit all of Fiona's accusations. Jamie also had to admit that his sister had always been mean and spiteful. As a child he had been punished for many naughty things Fiona had done and blamed on him.

As soon as his barrister gave him a date for the hearing, he shared it with Amanda. Having found a moment to retreat to her private salon, Amanda hastily jotted down the information Jamie had given her in a note to Mistress Brent. Amanda added a postscript to Melinda, or Lindy, saying she was anxious to see her again. She quickly sealed the note and pressed James Senior's ring into the hot wax she had prepared. She then rushed down the stairs.

"Arthur! Arthur!"

Arthur came running from the kitchen, afraid something had happened.

"Oh, there you are. Arthur, please take this note into Jamestown and see that it gets on the first ship to Maryland."

"Sure thing, ma'am. Everything all right?"

"It's about the adjudication. Mistress Brent promised to come and Melinda is coming with her. They need to know the date."

Arthur smiled and headed toward the door calling for Swen. Five minutes later, Amanda watched the carriage pull out of the carriage house and head down the drive at full speed. Amanda was happy that Swen still worked for the MacDougal's. He had finally saved enough to send for his family. They had arrived in Jamestown eight months earlier and Swen had settled them in a small house in Jamestown, but came out to work on the property every day.

Amanda breathed a prayer that the note would reach St. Mary's in time. She turned slowly and climbed back up the stairs to her room.

Amanda closed her bedroom door and went to her dresser. She sat before the mirror, noting the light shadows under her eyes and the small frown lines in her forehead. Whatever happens, she would be glad to have the struggle behind her. Amanda released her long hair from its bun, picked up her beloved brush, and slowly brushed her hair. As she did so she told herself that she was brushing away all of her fears and doubts about her future. She went to her bed, dropping down on the soft mattress. A good night's sleep would make her feel better.

However, three hours later she was still lying on her back staring sightlessly up at the cherubs and their clouds on Martha's ceiling. She finally fell into a worried slumber.

The next thing Amanda knew, she was waking up with the sun streaming through the window. She had neglected to close the drapes. On her bedside table she found a full glass of milk and an untouched scone. It cheered her that Cinnamon had thought of her, and the aroma of the scone made her hungry.

There was always something heartening about a new day.

15

Margaret and Lindy had made it on time for Amanda's case to be heard in the Jamestown House of Burgesses, which was the first legislative assembly in the New World, established in 1619.

In spite of the arguments Margaret offered, the fact that Amanda was a woman finally prompted a judgment against her. James MacDougal Junior had his inheritance. Since the marriage was ruled legal, Amanda was awarded a widow's stipend.

Lindy begged to stay in Jamestown and help her mother, but both Amanda and Margaret were against this. Amanda wasn't sure where she was now going to live but she knew that Lindy would be better off with Margaret. Margaret invited Amanda to join them in Maryland, but Amanda did not want to be a burden to Lindy. She graciously declined.

Margaret and Lindy took ship not knowing Amanda's fate. Through subsequent letters, Lindy learned that her mother was safe and content. So Lindy took a deep breath, threw herself into her studies, and prayed to Mother Mary to take care of her mother.

Amanda decided to stay with Aggie at the inn until she could make up her mind what to do with the rest of her life.

Prior to the trial, Fiona had again descended upon the household to make sure her dear brother had reclaimed his property. When he won his case, she left triumphant.

The next day Amanda, with Bertha's help, packed her belongings on the buggy and set off for Aggie's inn. Henry, Cinnamon and Esther agreed to stay on at the mansion with a good raise in salary. Bertha had threatened to quit, but Amanda talked her into staying due to her age. Addie also remained as cook.

At the inn, Amanda settled into Aggie's best room. It was large and clean. There was a bed with a soft mattress, an armoire, a wooden chair and a padded chair. A wooden chest with five large drawers gave her room to store her belongings. Aggie hovered around her like a mother hen.

"Don't worry, honey. We'll figure out some way for you to get by. This town is growing in leaps and bounds, and there are plenty of good men lookin' for wives."

"I do not want to think about anything right now, Aggie. I just want to rest and see if I can stop all these thoughts from going round and round in my head," Amanda replied.

But, as thoughts were prone to do, the heartrending ones that kept Amanda in a constant state of anguish did not abate. As for Jamie, her thoughts ranged from total hate, to confusion, and an odd feeling of loss. The remembrance of time spent together, thoughts shared, and a strong attraction haunted her. "Oh, why did he have to be my enemy?" she grieved.

Amanda knew she had to forget Jamie if she was going to be able to make a new life, but pictures of his handsome face, his roguish smile, and his lithe body kept intruding on her thoughts. After their truce, they had found they had much in common. Both loved the land and MacDougal House.

In those last days before the hearings, an easy friendship had grown between them. They had both refused to think about the ongoing unpleasantness. Instead, they spent time together discussing literature, history...especially that of Scotland...and many other interesting subjects. They walked together each morning in the gardens and Amanda pointed out her favorite flowers. They sat together in the evenings enjoying the warmth of the large parlor fireplace. Amanda had felt a sense of peace for the first time since Jamie came back to MacDougal House.

Even after the courts findings had been set down, Jamie had told Amanda that she could stay on as long as she needed, but Amanda knew how painful it would be to be a guest in her former home. She was determined to forget the past and go forward on her own.

In the weeks that followed, Amanda settled into Aggie's inn. Looking for something to do, she began to help serve food to Aggie's customers. It made her feel a little less useless.

The nights were the hardest. At first thoughts of MacDougal House warred with questions of her future. Surprisingly, she realized that the memories which haunted her the most were those of her enemy. She knew she would probably never see Jamie again, but she still remembered the feelings of warmth she experienced every time he accidentally touched her hand, or brushed against her as they worked at some project.

Those last two months before the adjudication had opened a small door in the most secret corner of her heart. Amanda had held out hope that Jamie would change his mind and give up his claims against her. When he had not, she had felt the pain of a double loss.

As for Jamie, he was experiencing feelings he had never before had to deal with. He had won. His inheritance was now safe, but where was the feeling of triumph and vindication he had expected? As the weeks flew by, Jamie grew restless.

Lying in bed at night, he would remember the Amanda he had learned to like. He tried to concentrate on the horrible things Fiona had said about her, however knowing Fiona better now, he wondered how much of her accusations were true.

He felt guilty about Amanda's departure. He had put thoughts of what would happen to her when he won his case at the back of his mind. He had to admit that he had often pictured Amanda near him no matter what happened. Her departure had been a surprise.

It had never occurred to Jamie that a woman could be a friend. He knew that he would wed one day to keep his bloodline active, but he had not given much thought to what that would be like.

Surprisingly, he found that he missed Amanda terribly. Even memories of the times they had been at war left him with warm feelings. He found he liked her spirit. In fact, he liked everything about her. Even the painful thought that she might have taken advantage of James Senior had begun to fade.

He finally decided to learn more about Amanda, so he called Bertha Curtin into his library.

"Bertha," he hesitated. "Bertha, as you know, my sister has told me her version of Amanda's arrival at MacDougal House. I am beginning to think that what she said might not be entirely true. I know I did not let you say much about her when I first approached you. I would appreciate it if you can now tell me what you know about Amanda."

"I wondered if you would ever get around to this. I can assure you, the picture of Amanda painted by your sister is quite distorted."

Bertha settled comfortably in her seat and recounted everything that had happened to Amanda, Melinda and the MacDougal's from the moment the two had appeared at the back door of MacDougal House.

When she finished, they both sat in deep silence. Bertha waited for a response from Jamie, whose face was expressionless. Finally Bertha spoke. "That is why we all love her so much."

Jamie finally moved. He gave Bertha a small, apologetic, smile. "Thank you, Bertha. You have helped me very much."

Bertha watched as Jamie rose from his chair, walked to the fireplace and stood looking into the flames, his arm resting on the mantle. Finally, she rose and left the room,

The direction of Jamie's thoughts had taken a drastic turn upon hearing Bertha Curtin's story. In the days that followed, he wrestled with his feelings of guilt and his burgeoning feelings of admiration for Amanda. Was it too late to make up for what he had done?

Jamie left the house early the following morning. When he arrived at Aggie's inn, Amanda was serving breakfast to some travelers. He stood for a long while watching her. She was smiling and joking with the travelers, looking happier and more relaxed than he had ever seen her. Doubts began to form in Jamie's mind. "Maybe she is better off here," he pondered.

Just then Amanda felt his presence. She looked up and saw him standing near the door. Her surprise was apparent, and he noticed, sadly, that her good mood quickly vanished to be replaced by a look of apprehension.

She came over to him. "Can I seat you, Master MacDougal?"

He smiled, "Yes. That will be fine."

When he was seated near the large stone fireplace, he ordered a mug of ale. Amanda also brought a warm scone. As she started to turn away, Jamie reached out and touched her arm. "Do you think you might be able to take a moment? I think we should talk," Jamie said.

"I will see if Aggie can take over." Amanda headed for the kitchen, her heart pounding. A few minutes later she returned. "We can talk in the vegetable garden behind the inn, if that is all right with you."

Jamie smiled, "That will be fine."

As they walked together down the garden lane, Amanda's emotions were a mass of confusion. Why was he here? What could he want of her now? She had been working so hard to get Jamie off her mind and here he was again. She was afraid to look at him.

"Here, we can sit on this bench," She said, nervously adding unnecessary information. "It is shady here, and no one much comes out here this time of day. They are all so busy. I really should be..." Realizing that she was exposing her emotions, she stopped mid-sentence.

"This is just fine. Please sit down Amanda," he said.

Fearing that he could hear her heart beating so loudly, Amanda sank onto the bench, examining her hands in her lap.

Jamie sat down beside her. He watched her for a moment, drinking in her beauty. The light shining through the leaves on the arbor overhead threw patches of color on her shiny black hair. She was so lovely that he found he could not talk past the lump in his throat. When he finally cleared his throat, Amanda jumped an inch or two off the bench.

Jamie lifted one very cold hand from Amanda's lap, and held it between his two warm ones. "May I?" he gently asked.

"Oh...Oh, yes, if you like." Amanda acquiesced, still avoiding his eyes.

"Amanda...my poor, dear Amanda, what can I say? I have treated you horribly. I do not know if you will ever be able to forgive me." Amanda remained silent. "I acted like a big bully. I listened to my sick sister...the moment I first saw you, I thought I had never seen a woman so alluring. When I found out you were married to my father it was like the old man had stolen you away from me. I was crazy in the head. All I could think about was another man touching you. It was my own father, and he was gone, but I was still wild with jealousy."

Amanda dared to look at Jamie's face, unable to believe what she was hearing.

"I made the decision then to harden myself against you. If I could blame you for the loss of my parents and my home, I could keep from falling in love with you. You *had* to be a fortune hunter. Fiona bolstered these misconceptions with her jealousy and hatred."

"That is why you would not let me tell you my side?" Amanda asked.

"Once I started blaming you I could not stop. I hated myself for the way I was treating you, but it is hard to admit that you hate yourself, so I convinced myself it was *you* I hated."

"That's too bad, Jamie, because I never hated you. I was happy you came home, and I would have been glad to turn MacDougal House and your legacy over to you. But, when you so badly misjudged me I was convinced that I had to protect myself."

Jamie squeezed her hand. "I finally began to know you, and I realized you were a good woman. You had become family and Bertha told me there was real love between you and my parents. That they had adored you and Melinda made my feelings even more conflicted. I held tightly to my convictions, because I was afraid I would not stand a chance with you."

Jamie lifted his hand and brushed a tendril of her hair back off her face. "When you moved out, I was sure it was over for good, and was probably for the best, but the things Fiona had said still bothered me. Bertha Curtin set things straight for me. When she finished her story, I felt a burning guilt surge through me. I thought I would drown in it."

Amanda looked away. "I am surprised you still want anything to do with me." Amanda pulled away from Jamie and fisted her hands on her lap.

Jamie turned her face toward him again. "I think you are the bravest, strongest women I have ever met. I know now that my heart was right from the beginning, and I wish I had listened to it. I am ashamed that put you through all that pain. Amanda, please let me make it up to you."

Jamie became silent for a moment, and then lifted her trembling chin with his hand. Looking into her eyes he said softly, "Do you know what I am trying to say, lass?"

Amanda managed a small smile. "I think so...I hope so." she whispered.

"I cannot live in that big house without you any longer. Please come home."

"I am afraid my living there now, even as your stepmother, would not look good."

"You silly little goose, you are much too young to be my stepmother, but you are the perfect age to be my wife. Amanda, please say you will forgive me and marry me."

Tears welled up in Amanda's eyes, and spilled over onto her cheeks. Jamie was not sure what kind of tears they were. "Do I have an answer? Do you care for me at all?" he pressed.

Amanda looked into his sincere face. She reached up and brushed her fingertips over his full, sensuous lips.

"Oh, Jamie, you have made me very happy. I have loved you for a very long time. I would love being your wife more than anything in the world, but..."

"Oh, no....not a 'but'..." He let his hand fall and turned his face away. "You can't forgive me. I have hurt you too much. I knew it, and I do not blame you."

"No, Jamie, that's not true. I do forgive you. It is something about me, about my past." Amanda hid her face in her hands. "I am not worthy of your love."

"Not worthy? Are you out of your mind? You are way too good for the likes of me. I promise you, Amanda, I will do everything in my power to make you forget our past troubles."

"No, Jamie. This has nothing to do with you. This is something that I never told anyone, not even your parents or Bertha, something that could turn your love to hate."

"Nothing in the world could ever do that, lass. Please, if you love me at all, tell me what the problem is. I promise, this time I will listen and understand."

"Jamie, there is more than one thing about me that may shock you. The first is that the only reason I was able to agree to marriage with your dear father is that we had agreed the marriage would be strictly platonic. James was a father to me. He married me to protect both Melinda and I from being thrown out in the world again with no support or protection. He was a saint, and I loved him dearly."

"I cannot believe this," Jamie said.

"Can't believe that the marriage was platonic?" Amanda queried.

"That is not what I meant. I can't believe that I put myself through all the painful jealousy, when my father never even touched you. It is hard to believe the depth of my own stupidity."

"That was the only relationship I could share with James, even if we had been better-matched age-wise. The second part of my past is that it would have prevented any other type of marriage with him, or any marriage at all, is how Melinda was conceived."

"Bertha said you came here from England, and..." Amanda took a very deep breath. "Please do not ask anything more, Jamie. Just listen. It is so hard to give up the thing I want most, but you have to know the truth, and you are not going to like it."

"I love you, lass. Nothing can change that."

"We will see." She turned her face to the garden, afraid to look at Jamie. "My story began when my father, who was an actor, went off to sea and never returned. Before my mother died, I was arrested for stealing a loaf of bread for her. I was thrown in a debtor's prison, and subsequently put on a ship for the New World as an indentured servant."

Jamie started to speak, but she put her hand up to his mouth to quiet his comment.

"Please, Jamie...When my ship arrived in Jamestown, I was auctioned off to a very ugly hunter named Hyrum Biggs. I named him what he was, 'Ugly'. He threw me on a pack animal, and took me to his small one room cabin in the forest."

Amanda shook her head hoping to stop the memory of her recurrent pain whenever the beast entered her body. "There he beat me into submission, and raped me at his discretion. The pain was terrible. As nature would do, she allowed one of his nasty seeds to get me with child."

Jamie tried to put his arm around Amanda, but she pushed it away.

"Indians killed Ugly when Melinda was three years old. I was with child again, but when the Indians set our cabin on fire, I lost a little boy. To make a long story short, Melinda and I escaped and with the help of some very kind people at a nearby trading post. They brought us back to Jamestown. The woman at the post gave me a letter to the MacDougal's and I was blessedly hired as a companion to your mother. So you see, I cannot give you my purity."

Amanda sat silently when she had finished her story. She knew all was lost, but for some reason a painful burden had somehow been lifted from her shoulders.

Jamie let her maintain the silence for a few moments and then again lifted her chin with his hand and made her look into his eyes. "Oh, my poor lass. What a terrible thing for you to go through. But, how can you think I would blame you for what that bastard did to you?"

"Forgive me or not, I am no longer a whole woman. I could not warm your nights or give you children."

"Why ever not, if we love each other, anything..." he started.

"Do you not understand at all? Each time he touched my body, I wanted to die. Many times I thought of killing myself, but the faint hope of escape stopped me. I am afraid that I could never let you touch me. What kind of a marriage would that be? I could not put you though that."

They sat silent for a long while, she knowing she had lost him; he not knowing how to comfort her. Finally, James put his arms around her and pulled her close to him, gently pressing her head to his chest with his hand.

"Do you think that is all I want from you, lass? I love everything about you, your mind, your spirit, and your strength. I can wait darlin'. We can take all the time in the world and let our love heal the past. Marry me and come home where you belong. We will face whatever happens together."

Amanda, still not convinced, looked up at him. "But, what if I never heal? What if I cannot learn to...? I do not want you to be stuck with an impotent wife. You need a son to carry on the MacDougal name."

"That is my problem. I believe that being touched with love cannot help but heal your fears, but if we never have a son, we will leave our legacy to Melinda. I will formally adopt her, so she will be a MacDougal. Now, sweet lass, say you will marry me and we will trust in our future."

Amanda gazed long and hard into the eyes of the man she loved, and was amazed that she felt no fear sitting there with his arms around her. Slowly she nodded her head.

"Oh, lass, let me seal our bargain with just one little kiss. I promise, I will not hurt, lass."

As Jamie moved his face closer to hers, she felt a jab of fear, but then she got lost in the beauty of his face and the sincere affection showing in his eyes. She slowly lifted her face to him. His lips touched her in a feather-light kiss, and she found herself relaxing in his warm embrace.

As his lips moved softly over hers, she was amazed to feel warmth spreading all over her body and she found herself returning his kiss. She had never been kissed by a man, and now she was being kissed by a man who loved her.

Feeling new hope spring up in her heart, she relaxed into Jamie's arms and felt the first of many thrilling moments the future would bring.

Made in the USA
Charleston, SC
21 July 2014